She staggered, slamming against a hard wall, which turned out to be a broad-shouldered body

The body had a pair of arms that caught and steadied her in a comforting embrace. The guy had blatant sex appeal in a lean body that scraped six feet and moved with a sexual, confident gait. Now, like half the female population in New Orleans, Christy found herself susceptible to this man, experiencing all these treacherous sensations. This dizzy breathlessness as the pair of brash green eyes continued to hold her gaze. This sudden heat in her insides as she stared up at the bold face under its thatch of dark hair. And this weakness in her limbs as the powerful arms continued to pin her against his chest.

"If you go around getting into trouble just to get my attention," Dallas said in a deliberately seductive voice, "things are bound to happen. *Really dangerous things.*"

Dear Harlequin Intrigue Reader,

Cupid's bow is loaded at Harlequin Intrigue with four fabulous stories of breathtaking romantic suspense—starting with the continuation of Cassie Miles's COLORADO SEARCH AND RESCUE miniseries. In *Wedding Captives*, lovers reunite on a mountaintop... unfortunately they're also snowbound with a madman!

And there's no better month to launch our new modern gothic continuity series MORIAH'S LANDING. Amanda Stevens emerges from the New England fog with *Secret Sanctuary*, the first of four titles coming out over the next several months. You can expect all of the classic themes you love in these stories, plus more of the contemporary edge you've come to expect from our brand of romantic suspense.

You know what can happen *In the Blink of an Eye...?* Julie Miller does! And you can find out, too, in the next installment of her TAYLOR CLAN series.

Finally, Jean Barrett takes you to New Orleans for some *Private Investigations* with battling P.I.'s. It's a regular showdown in the French Quarter—where absolutely anything goes.

So celebrate Valentine's Day with the most confounding mystery of all...that of the heart.

Deep, rich chocolate wishes,

Denise O'Sullivan
Associate Senior Editor
Harlequin Intrigue

PRIVATE INVESTIGATIONS
JEAN BARRETT

HARLEQUIN®

TORONTO • NEW YORK • LONDON
AMSTERDAM • PARIS • SYDNEY • HAMBURG
STOCKHOLM • ATHENS • TOKYO • MILAN • MADRID
PRAGUE • WARSAW • BUDAPEST • AUCKLAND

ISBN 0-373-22652-7

PRIVATE INVESTIGATIONS

Copyright © 2002 by Jean Barrett

This edition published by arrangement with Harlequin Books S.A.

® and TM are trademarks of the publisher. Trademarks indicated with ® are registered in the United States Patent and Trademark Office, the Canadian Trade Marks Office and in other countries.

Visit us at www.eHarlequin.com

Printed in U.S.A.

ABOUT THE AUTHOR

If setting has anything to do with it, Jean Barrett claims she has no reason not to be inspired. She and her husband live on Wisconsin's scenic Door Peninsula in an antique-filled country cottage overlooking Lake Michigan. A teacher for many years, she left the classroom to write full-time. She is the author of a number of romance novels.

Write to Jean at P.O. Box 623, Sister Bay, WI 54234.

Books by Jean Barrett

HARLEQUIN INTRIGUE
308—THE SHELTER OF HER ARMS
351—WHITE WEDDING
384—MAN OF THE MIDNIGHT SUN
475—FUGITIVE FATHER
528—MY LOVER'S SECRET
605—THE HUNT FOR HAWKE'S DAUGHTER
652—PRIVATE INVESTIGATIONS

Don't miss any of our special offers. Write to us at the following address for information on our newest releases.

Harlequin Reader Service
U.S.: 3010 Walden Ave., P.O. Box 1325, Buffalo, NY 14269
Canadian: P.O. Box 609, Fort Erie, Ont. L2A 5X3

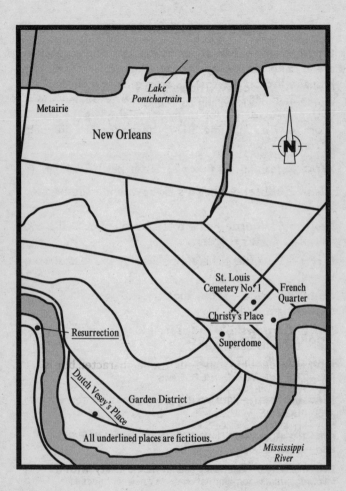

Lake Pontchartrain

Metairie

New Orleans

N

St. Louis Cemetery No. 1

French Quarter

Christy's Place

Resurrection

Superdome

Dutch Vesey's Place

Garden District

All underlined places are fictitious.

Mississippi River

CAST OF CHARACTERS

Christy Hawke—Both her heart and her P.I. agency are at risk.

Dallas McFarland—The sexy P.I. has more on his agenda than he is willing to admit.

Denise—Christy's assistant gives her a hard time, but she is a loyal friend.

Laura Hollister—Her death is shadowed by a web of lies and deceit.

Glenn Hollister—Christy's ex-boyfriend is desperate for her help.

Monica Claiborne—She trusts no one but Dallas to solve her sister's murder.

Daisy—The little girl is threatened by the loss of her father.

Camille Leveau—Does the voodoo queen have something to hide?

Marty Bornowski—The asphalt king is protecting more than his daughter.

Dutch Vesey—He's an undesirable character, but is he also a killer?

Buzz Purreau—The young jeweler has no secrets, or does he?

Alistair St. Leger—Christy's congenial neighbor is all too willing to help.

Edgar Evers—The lawyer startles Christy with a surprising revelation.

To new and used bookstores everywhere.
Your support is wonderful.
Bless you for caring.

The Altar

It was no more than a narrow shelf behind a hidden door in a darkened room, but it held all that he required to serve his demonic deity. A pair of black candles burned, their flickering light revealing on the shelf a tiny black coffin, the skull of a goat and several finger bones. There was also a flat dish containing oil. In it he placed the strands of auburn hair he had snipped from the head of his victim. He was ready.

Seizing one of the candles, he passed it back and forth over the dish before applying its flame to the oil. The hair slowly curled and burned in the ignited oil, filling his nostrils with a sickly sweet odor. As he watched the strands being consumed, he chanted a soft, rhythmic incantation.

When the hair was no more than a powdery ash on the surface of the hot oil, he began to pray. "You instruct us, Master, that those who transgress must pay for their transgressions. Hear me, Master, and know that she will trouble us no more…"

Above the shelf hung a small mirror. In the weaving light of the candles his face was reflected in the shadowy, distorted glass. A face that was lurid, glowing with triumph, for he knew now what it felt like to have taken the life of a human being. And, if necessary, he could kill again.

Prologue

New Orleans

Dallas McFarland was history. They had lost all swaggering, hot-eyed six feet of him at a fender bender over on Canal. McFarland had been trapped in the mob of gawkers that had gathered when a minivan had run a light and smacked into a panel truck. So much for his celebrated reputation as a private investigator.

Chortled wasn't a word that Christy Hawke ordinarily associated with herself, but on this occasion it seemed appropriate. She did feel like chortling. McFarland had been a thorn in her side from the day she had opened her own agency, robbing her of one client after another.

Not this time, thank you. She intended to demonstrate her worth, win this contest of skills, and secure the job she badly needed. Make that *desperately* needed.

But not by being overconfident, Christy sharply reminded herself. She and her subject might have accidentally shaken McFarland, but there was always the chance that Christy could also be given the slip. Not that her young target had manifested any sign yet of being followed. With all the negligent ease that only a teenager is capable of, she continued to wind her way through the tourists sauntering along Decatur Street, never once turning her head.

"Hey, my daughter is tricky," Marty Bornowski had gruffly cautioned them. "You wouldn't be the first tail this kid has managed to ditch. That's why I need the best and can afford to pay for it. So, providing one of you can show me whether she's still meeting this little punk on the sly, you get all the work I can throw your way."

Christy wasn't forgetting the warning as she kept her objective in sight. However, it did seem to her that if his daughter was determined to evade her father's surveillance, she was going about it all wrong. Because there was no way, *absolutely* no way, that Brenda Bornowski could blend with any crowd, not even here in the French Quarter where the eccentric were hardly remarkable.

From her chunky shoes to her black leather miniskirt, and cropped hair, with spiky tufts shaded from orange to silver-blond, Brenda proclaimed her presence. Then went on to confirm it with a lavender-blue mouth and a particularly vivid shade of green fingernail polish. And that didn't take into account her triple-pierced ears, pierced nose, pierced lower lip and conceivably other pierced areas not yet evident to Christy.

Interesting, she thought. It was just possible that Brenda was carrying more metal on her body than the heavy equipment her father used in his asphalt business, which had Christy wondering if she ought to start paving roads herself. Had to be a lot more profitable than private investigating, at which she was barely surviving. And that was on the good days. She had yet to determine if this would be one of them. That depended on Brenda.

Ah, the Jax Brewery! That was where they were going.
She watched Brenda cross the street and head toward the
blocky, multi-storied structure that had been converted
from an old brewery into a trendy shopping mall. Following
at a safe distance, Christy quickly checked the street behind
her before swinging onto the center after her subject. Wonderful! McFarland was still missing in action. Brenda Bornowski was hers!

Brenda started up on the top level and worked her way
down from shop to shop, Christy drifting after her. The girl
seemed in no hurry. She tried on an awesome jacket in an
explosion of colors, which she didn't buy. She chatted on
her cell phone, presumably to a girlfriend and examined a
selection of lingerie so blatantly erotic in nature it would
have made a Bourbon Street stripper blush. And as she
continued to aimlessly wander the mall, chewed her way
through a bag of licorice sticks acquired from a candy stand
near the elevator.

What Brenda didn't do was meet anyone, male or female.
Nor at any point did she indicate the slightest concern over
the possibility that she was being shadowed. Which, even
as careful as Christy was to remain unobserved, should
have been her first clue that trouble was on its way.

The problem wasn't Christy's lack of alertness, however,
but the mounting tension that accompanied it. This was
always a threat to concentration. She couldn't help it. She
had so much riding on this contest that she risked taking
the brim off her baseball cap from tugging on it, a habit
whenever her nerves were under siege.

Come on, Brenda. Make my day.

Things got a bit more interesting when they returned to
the ground floor and her subject took them into a bookstore.

A *bookstore?* It didn't strike Christy as Brenda's kind of scene. Had to be the young clerk and his eager smile. Sure. The two of them lost no time engaging themselves in a leisurely conversation, Brenda leaning against the counter as she flirted with him.

Christy went into action behind the paperbacks. From the shoulder bag that was far too large for her petite frame, but contained all her essentials, including her Glock semi-automatic, she removed a pocket-size tape recorder and dutifully reported the encounter in a low murmur.

"Don't think this can be the, uh, little punk she's meeting. No tattoos. At least none currently visible. I'd say he's harmless…"

By the time Christy replaced the recorder in her bag, her subject had left the counter and was strolling up one aisle and down the next. Christy followed, pretending to examine the titles. When they reached the end of the last aisle, Brenda abruptly swung around and faced her. Except she wasn't Brenda. Same chunky shoes, same black leather miniskirt, even the same hair, but definitely not Brenda Bornowski.

Christy must have clearly registered her shock since a gleeful grin appeared on the girl's face. And that's when she understood two things. The conversation on the cell phone upstairs had been a lot more than just gossip. A cunning Brenda, spotting Daddy's tail, had summoned Best Friend to the mall.

The second thing Christy understood was that she should never have taken her eyes off her subject. Not even for those forty-five seconds with the recorder, because that's all Brenda had needed to pull this switch on her.

Gone!

But maybe not. From the corner of her eye, Christy caught a flash of orange and silver blond through the expanse of glass at the side of the store. Brenda was outside and on her way to the top of the levee!

And I'll be damned if I lose her.

The little stinker was far too important to Christy, which was why she streaked out of the store, out of the building, toward the river.

Above the blare of a Dixieland band playing on the Brewery's restaurant terrace came the hoot of a steamboat whistle. It announced the imminent departure of one of the replicas of the old paddle wheelers that offered hourly excursions along the river. And Christy knew, just *knew,* that Brenda was making for that vessel.

Determined not to let her quarry escape, she struggled, squirmed and squeezed her way through the tourists that jammed the area. Progress, she was making progress. She caught a glimpse of Brenda racing up the stairs ahead of her. And then it all went wrong again.

A bevy of elderly ladies wearing badges that identified them as conventioneers swarmed around her, cutting her off, trapping her. One of them, who had an overbite and a raspy voice, demanded of Christy, "Okay, tell us how we get to the Streetcar Named Desire."

New Orleans always treated its out of town visitors with warmth and courtesy. Or tried to. But, myth or reality, Christy was in no mood for Southern hospitality. "Uh, I don't think it exists anymore, or else these days it's a bus; either way I don't know. Now if you'll just let me by—"

"Oh, not *that* one. I'm talking about the Streetcar Named Desire that's a club. You know, the one featuring exotic male dancers?"

Christy blinked at her. "No, I don't know, so if you'll excuse me—"

The raspy voice sounded injured this time. "But *he* said you'd be certain to know."

"Who?"

"That sweet man up on the levee who pointed you out to us."

That got Christy's attention. "What man? What did he look like?"

"Why, I'm not sure."

"I am," piped one of her eager companions. "He had a dynamite smile and a butt to die for."

Dallas McFarland! Jolted by the knowledge that she hadn't shaken him after all—because she didn't doubt for the space of a heartbeat that it was him, and never mind how he'd managed to catch up with them—Christy beat her way through the ranks of conventioneers.

There was another blast from the boat whistle. Frantic now, she sprinted up the stairs, arrived breathlessly on the broad top of the levee, but was too late. The paddle wheeler, passengers crowding the decks, was drawing away from the landing. Up near the prow stood a smirking Brenda Bornowski, not yet aware of the tall figure of Dallas McFarland stationed at the rail several safe lengths away from her.

The wicked grin that her infuriating rival directed at Christy down on the levee, informed her that not only had she screwed up what should have been an easy surveillance, but that he had somehow managed to snatch another potential client from under her nose. And just to be certain there was no question of that, McFarland stabbed a finger in the direction of a small figure who had arrived at

Christy's side. She looked down to see a boy in a Saints T-shirt extending toward her a rectangle of cream-colored pasteboard.

"Guy on the boat said to give you this."

He delivered the offering and melted away. And while the Dixieland band went on playing under the April sunshine, Christy looked at what he had placed in her hand. It was one of her own business cards printed with Hawke Detective Agency against a logo of a golden hawk. A bold, insolent black *X* had been struck across the face of the card from corner to corner.

Chapter One

It fronted on Royal Street, and it had just about everything
an old building in the historic district is supposed to have—
lacy wrought iron balconies, shutters at the long windows,
gas lanterns. A dream of a place, Christy would think
whenever she returned to it. Ordinarily, that is.

The carriageway that tunneled through the building
framed a view of the courtyard. Whenever Christy emerged
from the dim passage, she would find herself delighted all
over again by the fountain and vines and tubs of flowers.
Ordinarily, that is.

The old converted slave quarters were at the rear of the
courtyard. Christy occupied the small structure, her agency
on the ground floor and her apartment tucked above it on
the second level. It was a cramped arrangement, but, hey,
this was the French Quarter and rents were high. So she
would count herself lucky that the regular tenant, in a hurry
to take a job overseas, had subleased the place to her at an
affordable rent. Ordinarily, that is.

But not this afternoon. This afternoon Christy was oblivi-
ous to all this quaint charm—which she was in danger of
losing anyway, reasonable rent or not—because the only
thing she had time for as she stormed across the courtyard
and through the door marked Hawke Detective Agency,

was the image inside her head of Dallas McFarland sinking slowly in a bottomless pool of quicksand.

The office was silent. But since her assistant, Denise, was bouncing and swaying happily at her desk, Christy assumed that the jazz music she relished was pouring through the radio plug stuck in her ear. Fond though Christy was of the woman, she didn't consider her much of an assistant. However, as Denise was a retired bus driver with an adequate pension, she was willing to work cheap. This was because she had a regrettable longing for P.I. excitement, the kind of action that was in short supply lately at the agency, a situation Denise frequently grumbled about.

The radio plug came out of her ear with a jerk as Christy slammed over to her own desk and slumped in her chair. "Uh-oh. Looks like the Prince of Darkness beat us out of the running again."

"I don't want to talk about it!" Christy snapped. And then, surging to her feet, she proceeded to do exactly that as she prowled from one end of the small office to the other with Denise's gaze solemnly following her. "I didn't like the idea anyway! A controlling father wanting to spy on his daughter just because he thinks her boyfriend is no good and up to mischief! All right, so he's a *rich* father, and we needed the money!"

"Uh-huh."

"But a contest like that? Come on, it's dumb! I shouldn't have agreed to it!"

"Uh-uh."

"I mean, why didn't he just pick one of us, instead of pitting us against each other?"

"Maybe he gets his jollies that way."

"And McFarland—McFarland just loved it!"

"Sure, he's bad."

"Got that right! Arrogant, unprofessional, no principles!"

"And one sexy dude."

Christy rounded on her traitorous assistant. "What is it with you and the women in this town and that man? That—that bottom-feeder!"

"Guess by that you don't want to hear what happened here while I was out to lunch. Guess you're in no mood for it, huh?"

"What?"

"That the answering machine got itself full up with messages, the fax machine is spitting faxes all over the place, the computer is loaded with e-mail and they're all from your mama in Chicago lookin' to hear from you."

"I see. And all this happened while I was gone. Could it be possible, Denise, that you had a longer lunch hour than you planned?"

Denise thought about it. "Could be. Us full-figured gals need to keep up our energy."

"I don't suppose there's anything else on one of those machines. Like maybe someone needing to hire a P.I. with money no object?"

"Nuh-uh."

"In that case…" Christy returned to her desk and reached reluctantly for the phone. She hated having to call her mother, knowing exactly what she was going to hear before she heard it. No way around it.

She dialed home, or what used to be home for her, which was the main office of the Hawke Detective Agency founded by her mother and father back in Chicago.

"Hawke Agency." The familiar voice was cheerful, efficient. It belonged to her mother, Moura Hawke, the energetic doyenne of both the family and its agency, which had branches throughout the country operated by Christy and her four siblings.

"It's me, Ma. What's up?" As if she couldn't guess.

"A celebration, my darling. I hope. Did you win the Bornowski case?"

"Afraid not, Ma." Oh, how humiliating it was for Christy to admit her defeat. She was twenty-six years old and still regarded as the baby who had to be protected from the big bad world, still fighting to be recognized by her family as a P.I. in her own right.

"Oh." The eagerness faded from Moura's voice. "I suppose it went to McFarland?"

"Looks like it."

"I'm sorry." There was a pause, and then Moura's tone became very gentle. Christy realized what was coming. "The thing is, I've been doing all the accounts for the first quarter, and...well, basically, sweetheart, you don't have a quarter."

"I know, Ma. Things have been a little slow."

Slow? They had ground to a halt, and both of them knew it. The other phone in the office rang and Denise answered it. Christy paid no attention. She was too busy being heartbroken. She had done everything but promise her firstborn to convince her parents she was competent enough to open her own branch of the agency, and now she was on the sharp edge of losing it.

Moura had a suggestion. "Eden has a break between cases. What if she came over from Charleston and just sort of helped you to—"

"No!" Christy loved her family, Eden included, but she was damned if she was going to let her sister rush to New Orleans to try to save her agency for her. If she had to go down, she would sink on her own, thank you very much.

"Then what about Devlin?" Moura said, offering Christy's eldest brother.

It was Denise, bless her, who rescued Christy. She had lowered her own phone and, with a lot of head-bobbing and eye-rolling, was signaling Christy to take the call.

"Absolutely not. Look, Ma, I have to go. There's a call for me on the other line. I think it may be a new client. Love to Pop."

"But I haven't told you yet what your father—"

"Later, Ma." She hung up and eagerly whispered to Denise, "Is it a potential client? Do I get a miracle?"

"Now how'd I know if he is or isn't? But you'd better pick up. He sounds serious. *Real* serious."

Christy snatched up her phone, stabbed in the other line, greeted the caller with a brisk, "Christy Hawke speaking," and felt her heart lurch in her breast as the mellow male voice, from a past she thought she had buried, spoke to her earnestly.

"It's me, Christy. Glenn."

"How are you, Glenn?" Now how did she manage to sound so cool when her heart was still misbehaving?

"Not so good, actually." He seemed surprised that she could ask such a thing. "I need to see you, Christy."

"Personal or professional?"

"Professional," he said.

Should she resent him for contacting her like this? No, she decided, she had made peace with that particular episode in her past, forgiven him long ago. "Are you in trouble, Glenn?"

He paused. "Maybe."

"Like to tell me about it?"

"I think we need to get together as soon as possible."

Christy could appreciate his wish for a meeting. Clients rarely wanted to discuss their problems over the phone.

"I'm free right now." Oh, boy, was she free. "Do you know where my office is?"

"Uh, yes, but my lawyer doesn't want anyone knowing I'm worried enough to consult a private investigator, and if I'm seen going into your office…"

A lawyer? Just what kind of trouble were they talking about here?

"Look," he went on, "I'm already downtown. It was…well, necessary for me to be here." Was there an implication in that she was supposed to understand? "So if we could meet somewhere…."

"Name it."

"The Café Du Monde?"

"Give me fifteen minutes and I'll be there."

"See you then. And, Christy?"

"Yes?"

"The circumstances being what they are, I appreciate your willingness to offer your services."

Was that something else she was supposed to understand, she wondered as she put down the phone. She didn't, of course, but in fifteen minutes she hoped to. Denise was ready to pounce as Christy got to her feet.

"We got us a client?"

"I think so."

Denise grunted her satisfaction. "Maybe finally get some action around here. Where you goin'?"

"Upstairs. I need to change before I meet him."

"Must be some real important dude. Must be somebody you got to impress."

"Never mind."

Drat the woman and those shrewd jet eyes of hers, Christy thought as she tripped up the narrow stairway to her tiny apartment overhead. It was just like Denise to practically accuse her of wanting to look as attractive as possible when Glenn saw her again after all these years. All right, that's just what she wanted to do and she was a pathetic fool for caring. So what?

So what if Glenn Hollister had a wife now and was a father, as well, though she'd heard his marriage was foundering? And so what if he'd dumped Christy for the elegant Laura Claiborne, an episode which had left Christy's heart grievously scarred? Yeah, so what?

She didn't have an answer for that reckless *so what* until, about to burrow into the battered old armoire for an outfit guaranteed to please, she caught her image in the long mirror on the door. There was Christy Hawke in long shorts and running shoes, her honey-colored hair crammed under a Cubs baseball cap. Okay, so that much of Chicago was still a part of her. But, hey, it wasn't her fault. If New Orleans ever got itself a team, she was willing to switch her loyalty.

The brim of the cap shaded a piquant face and a pair of aquamarine eyes that defiantly said, "Here I am. This is what you get." So why was she getting ready to turn herself into some kind of baby doll? Forget it. Whatever dumb torch she might once have carried for Glenn Hollister, he would have to take her as she was.

And so much for all those *so what's,* she concluded as she firmly closed the door of the armoire, grabbed her bag and headed for the stairs.

THE CAFE DU MONDE was located on the river in the old French Market, which had once supplied the city with fresh fruits and vegetables. These days, the long colonnaded structure contained shops, most of them serving the tourist trade. The place was close enough to Christy's office to permit her to reach it on foot, but just far enough away to put her curiosity about Glenn Hollister into overdrive as she walked there.

That curiosity was at maximum speed by the time she arrived and stood searching the outdoor tables. They were crowded with the usual tourists hunched over beignets and café au lait. Christy was still looking for Glenn when he appeared suddenly at her side.

"I don't deserve this," he said out of nowhere in that kind voice that had always been a pleasure to hear. "Not after the way I let you go."

She turned to face him and realized immediately that she had probably made a big mistake. He was slender, fair-haired and had a face that could still soften her heart. Oh, yeah, not just probably but *definitely* a mistake for her to be here. On the other hand, with the wolf at her door....

The moment deserved something brilliant, witty, but all she had to offer was an inane, "Helping people is what I do, Glenn. Uh, where can we—"

"I have a table over here."

He conducted her to a shady corner and tried to seat her so that she faced the view. But since that view was of the nearby Jax Brewery, the scene of her recent defeat, Christy preferred to take a chair looking inward.

When Glenn had settled across from her, and they had ordered coffee neither of them wanted, Christy treated herself to a second examination of the man who had once meant—well, if not everything to her, pretty close to it. And she decided all over again that, yeah, he still looked good. He also looked like hell, which was something she'd missed the first time around. There was a grimness in the little smile he directed at her, a haunted expression in his eyes.

"The circumstances being what they are," she said,

leaning toward him. "That was what you said on the phone. Does that have an explanation, Glenn?"

His gentle gray eyes widened in disbelief. "You don't know? How is that possible when it must be all over the news?"

She'd been so busy fighting Dallas McFarland for possession of Brenda Bornowski that she hadn't watched a newscast or read a newspaper since early yesterday. And, of course, Denise couldn't have told her anything. All Denise ever listened to was her beloved jazz. "Sorry," she apologized. "I've been out of touch. Just how bad is it, Glenn?"

"Laura," he said, referring to his wife. "She's dead, Christy. And I'm about to be charged with her murder. That's how bad it is."

Beneath her shock, Christy felt a rush of affectionate sympathy for him. But it was one of those "What can I say? What *do* I say?" moments. The waiter helped her. He arrived to serve their coffee, giving her a few seconds to marshal her thoughts.

By the time he retreated, she'd found her tongue.

"Glenn, I'm so sorry. How awful for you. Your little girl—"

"Yes, this is going to be very hard on Daisy. She knows her mother is gone, but she's too young for the loss to really mean anything yet."

Christy faced a tough question, but it had to be asked. "Glenn, did you—" She couldn't bring herself to say it, but she didn't have to. He understood.

"No, I didn't kill her, Christy. And the cops haven't accused me of her murder. *Yet.*"

"But they suspect you of being involved, huh?"

"Oh, yeah, I know they do. I could feel it and my lawyer, who was with me when they asked all their questions, agrees that I may be this far from being arrested.'' He held up thumb and forefinger a scant inch apart. ''That's where we were before I called you, with the police.''

''What makes you their chief suspect?''

''I guess it's no secret our marriage was in trouble, that we'd been fighting a lot lately, mostly about money. And also—'' He hesitated, reluctant to impart the rest.

''I have to know everything, Glenn.''

''Yes. Well, Laura's best friend talked to the police. She told them she'd been worried about Laura, that she'd been acting frightened about something. When she'd asked her about it, Laura said it was me, that she was scared of me, and another friend backed up this story. Which is crazy. You know me, Christy. You know I'd never threaten anyone, least of all hurt them. But the police—''

''No, it doesn't look so good, does it? But come on, Glenn—''

He cut her off with a swift, ''I know what you're going to say, that the cops are thorough, that they'll look at every angle before they bring a charge. But how can I trust them to do that if they're already convinced they have Laura's killer, that all they have to do now is collect enough evidence against me?''

''Meaning,'' she said slowly, ''you want me to try to prove your innocence.''

''Yes. Will you?''

She appreciated his faith in her. But a case like this, aside from the obvious problems, presented another slight difficulty. The police did not appreciate P.I.s investigating their crimes. She'd have to be careful about that.

Have to? Whoa, when had she said *yes?* She hadn't. But *no* didn't look like much of an option, not with those lost gray eyes pleading with her across the table. Not with the memory of her mother telling her that her earnings this past quarter totaled to a nice round zero.

''All right, you'd better tell me the rest.''

He did and within ten minutes Christy had the essentials. How Laura, not for the first time, hadn't come home last night. How her body, skull split open, had been found early this morning in the old Claiborne cemetery out along the river road.

No, Glenn didn't know why Laura had this interest in what had once been her family's plantation, a property now reduced to a house in ruins on a worthless scrap of wilderness. But she'd been haunting the place lately. That's why he'd driven out there late yesterday afternoon, expecting to find her. He hadn't, but two witnesses reported seeing him speeding away from the scene in a state of agitation. Why wouldn't he be agitated, when his marriage had become as rotten as that crumbling house?

That was a particularly interesting portion of his story for Christy. On a personal level, anyway. Glenn was a teacher. That's how Christy had met him. She'd been attending the University of New Orleans, training for a career in education. Her semester of student teaching had been spent in his classroom where she had learned, after coping with a herd of fiendish sixth graders, that education was definitely not in her future but that Glenn Hollister could be. Maybe. Hopefully.

But before their relationship had a chance to develop into something permanent, Laura Claiborne had come back into Glenn's life. *The* Laura who had walked out on their affair several weeks earlier, but had now decided that Glenn was the man for her. And how could Glenn resist a woman so lovely, so enticing and so very pregnant with his baby?

End of episode. And, as it turned out a moment later, end of their meeting at the Café du Monde. There was a lot more information Christy needed from Glenn, but before he could supply it, his cell phone rang.

After speaking briefly to the caller, he pushed back from the table. "Sorry, Christy, but I have to leave. That was Monica's housekeeper." Monica being Laura's sister, Christy remembered. "Monica is expecting me to join her. There are arrangements we have to make."

The funeral, Christy guessed. She and Glenn agreed to meet again in the morning, then he paid the check and left.

Now what? But the answer should have been obvious to Christy, and it was. She finally had a job—thank God she had a job!—and since there were still several balmy hours of daylight left, why not begin performing it? She knew by then where she wanted to go and what she wanted to see.

Coming purposefully to her feet, she turned her back on the table and hurried away. Neither of them had touched their coffees.

THIRTY MINUTES LATER, having collected her vintage Ford Escort from where she kept it parked in an alley behind her office, Christy had crossed the Mississippi to the west bank and headed up the river road.

She knew how to get to where she was going. Some memories had a way of sticking with you, especially the painful ones. Wallowing in her misery after Glenn had parted from her five years ago, she had driven out to the Claiborne plantation. Why? Who knew. Maybe because she had expected to discover in its antebellum splendor, some satisfactory explanation for why Glenn had been so dazzled by Laura Claiborne. All she had found was a lost glory.

And how about today? What did she hope to learn by visiting the scene of Laura's murder? Probably nothing that the police hadn't already found and claimed. But you never knew what might turn up. It was a beginning, anyway.

Five years hadn't helped the property, other than to leave no doubt it had deteriorated beyond all hope of rescue. Christy saw that as she turned off the river road below the levee and bumped along the rutted lane. The Claibornes had abandoned the plantation in the hard times after the Civil War, selling off pieces of the land in the decades that followed. Now all that remained in the weed-choked wilderness were the family cemetery and the crumbling house surrounded by an industrial farm with its ugly storage tanks. So much for the romance of the Old South.

The grove of live oaks shading the place, and where she parked her car, was still magnificent, however. She admired its canopies of new green as she made her way to the cemetery. Better start there, she thought, even though she wasn't fond of cemeteries.

Yellow police tape marking the crime scene had been stretched along the wrought iron fence that enclosed the plot. The tape belonged to the New Orleans homicide division. Glenn had told her, because of its considerable facilities, it had been requested by the tiny local force to handle the case. Ignoring the tape's existence, Christy entered the cemetery and wandered among the whitewashed tombs of Claiborne ancestors. Her gaze combed the ground, as if she expected to spy a startling clue overlooked by the police. There wasn't one, unless you counted a couple of chicken feathers blown up against the iron fence. She didn't.

There probably hadn't been much for the police to collect either. She remembered it had rained heavily the night Laura's body had lain here and that would have obliterated evidence. Her gaze drifted toward the house. She considered the place.

Funny thing about gut-level instincts; when they were reliable, they could be so useful. Christy had those instincts, the kind that served a P.I. very well. Trouble was, they needed to be accompanied by the skills that only came from experience. That, unfortunately, she lacked, which meant her instincts weren't always dependable. At the moment, however, they were urging her to investigate the house. It was just possible it might produce something other than its ghosts.

Obeying her instincts, Christy turned her steps in the direction of the mansion. It really was a pathetic sight. The soaring brick columns that embraced the house on all sides were being eaten away by time and weather. Why had Laura repeatedly been drawn here?

The front door was gone. Boards had been nailed across the gap, but the widest of them had dropped, leaving a yawning hole. Christy didn't hesitate. Popping through the opening, she was inside the house. Or what was left of it.

Resurrection. That's what the plantation was called, named after the resurrection fern so common in southern Louisiana. But as Christy passed from room to room, she knew that this house would never be resurrected. It was a gray shell, stripped of everything but the dust bunnies.

Gone were the marble fireplaces, the paneling and carved moldings, the chandeliers, the floor tiles and silver locks. Vandals? If so, they had made off with what must have been some pretty valuable treasures.

Even the staircase was missing and if the outline of it in the peeling plaster on the wall was any indication, it had been a grand affair. But at the back of the house she located a plain service stairway that was still intact. Hey, why not check it all out? Which is why Christy found herself climbing the flight to the second floor where things got a bit more interesting. Or uncomfortable, depending on your point of view.

From behind a door that stood slightly ajar came a rustling sound. Spooks? Mice? Or maybe she was just imagining the noise. Either way, she took the precaution of removing the Glock from her shoulder bag. Of course, getting out of here fast would probably have been the smarter thing to do, but if you were a private investigator…well, you were supposed to investigate.

Semiautomatic firmly in hand, she spread the door wide. Behind it was another narrow flight of stairs leading to the attic. Saying a little prayer, she crept up the stairway, emerging at the top in the hollow vastness of the attic.

She could have sworn those instincts had been trying to tell her something. But, of course, they couldn't have been because there was nothing to find. No spooks. No wild-eyed lunatic leaping out at her. Not even a scurrying mouse. And she could tell because there was plenty of light. There was a reason for that. The neglected roof had opened up in one corner.

Nor had the damage stopped there, as she discovered when she went to look. The invasive rain had rotted the floorboards under the gaping roof both here and on the floor below, collapsing ceilings and leaving a cavity that dropped from the attic all the way to the first floor. A meteorite couldn't have fashioned a more perfect shaft.

There was an object above the deep well hanging from a rusted nail on one of the remaining roof rafters. It looked like a small bunch of dried plant material. Herbs of some kind? Leaning forward, Christy reached for it. That's when the rustling she had heard earlier revealed itself without warning in an explosion of sound and motion.

Suddenly, alarmingly, she came under attack. They swooped down at her, beat at her neck and shoulders, flew at her face. It was like a scene out of that old Hitchcock thriller, *The Birds*. Except these critters, a colony of swallows nesting up in the shadowy rafters behind her, meant her no harm. They were merely frightened and in a hurry to escape.

Intentional or not, however, by the time the last of them had streamed away through the opening in the roof, they had cost Christy her Glock and her shoulder bag. Her balance as well. She lost that just as her fingers snagged the dried plants, which immediately crumbled to flakes.

The next thing she knew, she was down in the hole itself where the flakes had drifted, hanging by her hands from an exposed pipe once buried under the missing floor. It must have been a gas line that had supplied a chandelier suspended from a second-floor ceiling, though explanations hardly mattered when her precarious handhold was the only thing keeping her from a broken neck.

It was a damn silly situation to get caught in, not to mention absolutely terrifying. The pipe seemed solid enough. Problem was, as hard as she tried, grunting, straining, swinging, she couldn't manage to pull herself up out of that shaft.

This was serious. Her arms were aching by now, her fingers numb. How much longer could she cling to this pipe before her hands began to slip, before she plunged— How far was it? She made the mistake of glancing down and was immediately so giddy that she closed her eyes. That's why she didn't see the long arm that reached down from over her head, didn't know it was there until a strong hand clamped around her wrist.

Eyes flying open, she issued a little yelp of surprise. The hand tugged, urging her to release her grip on the pipe. No choice but to trust him. She did and was hauled up with such force that when her feet touched firm floor again, they failed to support her.

She staggered, slamming against a hard wall which turned out to be a broad-shouldered body. The body had a pair of arms that caught and steadied her in a comforting embrace. At least it was comforting until, dragging her head back, she looked up and discovered that the pair of lady-killer eyes colliding with hers belonged to the Prince of Darkness.

"You have *got* to stop falling for me like this," he said.

Chapter Two

It was disgusting that, like half the female population in New Orleans, she should suddenly find herself susceptible to this man. Of course, there was a very good explanation. This was only a momentary reaction because she'd been so shaken by her predicament. Otherwise, she wouldn't be experiencing all these treacherous sensations. This dizzy breathlessness as the pair of brash green eyes, that didn't miss a thing, continued to hold her gaze. This sudden heat in her insides as she stared up at the bold face under its thatch of dark hair. And this weakness in her limbs as the powerful arms continued to pin her against his chest.

Okay, so the guy had a blatant sex appeal in a lean body that scraped six feet and moved with a sensual, confident gait. She'd give him that, whatever her earlier denials.

But Dallas McFarland? Come on, he was her rival, her sworn enemy. And nature was playing a mean trick on her, that's all, one Christy planned to correct just as soon as she recovered her wind.

"Because," he continued in a deliberately seductive voice, "if you go around dropping into holes just to get my attention, things are bound to happen. Really *dangerous things.*" And up came that grin again on his wide mouth, the sinful, mocking one.

"I suppose," she said, finding air at last, "there's an explanation for why you're not on a boat with Brenda Bornowski. Why you happen to be— Hey, let me go."

"That any way to express your appreciation to the man who just saved your shapely little fanny from getting flattened?"

"I'm forever grateful," she said sarcastically, and then amended it with a grudging, "Okay, I am grateful. Now let me go."

He released her and Christy moved back out of his reach. Better. Or it would be if those green eyes would stop trying to get intimate with her. "So what *did* you do with Brenda?"

"Turned her over to one of my operatives when the boat made its first stop. Routine stuff at that point," he boasted. "She did meet the punk onboard, by the way. I imagine Daddy will be subjecting her to a harsh punishment when he gets my report. Probably deprive her of her credit cards for at least a month."

He sounded so smug about it, so carelessly confident that Christy wanted to smack him. She had gone and busted her backside, that same backside he had just so familiarly referred to, to win the Bornowski case, and he'd reached out with ease and plucked it from her grasp. It was an outcome that still rankled.

McFarland had a pair of black eyebrows, thick ones that seemed to express his moods. Right now they were lifted in amusement. "Yeah, I know," he said, reading her thoughts, "you're wondering how I managed to catch up with little Brenda when you thought you'd left me in the dust back on Canal. It's called being resourceful—like slipping a couple of twenties to the subject's best friend beforehand to let you know by cell phone where she's planning to wind up. Hey, don't scowl at me like that. All's fair in love and private investigation."

"Which still doesn't explain what you're doing out here."

"Oh, didn't I say?" He leaned negligently against one of the attic's supporting posts. "See, my operative wasn't alone. He'd brought Monica Claiborne with him to the landing. She wanted to speak with me before she went on to meet her brother-in-law."

Oh, no, Christy thought with a sinking heart, knowing what was coming.

"Seems Monica isn't satisfied with what the cops are doing to find her sister's killer. And since, unlike her brother-in-law, she can afford to hire the best—that's me and my agency—she asked me to look into it."

It was worse than Christy imagined, because Monica must have told McFarland that Glenn meant to hire her for the same purpose.

He smiled that odious smile again. "News travels fast, huh? Hey, take it easy. Way you're reeling, you'll be sliding into that hole again."

Christy couldn't stand it. She *positively* could not stand it. This case was vital to her, probably her last chance to survive as a P.I. in her own right, and now here was Dallas McFarland again threatening to mess it up for her. Well, not if she could help it.

Recovering her gun and her bag from the floor, clutching them against her breasts, she fired off a livid, "I can't stop you from working for Monica Claiborne, but you keep away from me and my client or I'll report you to the licensing board for unethical practices! I swear I will!"

"Uh, actually, I was sort of thinking—"

"Don't!"

Pushing past him, she fled down the two flights of stairs

to the ground floor. McFarland was right behind her, as persistent as a dog barking up a tree. And equally annoying.

"I don't know what you're so mad about. If I hadn't come out here, just like you did, to take a look at the scene of Laura Hollister's death, where would you be? Still hanging from that gas pipe, right?"

Christy rushed on, not answering him.

"It's the truth, isn't it? So the least you could do—" He followed her through the gap in the boards and out into the yard. "—the least you could do is listen to me."

Ignoring him, she headed for her car under the oaks. He was still nipping at her heels.

"Look, grits, slow down long enough to hear me—"

This time she stopped, rounding on him so swiftly he almost collided with her. "What did you just call me?"

He backed up a safe distance away from her, his hands raised in mock innocence. "Hey, it's a compliment. Grits is one of my favorite foods. Really."

"Is it? Well, that's one Southern dish I can do without."

"You don't know what you're missing. With a little honey on top, it's downright irresistible." There went those eyebrows again, registering something far too suggestive.

"I'll bet."

Swinging away from him, she went on to her car. It was no longer alone under the oaks. McFarland's car was parked beside it. And wouldn't you know it would be a sleek, cream-colored convertible just reeking of success, making her own old red Escort look all the more inadequate by comparison.

Well, so what? It was dependable enough to take her out of here and away from McFarland, providing she could find the keys. Naturally, she couldn't. She had to stand there digging through all the junk in her bag while McFarland caught up with her. Trapped. Forced to listen to him as he leaned his rangy, tempting frame against the side of her car.

"Got a proposition for you, grits. Oh, you're gonna love it."

He spoke in a lazy, deep-voiced drawl, the country-boy variety. She suspected it wasn't altogether genuine and wondered how many women had been dumb enough to fall for it.

"What I was thinking," he went on, "is that you and I could work together on this case."

Now that took her attention away from her frantic search for the car keys. Boy, did it ever! She lifted her head and stared at him, not believing what she was hearing. Somebody here had just lost his mind, and she didn't think it was her.

"I can see by the way that sweet little nose of yours is twitching that you're just a tad upset by the notion. But think about it. Even if we do have separate clients, we're after the same thing, aren't we? The truth behind Laura Hollister's murder. So why not join forces and share our efforts? Make sense?"

"About as much sense as a cottonmouth getting cozy with a bunny rabbit." As she went on staring at him, Christy realized there was something intense behind this casual offer of his. "You're serious, aren't you?"

"Well, sure."

"It's never going to happen, McFarland. And why would an exalted P.I. like you, want it to happen when you know how I feel about you? Which, in case you've been wondering, isn't good. Besides—and correct me if I'm wrong—your opinion of me and my agency is—" She broke off with another sudden realization. "Oh, I get it. I'm a direct pipeline to the chief suspect. You want easy access to any privileged information my client might share with me. And that's about as underhanded as slipping a pair of twenties to Brenda Bornowski's best friend.''

"Why, when I'd be sharing anything Monica Claiborne knows with you?''

"I'll collect my own information, thank you. And move aside so I can get out of here." She had found her car keys, and now all she wanted was to put Dallas McFarland behind her. *Far* behind her.

"Sure you won't reconsider?" He stepped away from the Escort. "It would be an opportunity for you to work with an experienced P.I. Just think of how much you could learn."

There was one thing she had to say about this man, Christy thought, opening her car door and sliding in behind the wheel. He didn't lack ego or tenacity. As she fumbled with her seat belt, he poked his head through the open window of the driver's door.

"Okay, so you're going to solve this murder all on your own. But did you ever stop to think, grits, that the cops might be right and that Glenn Hollister did kill his wife?''

She turned the key in the ignition, started the car, and resisted the temptation to raise the window with his head in it. "Glenn is a decent, caring man, incapable of murder, and I'm going to prove that!''

"We're sensitive about ol' Glenn, are we? Interesting.''

Christy angrily tugged at the brim of her baseball cap and shoved the gear stick into Drive. Dallas McFarland leapt back from the window just in time to save himself from being decapitated as she sped away from the oak grove.

On the first half of the drive back to New Orleans, Christy fumed. On the second half she cooled down and thought about McFarland's reasons for wanting to work with her. And by the time she reached the city, she decided there was something wrong with those reasons. They weren't good enough. So what was he really after?

When she got back to the office and told Denise all about it, the woman agreed that McFarland's proposal didn't make sense. "Yeah, what's a hotshot P.I. like him need with you?"

"Thank you, Denise."

"Well, sure is funny."

On the other hand, Christy decided, they were probably assigning dark motives where none existed. And what did it matter, anyway, since she wouldn't be working with McFarland? No sir, she worked alone and starting tomorrow she was going to be much too busy helping Glenn to worry about anyone else.

However, at this moment, it was a little hard to concentrate on Glenn and her feelings for him with the memory of Dallas McFarland's hot eyes haunting her. And that was another thing. How could green eyes be hot? She didn't know, but *his* were.

THE OFFICE SUITE of the McFarland Detective Agency was located in a high-rise overlooking the Mississippi. Dallas's private office, as classy as his cream-colored convertible, had floor-to-ceiling windows that commanded a sweeping view of the New Orleans harbor, one of the busiest in the country with its barges, tugs and freighters.

At this moment, with a flaming sunset gilding the river and its traffic, the scene was particularly impressive. Dallas paid no attention to it. Tilted back in his comfortable chair, he occupied himself with something far more absorbing. His yo-yo.

Dallas was very good with the instrument, able to execute intricate loops that had been the envy of every kid on his block. Hell, he could make the thing actually sing when he tried. Right now, though, he was simply sending it out and back at a horizontal angle, an activity that permitted him to think. Unfortunately, whenever his frustration was considerable and he shot the yo-yo too far, it left marks in the designer wall covering.

That covering was taking a real beating this evening. The subject of his thoughts was Christy Hawke. Or, to be more accurate, how Christy Hawke had felt when she'd been plastered against him up there in that attic this afternoon.

Good. That's how she'd felt. Damn good, with those luscious little breasts of hers squeezed against his chest, that honey-blond hair all fragrant under his nose. The crazy thing was, he'd never thought of her before as anything but a small nuisance in a baseball cap and running shoes. Never found her remotely alluring. But up there in that attic, he'd just about lost all self-control.

So how smart was it that he wanted to hook up with her, place himself in a situation where he would be close to her on a daily basis? Not smart at all. He didn't need that kind of distraction.

The yo-yo in his hand flew out and back, out and back.

On the other hand, he did need what she was in a position to offer him. Needed it badly. Yeah, no choice about it. So all right, he would just have to resist temptation while he worked with her. He could do that. He could also live with the guilt of what amounted to using her. Couldn't he? Hell, he had to. There was no way he could reveal this secret that was eating him up inside.

The yo-yo bounced off the wall. He refused to see that as a sign of any dangerous emotion. But, just as a precaution, he rewound it and laid it aside.

Of course, she had no intention of working with him. None whatever. But Dallas had the solution to that. Not that it was something he wanted to do. She'd call him conniving, blow that baseball cap right off the top of her head. No choice about it.

Swinging around in his chair, he reached for the telephone on his desk.

CHRISTY WAS grabbing a quick breakfast in her apartment the next morning when Denise hollered to her from the office below.

"Girlfriend, you up there?"

Bowl of corn flakes in hand, she went to the top of the stairs. "I'm here. What is it?"

Denise stood at the bottom of the flight, hands planted on her ample hips. "You got you a surprise waiting down here. Want me to send it on up, or are you comin' down?"

"A delivery?"

"Uh, sorta."

"I'll be right down."

What now? she wondered, not certain that she cared for the ambiguous tone in Denise's voice. Spooning up the last mouthful of corn flakes, she dumped the bowl in the sink, snatched up her bag and flew down the stairs. As it turned out, straight into the outstretched arms of Denise's surprise.

"Pop!"

Christy was the only member of her family who shared her father's diminutive height. But what Casey Hawke lacked in size, he made up for in strength. She was reminded of that when he folded her in a hug that crushed her shoulder bag into her ribs.

When she was finally released, he demanded, "How are you, baby?" And before she could answer him, he turned to Denise. "How is she, Denise?"

"Got herself a case."

"Yeah, I heard about that."

How had he heard? What was he doing here? "Pop, what are you doing here?"

"On my way to help Roark with a client," he said, referring to one of Christy's brothers. "Didn't your mother mention that when you called?"

Had she? Christy didn't think so, but she kind of remembered Moura starting to tell her something about her father when she had to hang up on her. "Pop, this isn't San Antonio."

"Right, but I couldn't get a direct flight."

"So you're just here between planes?"

"That's all."

"Uh-oh," Denise mumbled ominously.

Christy didn't think she trusted her father's explanation either. "Have you had breakfast?"

"On the flight down. I could stand to stretch my legs though, before I grab a cab back to the airport."

He wanted to talk. He could have done that over the phone. This was beginning to sound more serious by the moment. "Let's go, Pop."

They left the office and crossed the courtyard, passing in the carriageway the side window of St. Leger's Antiques. Her friend, Alistair St. Leger, was arranging a display of snuff boxes and waved to her. Out on the street, carriages conducted tourists through the Quarter, and around Jackson Square, where Christy and her father ended up strolling, street artists set up their wares for the day. It was Christy's adopted city and she loved it all, even its seedier aspects, but her father's presence had her fearing she might be forced to say goodbye to it.

"All right, Pop, let's have it."

He wasn't gentle with her about it. Where business was concerned, he never was. "Your lease on the office comes up for renewal in ten days. We're not going to pick it up, Christy. The agency can't afford to carry you anymore.''

She stopped and turned her head to look at him. He had dark hair, liberally streaked with gray and a pair of blue eyes that at the moment were uncompromising. Beloved daughter or not, he was shutting her down. He was the senior member of the Hawke Detective Agency, who got tough whenever it was necessary. It was how Hawke's had been able to survive and prosper all these years.

Christy understood that even while she hated it.

''I'm sorry, baby. Maybe you just weren't meant to be a P.I. Anyway, it isn't as though you don't have a career waiting for you.''

Teaching. He meant she could come back home and go into the classroom. Never. Not without a fight. ''Pop, I have a case. Let me solve it. Let me prove to you that I am a good P.I.''

She started to tell him about it, but he held up his hand. ''I know all about Glenn Hollister and what you're trying to do for him. I heard it last night.''

Christy had another bad feeling. *Very* bad. ''How? Who?''

''Our competitor, Dallas McFarland, phoned me.''

''Why, that sneaky, low-down excuse for a—''

''Calm down, baby, and hear me out. McFarland had a proposition. Yes, I know. He already offered it to you and you turned it down. Well, I don't share your biases about the man. I listened to it and in the end, your mother and I decided it made good sense. McFarland is a seasoned investigator and it's going to take that kind of successful track record to save Glenn Hollister.''

''Oh, Pop,'' she pleaded, ''don't say it. *Please* don't say it.''

But he did. ''Look, your mother and I agree that you

have the kind of talent necessary to be a P.I. What you don't have is the know-how that comes either from experience or learning, and since you weren't willing to leave New Orleans to come home to us for that training— Anyway, here's the deal. You join forces with McFarland, who'll be kind of a mentor to you on this case and if before the ten days are up, the two of you, working together, have cracked the thing…well, then maybe Hawke's will be interested, after all, in picking up that lease for you."

"But that's blackmail!" Dallas McFarland's rotten blackmail. And why, *why* was he going to these extreme lengths to get her?

"Yes, baby, it kind of is. But you need a success and McFarland has what it takes to help you get it. Besides…"

A sly smile had appeared at the corners of her father's mouth. "What?" she demanded.

"You might get close enough to learn just how he's managed to steal all those clients from us."

Yes, she thought, there was that.

"What do you say, baby?"

Christy drew a slow, deep breath meant to steady herself. But with that breath came all the tantalizing aromas of New Orleans—the tang of the nearby river, the perfume of its flowers, the old, mossy smells of its damp earth, the odors of its famous cooking. They were all blended together on the warm, lazy air, and they made her ache inside, as did the sight of St. Louis Cathedral rising so majestically from the edge of the square where they stood. She couldn't bear to surrender them.

"All right, Pop, I accept your ultimatum. It stinks, but I accept it."

The crinkles deepened at the corners of Casey's eyes. "Don't think of it as an ultimatum, baby. Think of it as a challenge."

After putting her father in a cab, she went back to her office. "Call McFarland," she instructed Denise. "Tell him I'll meet him on the street outside the Claiborne and Hollister houses. He can talk to Monica while I interview Glenn. One hour and if he isn't there the deal is off."

Denise had one of her all-knowing looks. "Don't say it," Christy warned her. "Not one word."

Denise didn't, but it didn't help. The idea of Dallas McFarland as her salvation was infuriating.

THE TWO HOMES were situated side by side in the heart of the Garden District. Built by some eccentric Claiborne ancestor after the family had recovered its fortunes, they were something of a curiosity. Not just because they were identical, which they were, in nearly every respect, but because of their architecture. They were in the style known as Steamboat Gothic.

And you didn't have to wonder what that meant, Christy thought. Their galleries, embellished with elaborate scrollwork, were more like the decks of floating palaces than porches, while the cupolas crowning their roofs resembled wheelhouses.

Christy never passed them without slowing down for a look, partly because she'd known that Glenn and his wife occupied one of the houses, and that Laura's sister lived in the other. This morning, however, her attention was directed elsewhere.

He was already there, his cream-colored convertible parked at the curb in the shade of a glossy-leafed magnolia. If he was conscious of her arrival when she pulled up behind his vehicle, he was much too occupied to be interested in it. He'd left his car and was standing at the low wrought iron fence that framed both properties. There was an odd intensity in his manner, in the way he was so completely absorbed with the Hollister house, his eyes searching the windows.

What was he looking for? Christy wondered. What did he expect to see? And what was she doing sitting here at the wheel of her Escort watching him?

But the answer to that one was obvious, much as she hated to acknowledge it. She was admiring him, that's what she was blatantly doing. And, worse luck, there was a lot to admire.

McFarland's long, lean figure was clad in a trim, light gray business suit that accentuated the breadth of his shoulders. And wouldn't you know, she'd be dressed in her regulation knee-length shorts and baseball cap. Oh, they were going to make quite a team all right, a real contrast in styles.

As a concession to the warmth of the morning, however, he did have the jacket off and slung over one shoulder, the knot of his tie loosened, the sleeves of his deep blue shirt turned back over a pair of strongly corded forearms. Unfortunately, the effect wasn't as casual as it was downright sexy. Drat. Working with this guy was going to be even harder than she'd figured.

Tugging grimly at the brim of her cap, Christy left her car and joined him at the fence. He turned his head, favoring her with one of his cocky grins.

"So, grits, what's your take on your new partner?"

So he *had* been aware that she was checking him out. Great. "We are *not* partners," she informed him brusquely. "Not even remotely are we partners. This is a temporary arrangement, McFarland, and when it's ended—which can't be soon enough for me—we go our separate ways."

"Right. Anything else?"

"Oh, yeah. Rules."

One of those dark, aggressive eyebrows lifted. "Rules?"

"Rules. And either you agree to them, or I walk."

"Listening."

Christy used the spikes on the top of the iron fence to count them off. "First, we split down the middle all fees and expenses. I don't care what Monica Claiborne is paying you, it gets equally divided between us. Second, we share all information. No holding back and if I find out you have any hidden agendas—"

"Such as?"

"Just don't have them." She jabbed at the next spike. "Third, and this is very important, we stick to business. *All* business. No more touchy-feely stuff like up in that attic."

"Ow, that's a sharp one, grits. Painful."

He didn't know how painful. Those lethal green eyes of his were reminding her, all over again, of that brief, breathless intimacy they'd shared. Made it tough to concentrate on delivering her rules.

"And that's another thing. I want you to stop calling me grits."

"Well, now, see, that one might be a little difficult. It's kind of gotten inside my head."

"Then get it out."

"Does it qualify as a spike?" Her expression must have warned him that her aggravation was at a dangerous level, because he added a hasty, "I'll try. Is that all?"

"For now."

"Then shall we go to work?"

She watched him roll down his sleeves, button them, tighten his tie, slip into his jacket. And she wondered why she should be so annoyed that he was making himself gorgeous for Monica Claiborne?

THEY MET AGAIN by their parked cars to share the information they had gathered in their separate interviews.

"This could take a while," Dallas said. "We might as well sit while we talk. Your car or mine?"

Christy wasn't certain that she cared to get comfortable with him in either car. She preferred a neutral ground for their exchange. Where? The clang of an approaching trolley on nearby St. Charles Avenue provided the answer.

"How do you feel about streetcars?"

"Streetcars are good."

"Then let's ride one."

They reached the corner in time to board the old, olive-green car that served one of the last lines of its kind. Paying their fares, they squeezed into a slatted seat.

Dallas barely gave her a chance to get settled before he wanted to know, "And how is ol' Glenn holding up?"

The sarcasm in his tone whenever he referred to Glenn irritated her. He obviously considered him capable of his wife's murder, which was not exactly the best way to represent your client. All right, so strictly speaking Glenn was *her* client, but still…

"He's just dandy. Or would be, if he didn't have a murder charge staring him in the face."

"There's a little girl, isn't there? She okay?"

"I didn't see Daisy, but I imagine someone is taking good care of her."

Dallas fell silent as the trolley rumbled on through the Garden District with its classic mansions. His face was impassive and she wondered what he was thinking. Before she could ask, he had another question for her.

"And Hollister has no idea who might have wanted his wife dead?"

"Not a clue."

"What about Laura's car? It must have been parked somewhere near the old plantation house. If Glenn followed her out to Resurrection, why didn't he see it, know that she must still be there? Did you ask him about that?''

"Of course I asked him. He said it was there, that the police had found it parked out of sight behind this tangle of shrubbery. But since Glenn had no reason to suppose she might have hidden it or to check out the cemetery either, he assumed she wasn't there, after all, and he left.''

"In an agitated state. Why, if he never saw her?''

"He was upset about their marriage,'' Christy explained. "He'd been upset for some time. He'd counted on having it out with her about their problems and was angry that she wasn't available.''

"Seems a funny thing to do, going out there like that on the chance she'd be there. Why not wait until she got home to talk to her about it?''

"It was one of those spur of the moment things. An I've-had-it-and-I'm-going-to-settle-it-right-now emotion. We've all had them.''

"Yeah, but a couple of hikers didn't see us tearing away from the scene and a teenager out hunting rabbits the next morning didn't find our wife with her head bashed in.'' Aware of Christy glaring at him, Dallas offered a quick, "Hey, I'm just playing devil's advocate here, trying to look at all the angles. I'm not condemning the guy. I know that his marriage was in trouble. Monica told me that.''

"I hope she also told you that her sister had gotten very strange these past few months. Glenn said Laura had become withdrawn and wouldn't talk about it. Something was going on with her and I'm thinking it could have been another man, that she was meeting him at Resurrection, which would explain why she was out there so much and didn't come home some nights.''

"That would be a handy solution. Laura cheating on ol' Glenn and her secret lover doing her in.'' Dallas shook his head. "Except it doesn't work. And not because Laura Hollister wasn't the type to have an affair. She just wouldn't have been troubled about it."

"How do you know what type she was? Oh, Monica, I suppose. And would you please stop crowding me?"

Christy had grown increasingly aware of his disarming closeness. He was pressed so tightly against her that she could feel the heat of his solid body, smell the scent of his soap. His nearness was making her slightly woozy.

"Can't help it. In case you haven't noticed, these seats aren't exactly generous."

"Do you have to have your arm there?" It was draped along the back of the seat, not exactly around her but close enough to be threateningly cozy. She was beginning to realize the trolley hadn't been a safe choice.

"Nowhere else to put it," he said with an innocence she was learning not to trust. "And it's not about sex. It's about money."

"Huh?"

He chuckled. "Pay attention. The Hollister marriage. Money was the problem there. Laura liked to spend it, particularly on jewelry, and her husband earned a teacher's salary. Monica said they argued about that all the time."

"But there should have been plenty. Glenn told me that, though Monica controlled the sisters' inheritance, she doled out a generous monthly allowance to Laura."

"Not enough to suit Laura. Monica said her sister asked to have that allowance increased and was furious when she turned her down."

Dallas fell silent again. There was a faraway look on his face that Christy wondered about. Why did she have the persistent feeling he had some personal stake in this case, something he was unwilling to reveal to her?

"Hello," she prompted him.

"Sorry. You were saying?"

"Actually, I was hoping you would be saying it. You spent as much time with Monica as I spent with Glenn, but nearly everything we've got so far has come from Glenn. Didn't you get anything useful from her that could provide us with a strong lead?"

"Well, now that's interesting," he said with an exasperating casualness, "because it's just possible I did."

"Do I get to hear it?" she asked him impatiently.

"Would I hold out on a partner?"

Yes, if it suited you, Christy thought, but she didn't say it.

"It seems," Dallas went on with that same nonchalance, "that the police investigators went and turned up something curious in this little clearing behind the family cemetery where Laura's body was found. They questioned Monica about it. Wanted to know if she knew anything about her property having been used as a setting for voodoo practices."

"Voodoo! You mean the kind people don't kid about? The sick stuff?"

"Could be."

"And you're just now mentioning this? What exactly did they find?"

"Evidence that there may have been midnight ceremonies, the sacrifice of small animals. Monica was shocked."

Christy suddenly remembered the chicken feathers blown up against the iron fence enclosing the cemetery and how she had ignored them, which didn't make her happy about her detecting skills.

There was something else she remembered—that small bunch of dried plant material she'd been reaching for in the attic when the swallows had startled her. She told Dallas about it.

"So that's how you ended up down in that hole doing a trapeze act from a gas pipe. What happened to the stuff?"

"It crumbled to bits as I grabbed at it, and since by then I had, uh, a few other things to occupy me, I forgot about it. But it occurs to me now it could have been a voodoo charm. That means," she said excitedly, "Laura might have been involved with some kind of cult. And that could explain why she went out so often to Resurrection and didn't come home some nights. It could also explain her death."

"It could," Dallas agreed, "but since she died in the afternoon around the same time as her husband's visit out there, the police aren't ready to connect her murder with any late-night rituals."

"But *we* have to be serious about that possibility," Christy insisted.

"Right. Let's go."

He came abruptly to his feet, moving out into the aisle as the trolley slowed for one of its stops. Christy followed him as he headed for the exit.

"Where to?"

"Back to our cars."

"And then?"

He didn't reply. He was too busy making a path for them through a party of chattering tourists trying to board the trolley as they were leaving it. By the time she caught up with him, he had reached another trolley headed in the opposite direction.

"Lots of questions to be answered, grits," he said as he hustled her aboard the car. "Yeah, I know. Don't call you that. Look, don't think of it as food. Think of it as all the courage I admire in you."

Christy let that one pass. For now, anyway. "And just where are you taking us to get them answered?" she demanded again as she sank into one of the seats.

"Someplace that's going to fascinate you," he promised as he settled beside her. "Either that or scare you to death."

Chapter Three

Christy had always believed she knew the city and its environs so well that she could qualify as a New Orleans cab driver. That was before Dallas McFarland took her into a neighborhood so alien to her she would have sworn they were no longer in New Orleans, maybe not even Louisiana.

The houses, packed shoulder to shoulder along the tangle of narrow streets, looked like something Charles Addams might have executed in one of his more sinister cartoons. And their occupants, eyeing the cream-colored convertible as it passed, wore expressions that were even less cheerful.

"You sure we're not lost?" Christy demanded.

"Relax," Dallas assured her, negotiating the maze with perfect confidence.

"Well, I think we're lost."

"We're not lost."

"Then why won't you tell me where you're taking me?"

"Don't have to. We're there."

He pulled over to the curb, parking in front of a structure that seemed to be listing dangerously. Vines smothered its walls, climbing onto the mossy roof.

"It doesn't look safe," Christy decided. "Who lives here?"

"It isn't a house, it's a store," he said, sliding out from

behind the wheel. "And stop being so nervous. You're a P.I., remember?"

"I'm not nervous. I'm just cautious, that's all." She exited the car from the passenger side and followed him up onto the porch. "What kind of store?"

"The kind that sells voodoo supplies."

Which shouldn't have surprised her. This was New Orleans, after all, and they were after answers. But Christy was still a bit uneasy as she followed him into the store. With good reason, too, she thought as she gazed around the dim interior.

The place was like a wizard's cavern. Black candles burned on either end of a counter and shelves ranged along the walls were piled with dust-laden merchandise that didn't bear thinking about. There was a strong aroma in the air that seemed to be a combination of incense, fried onions and an old graveyard. Definitely on the creepy side.

"Everything but a smoking cauldron," Christy whispered.

Dallas chuckled. "She could probably produce one for you, providing the price was right."

"Who?"

"The reigning queen of voodoo in New Orleans. This is her store."

"Oh." Christy looked around. They were alone in the shop. "Where is she?"

"Patience."

"Maybe we should call out a hello, ding a bell or something to let her know she's got customers."

"She knows we're here. Look," he urged, "why don't you have a look around while we're waiting? You know you want to."

Christy had to admit she *was* curious. She wandered along the shelves inspecting masks, the skull of a goat, ritual altars, dolls and various powders and charms. "This is fascinating."

"All for the tourists," he said, trailing after her. "I suspect the serious stuff is in a private room by invitation only."

She leaned down, squinting at a label on a sealed jar. "What's High John the Conqueror's root?"

"How should I know?"

There were other jars, other labels. Stop Evil Floor Wash, Luck-in-a-Hurry Incense, Come To Me Oil, Mogo Love Drops, and something called Bendover that Christy preferred not to question. The instinct that promised to serve her well as a P.I. kicked in again without warning when she saw a jar marked Black Snake Root. The word *black* seemed to leap out at her.

"There's something that's just occurred to me," she told Dallas. "What if Laura Hollister's need for money had nothing to do with her expensive tastes? What if it was for something else?"

Dallas didn't seem to find it at all odd that she should start discussing a subject that probably had little or no relation to the voodoo supplies she was examining. "You don't mean voodoo, do you?"

"No, blackmail."

He was thoughtful for a second. "That's a possibility. *Definitely* a possibility. We'll need to look into that, too."

There was approval in his voice. Christy would have been pleased by it, had she not become suddenly aware of the silence in the store. It was unnerving. "I don't know about you, but I get the feeling there are eyes on me."

"We are being watched," he said calmly. "She just wants to be sure you're okay."

Christy refrained from shuddering as she peered at another label. "What on earth would you do with alligator teeth?"

"Bite your enemy?"

"Anyway," she went on, "maybe Glenn will turn up a connection. I asked him to go through all of Laura's personal effects as soon as possible and let us know what he finds."

"Good thinking."

This was twice within the same moment that he had complimented her. Did he mean it? Christy glanced at him, fearing he might be laughing at her again behind those compelling green eyes. No, she could see his praise was genuine, leaving her with a warm glow—a reaction that was definitely disturbing.

The situation threatened to turn awkward. Christy was saved from that by a sudden rattle of the beaded curtain hanging from the doorway behind the counter. She turned to see a stately African-American woman emerge from the back regions of the store, a smile of welcome on her handsome face.

The voodoo queen would have made Brenda Bornowski green with envy. She was a riot of color in a scarlet turban, a boldly printed caftan and heavy rings that covered the long fingers of both hands. Christy was impressed.

The voice that issued a delighted, "Sugar!" as she swept toward them was strong and deep. "What a wicked *coquin* you are to neglect us all these weeks! But I forgive you."

She expressed that forgiveness by wrapping Dallas in a lusty embrace. Christy groaned. Not another one! Wasn't there any female in this town immune to this brash devil?

Pecking Dallas on both cheeks, the voodoo queen released him with a quick apology. "I'm sorry you had to wait. I was in the back with a client."

Casting a spell? Christy wondered as the woman turned to her, luminous dark eyes registering her curiosity.

"Who have you brought with you?"

"This is Christy Hawke," Dallas explained. "We're working together on a case. Christy, I have the honor, the very *great* honor, of introducing you to Camille Leveau, a direct descendant of the famous Marie Leveau."

No one lived in New Orleans for any length of time without knowing that Marie Leveau had been a celebrated nineteenth century voodoo queen. Christy was no exception. She also knew that Camille Leveau wasn't the first voodoo practitioner to claim descent from Marie. There were even those who had boasted they were the reincarnation of the voodoo queen. How authentic was Camille's own assertion was anyone's guess. And as the glint in Dallas's eyes when they met Christy's gaze told her, what did it really matter?

All dignity now, Camille extended her hand. Christy took it, murmuring her pleasure as the beaded curtain parted again and Dallas swiftly rounded the counter to pump the hand of the new arrival, an elderly man with skin like seamed mahogany, who moved with the aid of a cane.

"Chester! I haven't seen you since that night at Preservation Hall," he said, referring to the French Quarter's famed jazz center, "when you had all of us cheering."

"Oh, I can still blow a mean horn all right, when my daughter here lets me."

Christy gazed at Dallas as he and Chester exchanged pleasant memories. She realized that these people were comfortable with him, obviously fond of him. It was understandable because this was an unexpected Dallas McFarland, one she hadn't discovered until now. Gone were the arrogance and the cynicism. In their place were gentleness and kindness as he listened patiently to the old man.

Christy found herself liking what she was seeing, and that worried her.

There must have been a softness in her expression that the voodoo queen observed and mistook for longing, because as the two men went on reminiscing, Camille drew her aside.

"You want him, huh?" she whispered. "And why not? He is one exciting man, that one. Those shoulders alone are—"

"Hey, hold on! You've got it all wrong!"

Ignoring Christy's objection, the voodoo queen went on earnestly. "I can make it possible, *chérie.* I can give you a potion that will not only put him in your bed, it will have him performing with great power."

"No, really I, uh—"

"And if the strength of the potion is right," she promised, "he will be your love slave for as long as you desire."

"No," Christy choked. "See, this is strictly a business arrangement with McFarland and me, nothing else, and, um…well, anyway, thank you, but, no. *Definitely* no."

Camille lifted her shoulders in a little shrug.

Dallas couldn't possibly have overheard them, but Christy could swear he knew exactly what they'd been talking about. One of those expressive eyebrows lifted suggestively as he cast a look in her direction that, if not exactly lewd, was positively hot with meaning. She could feel her face flaming. The worst of it was, when their eyes met she experienced something that was more than just embarrassment. She didn't care to define it.

Christy was relieved when Chester excused himself and they were able to address the matter that had brought them there.

"We need information, Camille," Dallas appealed. "Whatever you can tell us."

He went on to explain Laura Hollister's death, how they had been hired to clear her husband of her murder and the possible voodoo connection with the case. Camille listened without comment, her face betraying no emotion. She was silent when Dallas finished.

"Anything?" he implored.

The voodoo queen slid her gaze in Christy's direction, commanding softly, "This small bunch of dried plant material he says you saw in the attic out there at Resurrection where she died—describe it, please."

Christy did to the best of her ability.

Camille nodded wisely. "A gris-gris."

"What is a gris-gris?"

"A charm. Sometimes they are meant to keep away evil, sometimes they are meant to cause evil. Without seeing or touching this one, I can't know which."

"What else can you tell us?" Dallas urged.

"Nothing."

"There must be something."

"Only this. There is good voodoo and there is bad voodoo. Me, I practice the good. I am a conjure doctor. People come to me to have curses removed that were laid on them or to buy my cures for bad habits. I help people, I don't hurt them. You understand this?" She seemed anxious for them to believe that she performed only beneficial services.

"We understand," Dallas said smoothly. "Now tell us about the other voodoo, Camille. The kind that's evil. It's here in New Orleans, isn't it?"

"I tell you, I know nothing about it."

She's lying, Christy thought. She does know something, but she's afraid to talk about it. That was apparent in the way Camille held herself rigidly and in the way her mouth had tightened so stubbornly. Now why would a voodoo queen, with all her power, fear another form of voodoo?

Christy tried herself to reach the woman. "Would you tell us this then?" she probed gently. "Did Laura Hollister ever come to you?"

"Why should she?"

"Maybe just to buy supplies. Or maybe she needed your help. Maybe she was involved in something she was desperate to get out of."

Camille shook her head. "Your Laura Hollister was never a visitor to my store."

"But you do know something, don't you, Camille?" Dallas persisted. "There isn't much that goes on in this city that you don't know about. Come on, why won't you tell us?"

Camille turned her head, staring at him for a long, indecisive moment. Then, her voice solemn and low, she reluctantly admitted, "I hear things, yes. Things about a dark voodoo that I despise. A *destructive* voodoo. But it is dangerous to talk about these people and their activities. This I won't do. I know little enough anyway."

"Isn't there anything useful you can give us?"

She considered his request. "If you want to know more, you must go to the old St. Louis cemetery. Use your eyes and if you look hard enough, you may see for yourself."

"But which St. Louis cemetery?" Christy pressed her. "There are three of them, aren't there?"

"It doesn't matter which. Just be careful. The old cemeteries are no longer safe." She held up her hand as Dallas started to object. "No, sugar, I have nothing more to say, not even for you."

The voodoo queen conducted them to the front door. When Dallas tried to pay her for her service, she refused. "I don't want to be paid for something I want no part of. But, wait."

Leaving Dallas at the door, she drew Christy back into

the store. Reaching under the counter, she produced a small, simple red cloth doll and placed it in Christy's hand. "A gift," she murmured. "No charge."

Christy glanced at the tiny figure in her hand, not sure that she cared to be the recipient of what was, plainly, a voodoo doll. Her apprehension must have been evident, because Camille laughed softly.

"There is nothing to fear in a red doll, *chérie*. Red is for love." Her gaze slid briefly, but meaningfully, in Dallas's direction. "Believe in it, and it may bring you all that you desire."

Christy didn't know how to refuse the voodoo queen without offending her. Murmuring a quick thanks, she stuffed the doll into her shoulder bag.

When they got outside, Dallas wanted to know, "What was that all about? What did she give you?"

"Oh, just a little charm meant to bring me luck."

"Uh-huh."

He didn't believe her, of course. There was a wicked gleam in his eyes. Damn the voodoo queen for thinking she had a thing for Dallas McFarland!

"You know," he said as he guided the convertible through the traffic, heading them back toward the center of the city, "I caught a glimpse of it before you tucked it out of sight in that duffel bag you call a purse. Innocent little charm, my fanny. It was a voodoo doll. A red one."

Christy, taking refuge behind sunglasses and baseball cap, slouched down in the seat and didn't answer him.

"Hell, everybody knows what red voodoo dolls are for. So, grits, who are you planning to use that thing on?"

"Prince Charles."

His response took her completely by surprise. "Well, you know what I think? I think you've got the hots for ol'

Glenn. It's my guess that after a decent interval you'll be sticking pins into that poor little mite and chanting over it. Or whatever it takes to make syrup out of ol' Glenn. Why do you want to go and waste your money on junk like that? The guy isn't worth it.''

Christy should have been relieved that she was safe, thankful that Dallas hadn't realized it had been the voodoo queen's intention for her to lure *him* with the doll. But she was much too annoyed for that. ''In the first place, I didn't buy the doll. Camille insisted I take the silly thing as a gift. Anyway, it's none of your business who I might care for or not care for. And why do you keep picking on Glenn when you're supposed to be on his side? Furthermore, Camille meant the doll—'' Christy caught herself just in time ''—as, uh, just a kind of novelty.''

Too late. She couldn't see Dallas's eyes behind his dark glasses, but she didn't have to. The smug little smile on his bold mouth when she stole a quick look at his profile, told her that he had tricked her into revealing what he'd suspected all along. She had practically confirmed for him the voodoo queen's real purpose for the doll.

''Now see how you're already benefitting from my experience?'' The little smile widened into a maddening grin. ''I've just demonstrated how a skilled P.I. goes about getting information out of an unwilling subject. Useful lesson, huh?''

Smoldering, Christy tugged at the brim of her Cubs cap. ''Exactly what did my father tell you about me when the two of you put your heads together and came up with this little scheme of our working together?''

''That you've got a lot of promise. Just needs developing.''

She didn't care for the way his deep voice stroked the words *promise* and *developing,* as though he were suggesting something other than a knowledge of private investigation. "I see. Well, suppose you enlighten me now about what I'm really eager to know."

"And what instruction would that be?"

"The one that teaches me all about your big secret."

She watched the grin fade from his mouth. For a moment he concentrated on the traffic and said nothing. Then, a huskiness in his voice, and he asked a cautious, "Would you care to be more specific?"

"Don't play games. You know what secret I'm talking about. Come on, McFarland, just how have you managed to steal so many clients from me? Discounting, of course, the sneaky tactics you used to get Brenda Bornowski."

"Ah, that secret," he said, his manner careless again. "Only it's not. I just manage to offer the Big Easy the best P.I. services available, that's all. Your turn. Precisely what *did* Camille say to you when she gave you that doll?"

She wasn't falling into that trap again. "To regularly change its diaper. Watch the light; it's turning red."

Infuriating man, Christy thought, not wanting to admit to herself that she actually enjoyed sparring with him.

"Do you think this might be a waste of our time?"

Dallas, busy securing the top on the convertible, didn't answer her for a moment. They were parked outside the entrance to St. Louis Cemetery No. 1 on Basin Street.

Cemeteries weren't high on Christy's list of attractions. The sky didn't help. It was looking decidedly menacing with dark clouds piling up from the direction of the Gulf, which was why Dallas had raised the top. The failing light added to the eeriness of the place.

"I mean," Christy persisted, "what can we possibly expect to find in there?"

"Camille wouldn't have sent us here if there wasn't something for us to learn," her companion finally replied.

"Voodoo-related, I suppose."

"What else."

"The thing is," she said, following him reluctantly from the car, "I keep remembering how she warned us that the old cemeteries are no longer safe. Do you think she was referring to voodoo worshippers?"

"Nothing so sinister. Muggers. They've been known to hang out in the historic cemeteries preying on tourists."

None of which were in evidence this morning, Christy noticed. The threatening weather was keeping them away. They had the place to themselves. Odd that in the heart of New Orleans there should be an area that was so lonely.

And so fascinating, she decided, forgetting her qualms as she accompanied Dallas into the cemetery. A city of the dead. It was an apt description for the oldest New Orleans' cemetery, where the high water table had necessitated interment aboveground in endless rows of whitewashed tombs that resembled small houses. Lining the boundary walls were tiers of smaller graves known as oven vaults.

Whatever the form of burial, all of the structures had been embellished with stone carvings and ironwork so beautiful that they were treasures in themselves. However, the tombs had suffered greatly, partly because they were crumbling with age. But also—

"They're missing," Christy said, regret in her voice as she stopped abruptly on the weedy path along which they had been strolling. "A lot of the carvings and statues have been broken off. There's not a tomb that hasn't been defaced by vandals."

"Maybe not vandals," Dallas said thoughtfully. "Not entirely, anyway."

Christy stared at him. "Voodoo?"

"I think so. Worshippers who've chipped away pieces to use in their rites. Probably raided the tombs for skulls, as well."

Christy shuddered over the image of such desecrations. "That's not all," she said. "Have you noticed all the marks on the walls of the tombs, red crosses and the numbers three, seven and nine?"

He nodded. "Another voodoo connection."

"But what does any of it really tell us? Nothing. I can't imagine why Camille Leveau—"

Dallas held up one hand, silencing her. "Listen."

She heard a dull rumble. "Thunder."

"Not that. Try again."

This time she did hear it, the rhythmic sound of what must be a hammer striking a chisel. It was coming from a far corner of the cemetery they had yet to investigate.

"This ought to be interesting," Dallas said. "Let's see exactly how interesting."

If these *were* grave robbers, Christy wasn't certain how wise it was to spy on them. But she offered no objection, following Dallas as they crept silently toward the source of the steady chipping. The thunder rolled again, reminding her of the approaching storm.

Turning a corner, they spotted three figures at the end of a narrow avenue. The trio had their backs to them as they labored to remove a marble winged cherub from the face of a vault.

One of those young people was a female who complained nervously, "Hurry up, you guys, before someone comes."

As she started to look over her shoulder, Christy and Dallas ducked out of sight behind the blocky tomb they had just rounded. The two of them stared at each other, mouthing their surprise almost simultaneously. "Brenda Bornowski!"

"What's *she* doing here?" Christy hissed. "I thought one of your people was supposed to be tailing her."

"Managed to lose him obviously. That kid is as slippery as a bayou eel. Why isn't she in school?" he grumbled.

"Spring break. I can't believe she's involved in this voodoo mess. I suppose one of them is her boyfriend."

"Looks like Daddy Bornowski was right about the punk being a bad influence."

"What are we going to do about her?" Christy whispered, anxious on behalf of the teenager. "We can't just leave her here."

"Not when she and her friends may have some useful answers for us, anyway," Dallas said, moving out again around the corner of the tomb. "Let's see how willing they are to provide them."

They should have known the trio was not going to stand there waiting to be challenged. Brenda yelled a warning as Christy and Dallas approached. The tools were abandoned with a clatter, Brenda taking flight in one direction, her two companions in another.

"Not very willing at all, I guess," Dallas said. "You go after the girl, I'll take the guys."

They separated, Christy racing in the direction the teenager had fled. But Brenda was not a champion eel for nothing. Christy lost her within two minutes. And within three minutes, she was lost herself.

The cemetery was a bewildering maze of vaults and tombs, and she had taken so many twists and turns in pursuit of the now vanished Brenda that she no longer knew where she was. She stopped, trying to get her bearings, straining for a helpful sound. Except for the low growl of thunder, telling her she was at risk of an imminent drenching, the silence was total. Where was Dallas?

She experienced a sudden, pronounced discomfort. Maybe it was the deepening gloom or maybe it was the stone figure of a kneeling woman who seemed to be staring at her. And maybe she was just being a coward again.

You have to stop this, Christy. P.I.s are definitely not cream puffs.

Which was why, when she heard a low groaning coming from somewhere off to her left, she decided she couldn't ignore it. She headed in that direction. But when silence ruled again, she realized she could wander in here forever without locating the maker of that groan. Friend or foe? Either one, it had sounded like someone needing help. She'd have to chance it.

"Where are you?" Christy called out.

Another silence and then came a muffled response. "Over here."

Dallas's voice. He couldn't be more than a few rows away. Rapidly weaving her way through the monuments, she trotted around a corner and came upon him suddenly. He was sagging against the door of a tomb, looking ready to collapse. When she reached him, she was alarmed to see blood oozing from a wound in his scalp.

"You're hurt!"

"Damn little hoodlums bushwhacked me," he muttered. "Then to make sure nobody was going to catch them, they grabbed my cell phone and my gun."

"Oh, lord, you've been shot!"

"I wasn't shot. Did you hear a shot? What I was, was knocked silly when they jumped me, my head banged against concrete."

"You're injured, anyway. I'm going to call for assistance. And sit down before you fall down. You look all woozy. Here, let me help you.''

''Stop fussing. Just call. Brenda get away, too?''

''Afraid so.''

''Figures.''

By this time Christy had her own cell phone out of her shoulder bag. But when she tried to use it, all she got was an exasperating crackle. It was either the weather or the quality of the instrument. Her budget had long ago ruled out state-of-the-art equipment.

''Cheap thing. Useless,'' she grumbled.

''Never mind. All we have to do is get to the car. Here, you drive.''

He fished for his keys in the pocket of his suit jacket. He didn't find them. Beyond the far boundary wall of the cemetery, they heard the roar of an engine, then the squeal of tires as a vehicle sped away. Their eyes met.

''I'll be damned! They stole my car, too! What next?''

The heavens obliged him with an answer. It began to rain—a hard, soaking rain.

''Well,'' Dallas said, ''I'd say this case is going pretty well so far, wouldn't you?''

And before Christy could catch him, he slid down the side of the door into an unconscious heap.

Chapter Four

"What do you mean, help you out of here? I'm not helping you to go anywhere. You're going to stay put while I go and bring help."

"You'd leave me here all alone in this downpour? I could get pneumonia. You want that on your conscience?"

"Dallas, be reasonable. You shouldn't try to move. Damn it, you were unconscious!"

"For a lousy thirty seconds. And if you're wondering whether I have a concussion or I might be going into shock, stop wondering. All I need is shelter and an aspirin. Well, maybe a cold beer to wash it down. Now are you going to stop hovering over me and give me a hand up?"

Christy went on crouching there inches from his body huddled against the side of the tomb. She was concerned about his making any physical effort whatsoever, but he did have a point. They were both already drenched by one of those New Orleans' deluges that gave no sign of letting up. An unhappy situation that needed correcting. Besides, if she didn't lend him her support, he would just obstinately manage to stagger off on his own.

"All right," she relented, "but if you should feel at all light-headed again—"

"You'll be the first to know."

He used her shoulder as a lever and heaved himself slowly to his feet. Arm around his waist to steady him, Christy guided him carefully toward the exit.

"Lean against me if it helps," she encouraged him.

He did, and she immediately regretted her offer. Not because she was unable to bear his solid weight. The problem was the intimacy of his hard body squeezed against hers. She was far too aware of the sensual appeal of his warmth, of the provocative male scent of him in her nostrils.

This probably isn't smart. This probably is a large mistake.

She was convinced of that by the time they neared the gate. He had his arm slung around her shoulder, the tips of his fingers trailing along her arm. She became suddenly conscious that those fingers were doing things to her flesh. Alluring things. A slight action maybe, but it definitely qualified as stroking. When his swinging hand brushed against the side of her breast, striking sparks, she knew his attention was deliberate.

"Why, you sneaky—"

"Now what?"

"Taking advantage of the situation!" Realizing that she was the one who was light-headed, not Dallas, she abandoned him. "You don't need my support!"

He didn't, either. What had been a weak shuffle became a normal gait as he led the way through the gate with a relieved, "This place spooks the hell out of me."

So she wasn't the only one not fond of cemeteries.

Reaching the street, he stared glumly at the place where his convertible had been parked. "Yep, they took it all right."

Christy, searching for something else, gazed hopefully in both directions along the street. But, of course, there was no taxi to be had in this weather, no sign of a bus or a police cruiser they could hail.

"We have to find a phone."

"Don't worry," he said. "I have a plan."

She wasn't sure she liked the sound of that. But before she could question him, he was already moving along the sidewalk in the direction away from the Quarter.

"Just where are we going?" she asked, catching up with him.

"To shelter and a phone. It's not far."

But after two blocks, they were still trudging through the relentless rain. Sodden and miserable, Christy grumbled, "I don't know why I keep letting you convince me you know what you're doing."

They were in a neighborhood of old Creole cottages, some of which had been restored and others still in need of rescue. Dallas stopped in front of a shotgun house. The rooms of these single-story structures were in direct line with each other from front to back, an arrangement once popular in New Orleans. The narrow face of this particular shotgun was Italianate in style, with pedimented brackets along the roofline.

Under any other circumstances, Christy would have been enchanted. Now all she cared about was the refuge the cottage might offer.

"Who lives here?" she asked him.

"It isn't occupied."

She could see that for herself when, following him along a narrow passageway at the side of the house, they reached a small yard at the back. It was heaped with junk torn out of the interior, and a glance through an uncurtained window showed her that the place was in the process of being reconditioned.

"What are we doing here?" she wanted to know.

To her frustration, he didn't answer her. He was busy searching in the pile of discarded materials. "Aha," he pronounced in satisfaction, coming away from the trash with the broken end of an iron strap hinge.

"I think that knock on the head has affected your brain. What on earth do you want that for?"

"Tool," he said, approaching the windowed back door of the house.

Christy understood then what he intended. "Don't!" she cried. Too late. He'd already smashed one of the lower panes. As she watched him tap out all of the jagged pieces remaining in the frame, she understood something else. "You might have told me. This house belongs to you, doesn't it?"

"Yeah, and if I hadn't had my keys stolen—" He reached through the opening, unlocking the door and swinging it open. "Oh, well, it's only one pane. I'll fix it later. Watch the broken glass down here."

She was careful to step over the fragments as she followed him into the kitchen.

"Ah," he said, "a roof at last."

Christy silently echoed his appreciation. It was a relief to be out of the streaming rain.

Dallas gazed in the direction of the refrigerator. "Wonder if I've got any beer. You want a beer?"

"Don't you think you'd better forget that and take care of your injury?"

"Right. Think I've got some first aid stuff in the bathroom."

She trailed after him and stood in the bathroom doorway, ready to lend a hand if he should need it. Watching him at the sink as he began to clean and medicate the wound, she expressed her concern. "I still think you should have a doctor look at that."

"Naw, I'm fine."

She did have to admit he seemed fully recovered from the blow. Her attention strayed as she waited for him. Turning her head, she gazed with interest along the length of the deep house. Except for fixtures and appliances, there were no furnishings. The place was still in the process of renovation, with sawhorses, paint cans, lumber and tools scattered about. Was he camping out here?

"I thought you lived in an apartment over in the high-rent district," she said.

"I do. This is just for fun, though I might move in here after I finish it. Or maybe I'll sell it, like I did the others I rescued."

She looked at him in surprise. "You're doing all this work yourself?"

"In my spare time. Relaxes me."

"I'm impressed."

"I'll be sure to tell my daddy. He was a master carpenter, taught me what to do with wood and how to love it. Here." He tossed her a thick towel. "Start with this, and then we'll see what we can find for you to change into."

She caught the towel. He had finished at the sink, and now he stood there with one hand on the edge of the door, staring at her.

"What?" she asked.

"Just waiting for you to decide whether you're going to come in here with me while I get down to the skin or whether you'd, uh, prefer not to help strip off these sopping things of mine."

Christy hugged the towel protectively against herself and backed away from the doorway.

He chuckled. "Guess that's a choice. Too bad. It could have been interesting."

He was still chuckling when he closed the door in her

face. Turning away, Christy rid herself of the dripping base-ball cap and mopped at her wet hair, wandering from room to room as she waited for him.

Even with the house in this raw stage, there was a lot to admire. The black marble fireplaces looked original to the place, as did the transoms over each of the doors. But most of the wide moldings were new, as were all of the kitchen cabinets. The effect was simple but beautiful, nothing at all like the slick, image-conscious environment she would have associated with Dallas McFarland.

Enlightening, all these new and favorable facets of his character she kept discovering, and at the same time disturbing. It was much safer to go on thinking of him as an arrogant jerk. She was in the process of ordering herself not to further probe either his dimensions, or her feelings on the subject, when the bathroom door opened.

Christy prayed he wouldn't emerge naked. She believed he was capable of such an action. But although he was covered when he appeared, the result was almost as breath-robbing.

How a man managed to look incredibly sexy in baggy bib overalls was beyond her. It was the bib that was responsible. Or, rather, the lack of a shirt beneath it, leaving exposed a bare expanse of wide shoulders and a sleekly muscled chest.

"I snagged these for you from the hook on the back of the door," he said, thrusting toward her a pair of old jeans and a T-shirt. "Sorry they won't qualify you for the Mardi Gras, but it's the best I can do while your clothes go through the dryer."

The jeans and shirt, along with the overalls, had obviously been left by him in the house to wear when he was working here. Averting her gaze from all that hard flesh exposed at the sides of the bib, she accepted the garments with a murmured thanks and ducked into the bathroom. She had a feeling he might be chuckling again, *lewdly* this time, outside the door she swiftly closed behind her. Maddening.

So were the jeans and T-shirt. They were miles too big for her. And his male scent clung to them, making her squirm with images she had to obstinately resist.

When she joined him in the kitchen, the dryer was working on everything he'd worn but his suit. He leaned against the counter and, of all things, he was spinning a yo-yo. Working it like a champion, too. In those overalls that teased the senses, he could have posed for a calendar. One of those calendars that each month feature a riveting hunk in some revealing workman's garb.

Mr. January with his yo-yo.

Easy, Christy.

Offering no explanation for the yo-yo, he took her damp clothes and added them to the dryer. "Like a soda? Afraid I'm out of beer."

"All right."

Removing two soda cans from the refrigerator, he popped open the tabs and handed her one of the cans with an apologetic, "Sorry, I don't have any glasses here."

"It doesn't matter."

No chairs either, she thought, looking around for a spot to perch while she waited for her clothes to dry. The only place to sit was a window seat. She settled on one end of it and sipped from her can. The soda was cold and biting.

Dallas drank from his own can before telling her, "I phoned the cops to report my stolen property while you were in the bathroom."

"Did you tell them about Brenda?"

He shook his head. "She wasn't with the two punks when my gun, keys and phone were grabbed, and we don't know if she managed to rejoin them when they took the car. For now we'll keep her out of it.''

''Yes, but it looks like she may be involved and I've been asking myself just how and what connection, if any, it has to our case.''

''We'll sort it out.''

She wished she shared his easy confidence. She also wished he hadn't decided at that moment to amble across the room and squeeze beside her on the window seat. His closeness with all that bare muscle was disconcerting.

''What's the matter?'' he drawled. ''Do I worry you?''

''The only thing that worries me,'' she lied, ''is the case, because if we don't solve it in time, I have two parents in Chicago just waiting to snatch me back under their protective wings.''

''It can't be that bad.''

''You're obviously not the youngest of five siblings or you wouldn't say that. Actually, I did have a younger sister, but she died when she was an infant, which only made it worse, along with my being the smallest physically. My brother, Mitch, is the only one in the family who seems to realize I'm more than a blond doll.''

Dallas looked amused. ''That why you go around trying to look tough in the baseball cap and the running shoes?''

''I don't have to try to look tough. I *am* tough. But you try to tell my father that. Know what he calls me? Baby. He never calls my sister, Eden, that. But I'm *Baby* to him and always will be.''

''I think you're wrong. I think your father considers you a competent woman capable of being a P.I. in her own right. He just knows you don't have the experience yet, and he's practical enough to realize that I do.''

''Uh-huh.'' Christy tipped her head to one side, considering him with suspicion. ''Exactly how close did the two of you become in that phone call? Casey Hawke is not an easy man to convince. So just what did you say to persuade him we should pair up for this tournament?''

''Simple. I offered him what every father wants for his daughter—success.''

''And?'' Christy pressed him, knowing there had to be more.

''Nothing much. Just a promise that, while we were on this case together, I'd do everything in my power to keep his daughter safe. You can't blame him for needing to hear that. It was, uh, the last part that won him.''

She should have guessed that was the missing ingredient in this mix. She also should have resented their little arrangement. But somehow, dangerous though it was for her to feel this way, she experienced a certain pleasure in knowing that Dallas McFarland had offered to help her prove her worth while keeping her safe, even though self-interest *had* motivated his promise. She wasn't forgetting that she was his pipeline to Glenn.

Christy didn't tell Dallas any of this, however. What she said was, ''You see, that just proves my point. I'm good enough for things like surveillance or finding missing heirs, but when it comes to murder he doesn't trust me to take care of myself.''

''You have nothing to feel inadequate about.''

The way he said it, his voice slow and husky, and the way he looked directly into her eyes made her catch her breath. In the silence that followed, she heard the rain beating against the glass behind her and the rumble of the dryer across the room.

''On any level,'' he added softly, his gaze dropping to the area of her breasts.

She could feel those wicked green eyes burn a hole through the T-shirt she wore. And there wasn't much to penetrate. The fabric was worn and thin, and her bra—well, her bra was in that dryer. Even worse, far worse, she could feel the traitorous buds on her breasts go rigid under his hot gaze. What's more, she knew he could see it happening.

"This," she said hoarsely, trying to sound affronted and failing, "has nothing to do with my qualifications as a P.I."

"Maybe not, but it sure as hell has everything to do with your qualifications as a woman." He edged toward her, those seductive eyes mesmerizing her.

"You're breaking the rules again." She tried to scoot away from him, but there was nowhere to scoot. She was pinned in the corner.

"What rules?"

"The ones you promised to obey when I agreed to work with you."

"Did I?" He leaned toward her, his deep voice stroking her senses. "You'll have to remind me."

Christy swallowed. She was finding it difficult to breathe. "We were to keep it strictly impersonal. You weren't supposed to, um…" Her voice trailed away, the words lost with her self-control.

"What?" he whispered. His face was mere inches now from hers.

"I don't remember."

"Me, either. Guess they weren't important."

That's when she found out that his eyes weren't nearly as effective as his lips. He demonstrated this by capturing her mouth with his in a long, tantalizing kiss. It was a busy kiss that involved exciting little nibbles, his warm, clean breath mingling with hers and his patient, probing tongue urging her to taste him.

Christy's treacherous senses rioted on her. She couldn't get enough of his bold, enticing mouth. Their kiss deepened, robbing her of air, stealing her sanity.

Reality returned with a jolt, and reason with it, when she suddenly realized that his hands were under the T-shirt searing her flesh, cupping her swollen beasts. In another moment he would peel the shirt over her head and his mouth would be on her nipples. And, oh, it would be so easy to surrender to all the rest that would eagerly, mindlessly follow. And so very fatal.

Dallas McFarland was a man with a talent for pleasing people. It's why he was so good at what he did. He had proved that with individuals like her father and Camille Leveau. He pleased them, and then they were vulnerable, ready to submit. Like her in this moment. Only she couldn't.

Christy couldn't let herself be intimate with a man who must have loved and left scores of women without ever looking back. A man who—and she'd almost forgotten it—was still her rival. And who, if she wasn't careful, would ultimately hurt her.

He didn't resist when she broke their kiss and pulled away from him abruptly, but those expressive eyebrows of his demanded an explanation.

Finding enough wind, she muttered a blunt, "This isn't working."

The eyebrows climbed even higher. "Funny, I thought it was going great."

"Not that. Well, yes, that, too. Look, I'm calling it quits. I don't care what the arrangement was. From now on, I work on my own. Understand?"

"Yes. No."

"You'll have to. Excuse me."

She left the window seat and crossed to the dryer, removing her clothes. They were still slightly damp, but what did that matter? She had to get out of here. He didn't try to stop her when she went into the bathroom and changed.

Didn't argue when, emerging, she scooped up her shoulder bag and fled from the house.

It had stopped raining, and this time her cell phone worked when she reached the street and tried it again. She called for a taxi to pick her up at the corner.

She told herself while she waited for the cab that she didn't want to surrender her independence by working with Dallas. Then in the cab on the way to pick up her car in the Garden District, she told herself that if her worth was to mean anything, she needed to prove it on her own. And on the drive back to her office, she convinced herself that her reasons were honest ones and that she wasn't running away from Dallas McFarland because she was terrified of her feelings for him.

DENISE DIDN'T CARE for her decision. She wasn't exactly explosive about it, but she wasn't tactful either, which was no surprise.

"What are you saying, you're not gonna work with McFarland anymore? You go and lose your mind, girl-friend? You don't work with McFarland and your ma and pa shut us down."

"Not if I solve the case on my own."

"Huh. Guess that means I go back to driving that big old city bus, and just when we were getting us some action around here."

Christy stood over her assistant's desk, glaring at her. "Thank you for your confidence in me, Denise."

"Wasn't me who said you needed a coach." She peered at Christy suspiciously. "You sure it's not more than you and McFarland not getting along?"

"Isn't that enough?"

"Maybe." Denise got one of her sly looks. "Or could be the dude bothered you in another way."

Christy had no intention of revealing her chaotic emotions. She dismissed the subject with a brusque, "You've been watching those soaps again. Were there any messages while I was out?"

"Uh-huh. Glenn Hollister called up wanting to talk to you. Didn't say about what. There's his number on the pad."

This could be important, Christy thought, reaching for the phone. But when she dialed Glenn's home, there was no answer. Denise watched her as she replaced the receiver.

"What comes next, girlfriend?"

Christy wasn't certain what her next step ought to be. She'd have to think about that one and she might as well do it while grabbing some lunch. She gave Denise her noon break and went upstairs to her apartment.

When she slung her bag on the counter, it tipped over, spilling the contents on top. Among them was the small, red cloth voodoo doll Camille Leveau had insisted she have. Not wanting to be reminded what that silly figure represented, or the man it was supposed to lure to her bed, Christy tossed the thing on her desk and forgot about it.

She tried to concentrate on the case as she made herself a sandwich and poured a glass of milk. But Dallas McFarland kept getting in the way. Maddening.

She was still in a state of indecision when she finished eating and returned to the office where she tried again to phone Glenn, hoping he had some development to share with her. Anything to give her a lead.

She was punching in his number when, through the window in front of her, she saw a tall, slender figure coming through the carriageway from Royal Street. It was Glenn himself. Lowering the phone, she hurried out into the courtyard to meet him.

"I hoped I'd catch you in," he said.

He looked like he needed to talk. "Come on into the office," she invited him.

Glenn shook his head. "I can't stay. Monica is waiting out front in the car. We're on our way to Laura's wake."

Which explained the dark suit he wore, she thought. There was an anxious expression on his face, and his gray eyes were melancholy. Even so, he had never been more handsome, his fair hair brushed smoothly back from his high, classic forehead.

Christy's heart should have been missing a beat at the sight of him. There was everything to justify such a reaction. But somehow Glenn's old luster had dimmed for her. All she felt was friendship and sympathy. She acknowledged this, but she refused to question her feelings any further.

"Denise said you've been trying to reach me, Glenn. Have you learned something?"

He nodded. "That's why I stopped by. I've been sorting through Laura's things as you suggested. There was something unexpected when I got into the safe in her bedroom where she kept her jewelry."

Christy could guess what was coming. "Her valuable pieces were missing, I suppose." Sacrificed to pay for blackmail, she thought, which meant she had been right.

But Glenn surprised her. "No, just the opposite. All her old jewelry was still there, but there were several more expensive-looking things. The collection is bigger than ever now. Laura must have been secretly buying pieces. No wonder," he added bitterly, "we were always battling about money."

Not blackmail then, Christy thought in disappointment, realizing she had just learned another valuable lesson about private investigation—one she hadn't waited for Dallas to teach her. Never assume anything.

Except for the soft splash of the fountain, there was silence in the courtyard while Christy examined Glenn's information. She had been so certain that blackmail was the explanation. But this time her instincts had failed her, sending her back to square one. Frustrating.

"Glenn," she questioned him, remembering that Laura and her sister had also argued over her spending habits, "what does Monica say about these new pieces?"

"She was angry when I showed them to her. Monica doesn't have any interest in jewelry herself, not the valuable stuff certainly. She thinks it's a waste of money."

"Have you discovered anything else?"

"Not yet. There's a lot of stuff in her desk to go through. I'll keep looking, but it takes time. Christy, are you making progress in solving her death? Anything at all?"

He sounded so desperate that she immediately realized it was more than his discovery of the jewelry that had brought him here. "What is it, Glenn? What's happened?"

"The police," he said. "They're trying to get a warrant to search my house. So far my lawyer has blocked it, but he thinks they'll succeed in the end."

"What does it matter if they do search?" She peered at him sharply. "Glenn, you don't have anything to hide, do you?"

"Of course not." He raked his fingers through his hair, the gesture expressing his deep concern. "It's just that it's one more example of how stuck they are on me, of how they keep trying to turn up evidence. Christy, you've got to find Laura's killer before they charge me."

"I'll do everything I can to prevent that happening," she promised him gently, and then she reluctantly added a hopeful, "Remember that Dallas McFarland is also working to clear you."

Glenn took her hand, his earnest gray eyes pleading with

her. "Monica is McFarland's client, not me. Oh, I know he's good, but it's *you* I trust, Christy."

He squeezed her hand with a sudden rush of warm affection. It was a simple intimacy that should have meant everything to her. But, pleased though she was by his faith in her, the gesture made her feel uncomfortable, especially when Glenn's daughter found them like that.

The four-year-old charged through the carriageway, arriving at Glenn's side with a breathless, "Aunt Monica sent me to find out what's keeping you, Daddy."

If the little girl had noticed her father holding the hand of a strange woman, which to Christy's relief he was no longer doing, she didn't seem in the least concerned about it. She gazed up at Christy with a lively curiosity.

"Daisy, this is a friend, Christy Hawke."

Christy crouched down so that her face was on a level with the child's. "Hello, Daisy." She smiled at the girl, seeing that she clutched a stuffed animal. "Is that a panda bear?"

"Uh-huh. He was my mommy's when she was little. Wasn't he, Daddy?"

"I found the bear tucked away in Laura's things," Glenn softly explained. "I thought Daisy might like to have it."

Christy understood what he was telling her, that he'd offered the toy to his daughter as a kind of comforting link to the mother she'd lost. She resembled her mother, Christy thought, remembering a newspaper photo she'd once seen of Laura attending a society function. Daisy had the same auburn hair and delicate features, which made the sight of her treasuring the stuffed animal all the more poignant.

"He's a very handsome bear," she solemnly assured the child. "What's his name?"

"George."

"That's a good name. Hi, George."

"She likes you," Glenn murmured. "She's usually very shy with people until she gets to know them."

"That's because we both know how to talk to panda bears. Right, Daisy?"

"Right."

"We'd better go," Glenn said as Christy rose to her feet. "Why don't you walk out to the car with us? You've never met Monica."

"All right."

She accompanied father and daughter to the carriageway. None of them were aware of a figure on the balcony above the back side of the antique shop. Screened by the lush thickness of a bougainvillea, he had been there in the shadows the whole time listening and watching.

Chapter Five

Shame he didn't have one of his yo-yos with him, Dallas thought, staring at the three figures below as they disappeared into the carriageway. He could have used the instrument to relieve his present tension. Instead, he leaned against the railing of the balcony, drawing a slow, deep breath and willing himself to relax. But his emotions still had him all tight inside.

Dallas hadn't counted on Hollister's arrival on the scene. Nor the sudden appearance of the little girl. His overhead position, plus the obstruction of the bougainvillea, hadn't permitted him to catch much more than frustrating glimpses of the top of the child's head. He hadn't been able to see her face. Not clearly see it.

Daisy. He liked the name. It was old-fashioned, but it conjured up pleasing images.

And then he thought about Christy. Now there was an image—honey-blond hair, aquamarine eyes, and a mouth meant for kissing. Except he had an idea she wouldn't be in any mood for kissing when she learned he'd been here in the courtyard the whole time. She was sure to accuse him of deliberately eavesdropping on that tender exchange between ol' Glenn and her.

Well, hell, he hadn't meant to spy on them. He had

meant to announce his presence up here and then explain his very sensible reason for it. Only things hadn't worked out that way. He'd found it more useful to remain silent.

Dallas frowned. It was getting increasingly harder to keep his secret from Christy. The whole thing was complicated by a lot of confusing feelings where she was concerned. Tantalizing feelings he hadn't anticipated. He wondered how much longer he could handle them. Or the guilt that was growing inside of him. He hadn't realized how difficult it would be to maintain his silence, how conflicted it was making him feel.

He glanced at the door of the upstairs apartment that faced him. There had been no answer when he had rung its bell earlier. No point in his hanging around. But he went on leaning against the railing, reluctant to go down into the courtyard and face the music.

THE CAR WAS an expensive one, its owner waiting by it impatiently. Christy found Monica Claiborne to be a slightly older version of her late sister. She had the same elegant features and bearing, only her taste in dress seemed much more restrained, her manner completely self-assured.

After Glenn introduced them, Christy, mindful of Daisy's presence, offered a comforting but careful, "This is a difficult time for you, Ms. Claiborne, but I want you to know that I'm going to do everything I can to clear up this situation for your family."

Monica nodded. "I know that Glenn is relying on you, Ms. Hawke, and I appreciate that. But I hope you'll forgive me for continuing to put my own faith in Dallas McFarland. He is, after all, more experienced."

Christy was getting awfully tired of hearing that. She also wondered if Monica had a personal interest in Dallas. It wouldn't be surprising, considering the appeal he had to the greater portion of New Orleans' female population. And she was not, *not,* going to let herself experience any pangs over the possibility of Monica Claiborne and Dallas McFarland.

"Glenn, we really need to go."

Christy leaned down to Daisy. "Bye, Daisy. Take good care of George."

It occurred to her that the child was awfully young to be taken to her mother's wake, but it was none of her business. She stood at the curb and watched the car draw away along Royal Street. She was about to turn back into the carriageway when her gaze was caught by a familiar sight. There, parked across the street, was a cream-colored convertible. She could just make out the letters on its plate.

It was Dallas McFarland's car! What's more, Christy didn't think the young men who had stolen it would have left it here. The convertible was too distinctive a vehicle to abandon it on such a busy street without causing notice. Which, she decided, meant that Dallas had managed to recover his car and drive it here himself. He was somewhere close by, and she had a strong suspicion of just where that *somewhere* might be.

Wheeling around, Christy marched back through the carriageway. When she reached the center of the courtyard, she lifted her head and shouted a defiant, "Either you come out of hiding or I send for the police and report you for a prowler!"

There were a few seconds of silence while she scanned the four sides of the courtyard. Then there was a movement behind the bougainvillea that sprawled along the balcony of Alistair St. Leger's apartment over his antique shop. The tall figure of Dallas appeared, descended the stairway, and joined her at the fountain, all without hurry or concern.

"I see you got your car back," she said dryly, jerking her head in the direction of the street.

He treated her to one of his impudent grins. "Would you believe the cops found it not more than three blocks from the cemetery? And the thieves were considerate enough to leave my keys, cell phone and gun in the glove compartment. I call that real lucky, though the cops went and confiscated my piece. Something about my permit to carry concealed not being in order."

She smiled at him sweetly. "And so timely, too. Gave you the opportunity to spy on me down here."

"You mean that performance with you and ol' Glenn. Not much fire in him, is there? Of course, he might have made a better effort if his daughter hadn't come along. Cute little girl. I'd say she's handling her mother's death pretty well, wouldn't you?"

"I am not discussing Daisy with you. Why were you snooping on us?"

"It's what P.I.s do, remember? That is, if I had been snooping, which I wasn't."

"Uh-huh. I suppose you're going to tell me it was purely a coincidence you were up there behind that bougainvillea."

"Well, yeah, it was."

"And, naturally, you didn't speak up because you didn't want to intrude on a private moment."

"Something like that."

"I see. And just what particular coincidence put you up on that balcony?"

"The one that brought me to call on your neighbor, Alistair St. Leger. Only his shop out front is closed, and no one answers upstairs. I don't suppose you, uh—"

"He and his assistant are probably out on an appraisal or attending an estate auction." Christy examined his face.

"You're serious about having come here to see Alistair, aren't you?"

"Said so."

"Let's just say then, to save further argument, I accept your excuse for being up there. Now would you care to explain the reason behind it?"

"Could we sit while we do this? It's been a long morning."

Without waiting for an invitation, he settled himself on the raised stone coping of the fountain's small pool. He gazed up at her, expecting her to join him. Considering how proximity to Dallas McFarland always seemed to lead to trouble for her, Christy wasn't sure it was a smart idea. Not that he was anything like half naked this time. He had traded this morning's outfit for tan slacks and a black knit shirt. Very casual, but no less sexy. However, as she didn't want him to think his closeness worried her, she perched beside him, keeping several safe inches between them.

"Comfortable?" he inquired.

"I will be as soon as you stop stalling and tell me why you need to see Alistair."

"You're responsible for that."

"I am?"

"Indirectly, anyway. See, I thought about how you weren't satisfied with Camille's reason for sending us to the cemetery."

"I wasn't?"

"No, you questioned it. So I decided I'd better start paying attention to this instinct of yours and that maybe what Camille meant for us to discover wasn't the robbing of tombs for relics to be used for voodoo."

"But that is what we saw—Brenda and her friends plundering one of the tombs."

"And we go and assume it was for voodoo purposes."

"What else could it have been for?"

"Profit from cemetery art. Think about it."

Christy did for a moment. "So what you're saying," she said slowly, "is that all those wonderful old stone carvings and ironwork pieces are valuable works in their own right. Valuable enough to be looted to supply illegal collectors. That's it, isn't it? Wait a minute. I hope you're not thinking Alistair could be connected with such a market. He's one of the most respected antique dealers in New Orleans."

"Which is exactly why I'm here. With St. Leger's knowledge, he'd have heard if there actually is such a traffic and who might be involved in it."

Christy shook her head. "Maybe, but what has any of this got to do with Laura Hollister and her death?"

"She had a passion for expensive jewelry, didn't she?"

Christy nodded. "And not the funds for acquiring it. Except, as Glenn said, she *had* been acquiring it. How? By trading in stolen cemetery art? And did that get her murdered?"

"It's possible. She was found in a cemetery, after all, even though there was no sign of that one having been pillaged."

"None of this is enough to interest the police. It'll take real evidence."

"We'll get it."

"We?" She stared at him. "Have you forgotten we're no longer working together?"

"Now, see, that's another thing."

"Don't say it."

But he did, and in persuasive terms. "Grits, with your instincts and my know-how, we make a great team. Does it make any sense to spoil that because of a little misunderstanding, and just when we could be on the point of a real breakthrough?"

"Yes."

He paid no attention. He went on with his pitch. He flattered her, challenged her, coaxed her. He must have been very good with these sales techniques since, without knowing quite how it happened, Christy found herself agreeing to work with him again. Well, after all, she did need to save her agency.

"*But,*" she emphasized, "this time we stick to the rules. No more physical stuff."

"It's a promise."

"Business only."

"Absolutely."

"Okay then."

But it wasn't okay. She was already regretting her surrender, probably because as she sat there briskly demanding that he behave himself, she found herself fascinated by the pulse beating in the hollow of his deeply tanned, very male throat.

This time she had only herself to blame. And she might have changed her mind again about teaming with him, but a movement in the rear window of St. Leger's Antiques, someone adjusting a blind, prevented that. Dallas surged to his feet.

"Looks like they're back and the shop is open again. Let's see what your friend has to offer us."

They went around to the front door on Royal Street and entered the store. Alistair's assistant met their inquiry with a nod in the direction of the office. "He's on the phone with a client. I'll tell him you're here."

Christy never tired of admiring the merchandise in the shop. All of it was of the finest quality, and she could afford none of it. But she could drool over it, which was what she was doing with an attractive antique brooch in a glass case when Alistair arrived from the back.

"How's my favorite neighbor?" he greeted her warmly.

The word *distinguished* could have been coined expressly to describe Alistair St. Leger. He was tall and thin, with a lined, aristocratic face, thick silver hair and a pair of congenial blue eyes. The blue eyes turned sober after Christy introduced Dallas and they explained their errand.

"Yes, it's true, and no secret in the antiques trade," he said with both disgust and regret in his tone. "There is a lucrative black market in cemetery art. The thieves know better than to offer any of these stolen pieces to me or the other reputable dealers, but unfortunately there are unscrupulous dealers willing to traffic in these lost treasures."

Alistair was sorry, but he had no knowledge of their identities. No, he had never met Laura Hollister, though her sister had once bought a Prudent Mallard chair from him.

Dallas was satisfied by Alistair's information when they came away from the shop. He hadn't expected any startling revelation. But Christy was bothered as they stood on the sidewalk in the glare of April sunshine.

"What are your instincts telling you this time, grits?"

It was scary the way he kept reading her like that. "I don't think they can be very reliable because I'm back to feeling that voodoo still has something to do with Laura's death."

"Not according to the police," Dallas said. "I asked them about it when I reclaimed my car. They were only mildly interested when they found possible evidence of midnight ceremonies at the Claiborne plantation. Since then, having asked in the neighborhood, they've dismissed it as kids fooling around. No connection to Laura."

"So where does that leave us? Pursuing voodoo or stolen cemetery art?"

"Let's put voodoo on the back burner and concentrate on the cemetery art."

"How?"

"Know what would be fun? Paying a visit to Brenda Bornowski. If she can't recommend a good body-piercing parlor, bet she can tell us who's buying and selling cemetery art."

THE BORNOWSKI HOME was in Metairie on one of those residential streets where the property values are astronomical. Spacious, brick and traditional, the house was embraced by azaleas, some of which still blazed with pink bloom even though the season was late for them.

Christy had a suggestion as the convertible turned into the driveway. "If she is here, I doubt our Ms. Bornowski will be in any mood to receive callers. She might even, uh, suddenly decide not to be at home. Of course, if one of us slips around to the back while the other goes to the front door…"

"Sounds right to me," Dallas said.

Christy's hunch was confirmed when she stood at the front door and no one answered her ring, although a curtain moved at one of the windows. A moment later she heard the crash of a door somewhere toward the rear of the house, followed within seconds by a loud yelp. When she got to the corner of the house, Dallas had an outraged Brenda firmly by the arm and was leading her along the brick path at the side.

"Let me go! You got no right to manhandle me!"

Dallas was shocked. "Manhandle you? Why, Brenda, how can you say that when all I was doing was rescuing you from that shrubbery you'd tumbled into?"

Which had happened, Christy surmised, when a fleeing Brenda had tried to get away from Dallas. He released her when the three of them reached the front door. Brenda rubbed an imaginary bruise on her arm and glared at

Christy, a surly expression on her mouth. The mouth was no longer lavender, as it had been in that episode at the Jax Brewery. Brenda had switched to a black lipstick. A nice vampire touch, Christy thought.

"Talk to us, Brenda," she encouraged the teenager.

"Like?"

"You could start with voodoo," Christy suggested. "Know anything about voodoo, Brenda?"

Brenda laughed. "You're crazy if you think I'm into that junk."

Christy was inclined to believe her. There was the ring of truth in her voice.

"How about stolen cemetery art then?" Dallas said. "You sure know about that, don't you, Brenda?"

A sly look came into the girl's eyes, heavy with mascara. She shrugged. "I don't know what you're talking about."

"Fibbing?" Dallas made a tsking noise. "Shame on you, and after we caught you red-handed at St. Louis Cemetery this morning robbing that tomb."

"Stuff it."

"Hey, Brenda, know what? I bet if you don't talk to us, you talk to the cops. Suppose we call them, huh?"

Dallas removed his cell phone from his pocket. Though his action had her looking less rebellious, Brenda remained silent. Christy hoped the girl wouldn't end up calling his bluff, because if the police did come, they were more apt to charge Dallas than Brenda. He had admitted to Christy on the way to Metairie that the police, when returning his car, had used the opportunity to express their unhappiness with his activities. They had only shared their decision about the unimportance of the voodoo in hopes of discouraging his involvement in the case. Dallas wasn't worried, however. Police warnings were nothing new to him.

"It's a shame, Brenda. So far we've managed to keep you out of it, but it looks like that's about to change."

Popping open the cell phone, Dallas held the instrument out in front of him ready to dial. Brenda caved.

"All right, so I was there. But me and Troy weren't robbing any tomb."

"That's funny, Brenda, because it sure looked like that's exactly what you and your boyfriend were doing."

"Well, we weren't," she said defiantly. "It was Troy's buddy, J.J., who was swiping the statue. All we were gonna do is help him carry it out of there."

"And what was J.J. going to do with the statue?" Christy asked.

"I dunno."

"Dallas, it looks like you'd better make that call."

Brenda relented again. "Okay, so he sells the stuff to some guy. Don't ask me who, because he never said. It's no good your looking for J.J., either. He's scared now and gone into hiding someplace. And, no, I don't know where, and neither does Troy."

"Are you being straight with us this time, Brenda?"

"Yeah, I swear." The defiant look came back into her eyes. "Anyway, if you're looking for answers about all that cemetery crap, you'd better get them from my old man. Anyone knows, he does."

Christy and Dallas exchanged glances. "What does that mean, Brenda?"

"You wanna see? Come on, I'll show you."

She led them into the house, along a wide hall, and down a stairway. At the bottom she opened a door. They followed her into a cavern of blackness. Brenda's hand groped for a switch on the wall.

"There!" she said as overhead spots flooded the large room with light.

On all sides, either mounted against the walls themselves or ranged on floor pedestals, were marble and wrought iron treasures. The relief of a weeping woman under a felled tree, a winged hourglass, an angel bearing a cross, the portrait in stone of a beloved pet. The figures were everywhere. They gazed in shocked silence at Marty Bornowski's secret collection of cemetery art.

Brenda laughed. "And he tells me *I'm* gonna turn into a delinquent if I don't shape up?"

Christy experienced the kind of sympathy for the girl she hadn't felt before. No wonder Brenda didn't have any respect for her father, not when he had this code of double standards. "Brenda," she asked her gently, "how long has he been collecting these things?"

"A couple of years, I guess."

"Do you know who he buys the stuff from?" Dallas asked.

"No. All he says is not to talk about his collection to anyone."

"Then we won't ask you any more questions. We'll save them for your father. Any idea where he's working today?"

"As if I'd know. Check with his office." She hesitated. "Uh, does he have to hear I was with Troy and J.J. in the cemetery?"

"I'm afraid so, Brenda," Dallas said.

"But we'll do all we can to soften it," Christy promised her.

They parted from the teenager, and when they got back to the convertible, Dallas used his cell phone to call the office of Marty Bornowski's asphalt company.

"Yes?" Christy asked when he ended the call a moment later.

"How would you like to pay a visit to the Super Dome?

They're laying a new surface on one of the parking lots there.''

THE TEMPERATURE had been climbing since this morning's rain, and by the time they drove back into the heart of the city, Christy felt the heat. As sultry as it was, it was nothing compared to Louisiana's oppressive summers. But the vast parking lot where they found Marty supervising his crew could have matched New Orleans in August. The steaming asphalt under the rollers of the heavy paving equipment turned the area into a sweltering dark sea.

It was cooler when the contractor led them away from the noise of the machinery and into the shade cast by a trailer. "Something up with Brenda?" he asked them, surprised by their visit and with an expression in his eyes that wondered if he should be worried as well.

"You could say that," Dallas said.

Christy watched Marty Bornowski's face as Dallas went on to explain their errand. Burly, with a gruff manner and at the moment needing a shave, he didn't look like a man who'd collect art of any kind. But then people were never what you expected. It was one of the things that fascinated her about private investigation.

"Yeah," he said when Dallas had finished, "I was afraid that punk Brenda keeps hanging out with would get her into trouble, but I never figured something like this."

"You could help her," Christy said, "by giving us the name of the dealer who's selling you stolen cemetery art."

Marty was suddenly both wary and reluctant. "Who said it was stolen? And what's that got to do with helping my kid?"

"Oh, I don't know," Dallas said, leaning nonchalantly against the side of the trailer. "Maybe it would keep us from reporting your daughter's activities this morning to the police. What do you say, Christy?''

"We could do that."

Marty gazed at them in silence for a moment before he made up his mind. "All right, but my kid is kept out of it."

"That's a promise," Dallas agreed. "But if there's a next time…"

"I'll make sure she keeps her nose clean from now on." He took a small pad and pen from his shirt pocket, holding the pad against the wall of the trailer as he wrote down an address. "Vasey Antiques and Architectural Salvage. You'll find it over on Magazine Street. Guy name of Dutch Vasey runs the place." He tore off the sheet and handed it to Dallas. "Guess I won't be buying any more cemetery art."

Dallas pocketed the paper. "Doesn't look like it, Marty."

He and Christy were halfway back to the convertible when she stopped him. "Hang on a minute. There's something I need to do."

Mystified, Dallas watched her swing around and march with determination back to the trailer. She caught the contractor just as he was starting back to the job. He stared down at her small figure in surprise as, no longer able to hold back, Christy vented her anger.

"Mr. Bornowski, I'd be as wrong as you are if I left here without telling you that, under all that makeup and mutiny, your daughter is probably a very decent young lady! But you're going to lose Brenda if you don't start paying attention to her."

"I beg your pardon."

"Don't beg *my* pardon! Beg Brenda's! Let her know the mistakes you've made and that you're sorry for them and that from now on you're going to be a more sensitive father. She deserves to hear it." She started to turn away. "Oh, and try trusting her. Works miracles with teenagers. No need to thank me."

She left him with his mouth hanging open. Dallas was grinning when she rejoined him at the car. "Grits," he said, with pleasure in his voice, "you just keep getting better and better."

MAGAZINE STREET paralleled the river for endless blocks. Much of its length was occupied on both sides by antique shops, few of them as grand as those in the French Quarter, but many of them offering high-quality merchandise.

Vasey Antiques and Architectural Salvage was located away from that popular district. Eyeing the structure as Dallas parked opposite it, Christy thought it had a lonely, run-down appearance. It looked more like a junk shop than an antique store. There was no one in sight. The area was very quiet.

"What are we waiting for?" she wondered as Dallas continued to sit behind the wheel. He had scarcely glanced at the building.

"I want to talk for a minute before we go in there."

"Now?"

"It's as good a time as any."

Christy couldn't imagine what he wanted to discuss. They had already settled what questions they were going to ask Dutch Vasey on the way from the Super Dome. "You choose the darndest moments for conversation. What's this about?"

"Us."

She stared at him. He was serious, and that made her nervous. "I don't think we'd better do this."

"We need to do it, Christy. See, there's this thing that's

been thrumming between us all day. You know, a wire that just keeps getting tighter and hotter. What I want to know is why do you keep denying it?''

''Excuse me if I'm wrong, but didn't you swear less than an hour ago, *faithfully* swear, there would be—''

''No more physical stuff. Is this being physical? I don't think so.''

He leaned toward her as he said it, careful not to touch her. But that didn't matter, when the heat he radiated from his powerful body was as effective as a caress, promising sensual pleasures. And there it went again, the breath sticking in her throat. She swallowed past it, managing to answer him.

''What is it with guys like you, that you have to score with every female you encounter?''

''Only the small, blond ones in baseball caps. And you're still trying to run away from that hot wire. Come on, why can't you admit it? You want me as much as I want you.''

''If egos were gold, you'd be fabulously rich, Mc-Farland.''

But, of course, he was right. She did want him. Then why did she keep on resisting him? Her earlier arguments weren't enough to explain it. Maybe it was because, whenever he got too close, she felt like one of his yo-yos, suspended from some taut string that bounced her from emotional highs to emotional lows. It was a feeling that robbed her of self-control, something she didn't like, didn't trust. In fact, she was plain scared of it.

''So does that mean we're not going to do anything about the thrumming?''

She tugged at the brim of her cap in a gesture that conveyed finality. ''Not only are we not doing anything about it, we're not even going to discuss it any further.''

''Goes along with no more physical stuff, I suppose.''

He nodded, accepting her decision. But although he was willing to drop the subject, there was a relentless glint in his eyes that said *For now*. "Come on, let's go see what subjects Dutch Vasey is prepared to discuss."

None, as it turned out, because when they left the car and crossed the street, it was to learn there was a good reason why the place looked lonely. There were no lights behind the windows, and the shop door was locked. Christy peered through the glass. The store was jammed with secondhand furniture, nothing that resembled a genuine antique.

"I don't see any cemetery art in there, but then I suppose he wouldn't keep it in plain sight."

"Let's see if he keeps his graveyard out back," Dallas suggested, leading the way along a blank-walled alley at the side of the store.

They found another door at the rear of the brick building. It, too, was locked and the windows on either side dark.

"Now that looks interesting," Dallas said, indicating a large barn-like building at the back of a weedy yard. "Warehouse?"

They approached the structure and tried the door. Also locked.

"What do your instincts tell you about this place, grits?"

"Not to mess around with it."

"Well, mine tell me," he said, moving toward a window, "that when you paint windows over from the inside, like this one, it means you've got something to hide. And I just can't stand that."

"You're not going to break another window!"

"Don't think I'll have to," he said, eyeing the peeling wooden framework that was crumbling with age. He extracted a penknife from his pocket, opened it and inserted the blade between the upper and lower sash.

"Oh, great," she said. "Why not just leave your business card while you're at it?"

He didn't answer her. He was busy with the tip of the knife, probing for the catch.

"I don't suppose it's occurred to you that, if you do manage to work the catch open, it's apt to set off a security alarm?"

"Not likely. If you were storing illegal wares, would you want to bring cops swarming onto the scene? Ah, that does it."

The catch released, he raised the sash to its full height. "I'm going in. Stand by the door. I'll see if I can unlock it from the inside."

She watched him heave himself through the opening. Seconds after he disappeared, she heard a loud thump followed by a muffled curse. By this time she was at the door. "What's wrong?" she called out.

"It's like midnight in here. I walked into something. Hold on."

She could hear him fumbling with the lock on the other side. The first thing she noticed when he succeeded in opening the door were the cobwebs in his hair. "Looks like what you ran into was a spider."

"Get in here before the neighborhood starts wondering about us."

Christy scooted inside. While he closed the door behind her, she groped along the wall. "Must be light switches somewhere along here. Ugh!"

"What?"

"More cobwebs. Dutch is not a good housekeeper. Here we go."

Locating a bank of switches, she flipped them up. Lights in the lofty ceiling illuminated the vast interior of the warehouse. Dallas's long whistle expressed how impressed he was as they stood gazing at the contents on the end nearest them.

"It's a regular cemetery all right," he said. "All but the bodies."

They walked along the rows of marble statues and markers that composed the trove of stolen cemetery art. The pieces were all tagged, waiting for the customers who would be admitted here only by special arrangement.

Even with the lights, the warehouse was shadowy, its air stale and warm without circulation, bearing a strong musty odor. Christy had had enough. Having reached the end of a row, she started to turn back. "Let's get out of here. We've seen what we—"

She didn't finish. Her attention was suddenly captured by what occupied the other end of the warehouse—a collection of another sort. For a full thirty seconds she gazed at the bulky assortment, struggling to understand what was so familiar about it. Then, as recognition struck her, she ran toward the collection with a cry of excitement.

Dallas stared at her in astonishment as she raced from piece to piece, touching them, announcing each discovery.

"The fireplaces. The chandeliers. And these are the doors and paneling. Even the main staircase! They're here, Dallas, all of them!"

Chapter Six

"There must be a cure for it," Dallas assured her in a soothing voice. "Don't worry. We'll get you to a good shrink."

Christy ignored his sarcasm. "No, don't you see? My instinct was right when it urged me to go into the house and investigate. It was all there for me to discover. Only, naturally, I didn't understand what I was seeing. Not at the time."

"Naturally. Uh, just what house are we talking about?"

"Resurrection, the old Claiborne plantation where Laura Hollister's body was found. All these architectural gems were stripped from the place."

Dallas eyed the collection with the first sign of interest. "How can you be certain of that? There are any number of old houses in Louisiana. This stuff could have come from any one of them."

"I tell you it came from Resurrection. All of these things fit the spots they were taken from. Like this, for instance." She began to circle the magnificent curving staircase. "It has the exact same shape as the outline it left behind on the wall in the mansion."

"How can you remember it that accurately? All right,

don't look at me like that. Let's suppose it's true. What does it prove?''

"That Dutch Vasey had a connection with Laura Hollister."

Dallas nodded. "Maybe."

"And that he could have kill—" She broke off, her attention caught by another discovery at the back of the staircase. "Look at this if you don't believe me."

He joined her where she stood staring up at the underside of the staircase. There, attached to a nail driven into one of the risers, was a small bunch of dried herbs bearing a bittersweet odor. Dallas reached up and touched the black ribbon that was wound around the clump. "This the same kind of gris-gris as the one you spotted up in the attic?"

"Identical. Do you suppose they were placed in the house to keep intruders from discovering its secret, either that voodoo was being practiced there or that it was being stripped of its treasures? Maybe both."

He looked down at her with a new respect in his gaze. "Hanging out with me is definitely improving your detecting skills. What do you say we go and talk to the police? Maybe now they'll be interested in a new explanation for Laura Hollister's murder."

Christy thought that was an excellent suggestion. She continued to think it all the way back across the warehouse and was still thinking it when they doused the lights. She stopped thinking it when they opened the outside door and found a very lethal revolver pointed at them.

The gun was in the hand of a rather nasty-looking small man with slicked-back hair. What there was of it, that is. His scalp was visible through the oily strands. Dallas considered him before asking, "What do you want to bet, grits, that we have the pleasure of meeting Dutch Vasey?"

"What were the two of you doing in there?"

"Just browsing," Christy said.

"Yeah? You always do your shopping by forcing open a window to get inside?"

"Why don't you call the police then?" Dallas challenged him.

"Shut up!" he snarled. "And while you're doing that, get your hands in the air and move back inside. *Now.*"

Christy had no intention of arguing with him and hoped Dallas felt the same. Dutch not only had an unpleasant disposition, he also had a nervous tic at the corner of one eye that told her he was worried by their presence. And a man that upset was capable of getting reckless with the gun in his hand.

To her relief, Dallas must have agreed with her since his hands went up at the same time as hers while they backed away into the warehouse. Their adversary joined them inside, slapping up the light switches with his free hand and kicking the door shut behind him. Not a good sign, Christy thought.

"I wanna know who you are," Dutch demanded.

"Understand you're in salvage," Dallas explained. "The little woman and I are interested in a fireplace mantel, but I have to say you drive a hard bargain."

"You got a smart mouth. Okay, we're gonna do this real careful, no sudden moves. Drop that shoulder bag," he ordered Christy.

And there, thought Christy, easing her bag to the floor, went any opportunity of getting her hands on her Glock, and Dallas's own weapon was still with the police.

"You next," he commanded Dallas. "Empty your pockets and throw it down, everything."

"Look, why don't you let the lady go?" Dallas tried to persuade him. "She isn't involved in this. She just came along for the ride."

Christy was touched by his effort to protect her, even if it was out of an obligation to her father. At the same time, she found it annoying that his request seemed to dismiss her as a professional equal. In any case, Dutch ignored his appeal.

"The pockets," he barked.

Glancing sideways at Dallas, Christy could tell by the tightening of that perfect jaw that he was angry now. For both their sakes, she hoped he wouldn't vent that anger by trying to attack the vermin holding them at gunpoint. To her relief, Dallas began to reluctantly unload the contents of his pockets. Down went his cell phone, penknife, keys and wallet.

"Now back off some more and get those hands in the air again."

No choice about it. They obeyed. Keeping both his gaze and the revolver on them, Dutch squatted on the floor and began to examine their belongings, permitting himself brief little glances at what his fingers discovered.

Must have found the Glock, Christy figured as, hand burrowing into her bag, he uttered a savage oath. When his thick-waisted figure finally came erect again, he was holding their open wallets. And that eye with the tic, which had squinted at their identifications inside, was twitching like mad. Not encouraging, she realized.

"P.I.s! You're a couple of damn P.I.s! Who sent you here?"

"We're working for the police," Dallas lied, trying to scare him into releasing them.

Dutch laughed harshly, the hand gripping his revolver trembling noticeably. Also not encouraging, Christy decided. "Bull! The cops don't hire P.I.s." He was silent for a tense moment, then made up his mind. "Turn around."

"You're not going to shoot us in the back?" Christy

objected, thinking that if he had killed Laura Hollister, probably two more deaths wouldn't bother him. Up to this point, she had been only moderately frightened. Now she was *very* frightened.

"You'll get it in the front if you don't move. Up there, both of you." He indicated the other side of the warehouse where a shallow flight of steps mounted to a door.

Seconds later they were on the landing in front of that door.

"Inside," he growled behind them.

Dallas stalled, his anger surfacing again. "I don't like surprises. How about telling us first what's on the other side?"

"How about I coax you in there with a couple of bullets?"

"Like I say, I love surprises."

But there were no surprises waiting behind the door Dallas opened. Unless, Christy thought, following him inside, you counted a hollow storeroom as a surprise. There was not so much as a stool in evidence. Before either she or Dallas could ask their captor what he planned to do with them, the door had slammed behind them. They wheeled around in time to hear a key on the other side being turned in the lock. Then there was silence. Dutch had gone away, leaving them prisoners in the storeroom.

"It would take a bulldozer to batter it down," Dallas grumbled, examining the heavy door. "You got a bulldozer on you, grits?"

"No, and I don't have my gun to shoot the lock off or my cell phone to call for help, either. He's left us with nothing."

"Could be worse."

"How?"

"We could be in the dark."

That was true. Although there were no windows in the solid walls, there was a skylight overhead admitting sufficient daylight. It didn't offer a likely escape route, however. Even though the storeroom was higher than the ground floor of the warehouse, the ceiling was still a good twenty feet above them.

"Ah," Dallas said, spotting a second door on the other side of the storeroom. "Must be the emergency exit."

"Or where he keeps his pit bulls."

But when they investigated, hoping to at least discover tools behind that second door, all they found was another storeroom, this one without so much as a skylight. The place was crammed with packing crates, all of them disappointingly empty.

A discouraged Christy sat on one of the upended crates. "I am not a happy camper. Did you notice how scared Vasey was when he found us in his warehouse? And when he learned we were P.I.s, he was positively alarmed under all that bluster."

"Uh-huh," Dallas said, perching on the other corner of the crate, "I see what you mean. If Dutch did kill Laura Hollister, and it's beginning to look like he could have, then he's probably in a panic about us getting too close to the truth."

Christy shuddered. "Desperate enough to kill again to protect his secret. Where do you suppose he went off to?"

Dallas shook his head. "Maybe just to think, try to decide what to do about us."

"We have to get out of here. We can't just sit around waiting for him to come back."

"Don't plan to, not when I got us into this mess." He turned his head, casting his gaze over the stacks of crates behind them. "How are you at building pyramids, grits?"

For a moment she was puzzled. Then, twisting around to

look at the crates, she understood his intention. "You think we can?"

"Only way to reach that skylight."

He made it sound much simpler than the job proved to be. There were plenty of stout crates, and they weren't particularly heavy. Dragging them out to the other storeroom wasn't difficult. The rigorous part came in piling them into a mountain high enough to gain them access to the skylight. Each succeeding level became harder to raise than the one beneath it.

At the beginning of their effort, Christy worried about Vasey. Would he return before they could reach the skylight and stop them? Where was he? What was keeping him from dealing with them? And then she forgot about Vasey because she had a much more daunting concern to occupy her.

It had been stuffy enough down in the warehouse. Up here the air was absolutely sultry. They were soon perspiring freely. Christy had no choice but to bear it. After ten minutes of laboring, Dallas figured otherwise.

"What are you doing?" she challenged him, her voice cracking in panic.

"What's it look like I'm doing? Trying to cool myself down by a few degrees."

Gulping, she watched him peel the black knit shirt over his head. He wore nothing underneath. His bib overalls this morning had merely teased her. But this display of fully naked chest positively taunted her with its slabs of rippling muscle slick with sweat.

"Much better," he pronounced, tossing the shirt to one side. "Why don't you do the same and get rid of that top?"

She could swear that was a leer on his face. "I'm fine."

She wasn't, but she might have endured the situation if it hadn't worsened in the following moments. True, the nature of the job demanded that they work closely side by side. Brushing against each other as they shoved and tugged at the bulky crates was unavoidable. The first time it happened, his bare flesh coming in warm contact with her arm as they struggled to position a crate, was like a flame searing her skin.

"What?" he asked when she jerked away.

"Nothing," she muttered, trying to look anywhere but in the direction of that alluring male chest.

When it happened again seconds later, her nostrils were assaulted by such a potent whiff of his musky scent that it made her light-headed. She also suspected that this time their contact was no accident.

"Are you doing that deliberately?"

"I don't know what you're talking about." His voice was all innocence, but she didn't trust those wicked green eyes that regarded her. Every time he looked at her like that, she felt as if he were trying to see into her soul. "Come on," he urged. "A couple more layers should do it."

Giving him the benefit of the doubt, she resumed work. But when his shoulder scalded her cheek, practically stroking it as he reached around her unnecessarily, that doubt vanished. He *was* taking advantage of their circumstances. How could the lout have sex on his mind at a desperate time like this? And how dare he have it on his mind?

"You *are* doing it deliberately!" she accused him.

He pulled back, shaking his head and looking infuriatingly mournful. "We've got to get you out of here. All this heat and strain is giving you delusions."

"Don't you play that game with me! No physical stuff! Isn't that what we said? And every chance you get, you go and break your promise!"

"Hey, is it my fault you keep bumping into me? Are we

going to finish this, or are we going to continue arguing until Vasey gets back here with that gun?''

"No more funny business. Just keep that body away from me."

Grumbling something under his breath about just how many women, given the chance, would appreciate *that* body, he attacked another crate.

Minutes later, to Christy's panting relief, the last crate had been hauled to the top of the stack where they stood. The skylight was now within Dallas's reach. To her further relief, he had recovered and donned his shirt, making him much safer even if the fabric, damp from his perspiration, did mold itself provocatively to his hard contours.

With a silent prayer, she watched him struggle with the stiff catch on the old skylight. "Do you suppose you could hurry?'' she finally asked, beginning to think their position was a precarious one. The pyramid of crates no longer seemed steady to her. She could swear the summit, anyway, was beginning to sway. "I don't know about you, but it feels like this whole pile under us could collapse."

"Stop worrying. It's rock solid."

"If you say so."

"Here we go," he said, succeeding at last with the catch and flinging open the window panel.

Christy welcomed the rush of cooler air from outside, but she was still anxious. "Really, Dallas, I can feel it shifting. Can't you?"

"You're just imagining it."

Imagination or not, she was thankful when, gripping the edges of the skylight's steel frame, he heaved himself through the opening and onto the roof. Turning around, he poked his head back through the opening. "Come on up. The view is pretty decent, if you don't mind the trash cans down in the alley."

But Christy had neither his height nor his strength, and on her own she wasn't able to swing herself up through the gap.

"Here," he said, stretching one arm down to her, "take my hand."

Circumstances being what they were, she didn't concern herself this time with any physical contact. She seized his hand.

"Always seem to be pulling you up out of holes, don't I?" he said, and she knew he referred to their first encounter at Resurrection when he had rescued her in the attic.

"Just get me out of here, will you? This thing is really shaking."

"Not that again."

He pulled, and she scrambled, and together they put her on the roof beside him. She drew a deep breath to thank him, and in that instant there was a crash below them as the stack of crates went tumbling down to the floor of the storeroom. She looked at Dallas. "Uh-huh," she said dryly.

"I'll be damned."

"I think I already have been." Grimacing, Christy put a hand to the back of her neck.

"What's wrong?"

"With all that straining to get up here I must have pulled a muscle. And there will be no pain-in-the-neck cracks, please. Okay, now what?"

"We get off the roof. If we have to, we'll slide down a drainpipe."

Funny man. He kept thinking she was an acrobat. She certainly didn't welcome the idea of any drainpipe, not when they were at this dizzy height above the ground. On the other hand, shouting for help didn't seem to be an option. Suppose Dutch Vasey answered her call with his gun?

"Think," Dallas said, surveying the expanse of roof,

"that we ought to do this on hands and knees. The pitch is fairly low, but walking around up here would be a little risky."

A *lot* risky, Christy decided. She had no intention of getting to her feet. "Lead on."

She started to crawl after him, but the asphalt shingles under the heat of the sun were like burners on a stove. Her hands could take it, but her bare knees protested.

"Another crisis?" Dallas asked, turning his head when she yelped with the pain.

"Sorry, but my knees need protection."

"Happy to oblige."

She couldn't afford to object when he stripped off the black shirt again and pitched it to her. Accepting it, she snugged it around her right knee.

"Still leaves you the left one," he said. "I could give you my pants, but I don't think it's fair I'm the only one here sacrificing to the cause." He gazed pointedly at her own top.

She could either surrender her modesty or suffer a blistered knee. She chose to protect the knee, but she didn't like the familiar way he stared at her bra as she removed her top and tied it around her leg.

"Nice lingerie," he commented.

She just knew he was waiting for her nipples to harden, like they had this morning. Well, not this time. "Stop gaping and start crawling."

Maybe I don't want to be a P.I., after all, Christy thought as she followed Dallas along the slope of the roof. Maybe teaching would be more comfortable. In fact, she was convinced of it a few minutes later when she realized they were being observed.

She drew Dallas's attention to that fact. "Uh, I don't know if you've noticed it, but there's an elderly woman in the upstairs window of that house over there. She seems to be watching us through a pair of binoculars.''

''Oh?'' He turned his head, looking in the direction she indicated. When he discovered the woman in the window, he smiled and offered her a salute. ''Pays to be friendly to the neighbors, I always say.''

The old woman was too far away for Christy to detect the expression on her face. She wasn't certain whether the poor thing was alarmed by the sight of a half-naked couple wandering around a rooftop on all fours or whether she was enjoying their performance. Thinking maybe it was better if she didn't know, she hurried to catch up with Dallas.

Guided by the route of the rain gutter at the edge of the roof, he had now reached a corner of the building. ''Should be a downspout along about here,'' he said, leaning out over the eaves.

''Careful,'' she cautioned, entertaining a vision of him pitching headfirst into the alley below. ''Is it there?''

''No downspout,'' he reported, drawing back from the edge.

''Great. We've just left one trap for another.''

''No downspout,'' he repeated. ''Something much better.''

''Uh-huh. A ladder, I suppose, just waiting for us.''

''Actually, it is. Or the next best thing. Metal rungs attached to the side of the warehouse.''

Christy lifted her gaze heavenward. ''Thank you, God.''

''Open heights bother you?''

''Only anything above the level of a step stool.''

''You'd better go first then so I can lower you over the edge. Scoot around.''

Christy tried not to think about what was happening while, flat on her stomach, he gripped her by the wrists and eased her over the eaves. She had a panicky moment hanging there in midair before her scrabbling feet found the first rung. It was easier after that. Not good, but easier.

"Don't look down," Dallas coached her as she descended carefully rung by rung. "Just keep looking up."

It was good advice, except it failed to prepare her for what was waiting for them in the alley below.

"I'm doing that myself," Dallas called out as he followed her down the ladder.

Christy, stepping off the last rung, tried to warn him. "Uh, Dallas—"

"They say you don't get vertigo if you keep looking up. You on solid ground yet?"

"Yes, but I think you should know—"

"Didn't I tell you everything would turn out okay? You gotta start trusting me, grits."

Satisfied with himself, he reached the floor of the alley and swung around to face the two uniformed police officers who stood on either side of Christy eyeing him.

"How are you, McFarland?" the elder of the two greeted him. "Tired? Kind of feel like I have to ask, seeing as how you and the lady here seem to have had a real busy day for yourselves."

"I'm good, thanks. I suppose the, uh, old woman in the window—"

"That's right. You hear a racket, then you go and see a man and a woman minus their clothes playing games on a rooftop... Well, that's bound to have you dialing the police."

Christy tried to offer an explanation. "Officer, there is a very good reason why—"

"We'll save it for the station, ma'am."

"Is that necessary?"

"Let's see. There was the episode involving the cemetery this morning, and now indecent exposure while trespassing. Maybe even a charge of breaking and entering. Oh, yeah, I think that deserves a trip to the station. This way, folks.''

He jerked a thumb in the direction of the police cruiser waiting at the mouth of the alley.

IT WAS A GRUELING SESSION. Which it wouldn't have been, Christy thought, if New Orleans' finest hadn't been so infernally obstinate about everything.

No, they weren't going to arrest Dutch Vasey. Why? Well, that would be a little difficult since he seemed to have disappeared. All right, maybe he was on the run and maybe that collection of cemetery art in his warehouse had been illegally obtained, though there was no absolute evidence of that. Yes, they'd certainly question him about it, providing he ever turned up.

But maybe Christy and Dallas ought to be glad Vasey wasn't around since he would have been entitled to press charges against them, for both illegal entry and damage to his property. It was an argument that infuriated Christy, considering Vasey had held them at gunpoint and then locked them up in his storeroom. If she hadn't been so exhausted by then, she would have lost her temper, which probably wouldn't have been at all smart.

They didn't fare much better with the paunchy homicide detective in charge of the murder. He wasn't interested in their theories. Nor did he consider the contents of the warehouse a sufficient reason to connect Dutch Vasey in any manner with Laura Hollister. Furthermore, if they didn't start obeying warnings about keeping their noses out of his investigation, they faced serious consequences.

They were also told by the officer who returned their possessions to them, after recovering them from the warehouse where Vasey had dumped them, "Twice in the same day. This is getting to be a bad habit, McFarland."

"Hey," Dallas defended himself, "can I help it if people keep snitching my belongings?"

The officer glared at him. "You're just lucky we're releasing you—this time. Take your stuff, the both of you, and get out of here."

Christy was glad to do just that. She felt like she was staggering when she came away from the police station. "I'm tired, I'm dirty and I'm discouraged," she complained. "I also think I'm hungry, although I'm not sure about that."

"Come on," Dallas said, perpetually cheerful, "I'll drive you home."

It was late by the time they got back to her office. Denise had long since left for the day. Christy checked for messages from her. There were none.

"You make up your mind yet whether you're hungry?" Dallas asked.

She didn't remember having invited him in, but he was there just the same. "I'm sure." But neither the prospect of cooking a meal for herself nor trudging off to the nearest fast-food counter was at all appealing. Dallas seemed to understand that.

"Make you a deal," he said. "Give me five minutes in your shower, and I'll fix us dinner. You have any groceries in the house?"

"Uh, maybe." *This is not wise, Christy. Not wise at all.*

"I make a hell of a Cajun chicken. Fresh meat is better, but frozen will do."

"So let me get this straight. You're a hotshot P.I., a master carpenter on the side and, in between, a gourmet cook who also happens to spin a mean yo-yo?"

"That's about it."

"So when do you find the time to make all these New Orleans beauties happy?"

He heaved a much exaggerated injured sigh. "Christy, Christy, what do I have to do to convince you I'm not a serial lover, that I'm just a regular guy?"

She angled her head, considering him. Maybe she had misjudged him. Maybe he wasn't a womanizer. Not a serious one, anyway. "Cajun chicken, huh?"

"With steamed rice."

The hell with wisdom, Christy thought.

Fifteen minutes later in her upstairs apartment, Dallas having relinquished the bathroom to her after taking his turn under the shower, she soaked in a scented tub. When she emerged, she was no longer ready to collapse. A change of fresh clothes in her bedroom—well, actually, it was more of a cubicle than a bedroom—further revived her. And when she returned to the main room and sniffed the air, which was rich with a savory aroma, she felt positively regenerated.

Dallas was in the kitchen alcove applying herbs and spices with a reckless confidence. Mysterious seasonings she hadn't even known were in her cupboards. He had already set the table, and in the center stood a plate with dessert on it.

"Pralines? I didn't have any pralines."

"Your assistant did. I spotted a box of them on her desk when we came in."

"You went down to the office and swiped Denise's energy boosters? She is not going to be happy about that."

"Promise her a nice Christmas bonus."

"I may not be in business by May Day, never mind Christmas."

"Sure you will. We're going to take care of that while we eat. Sit down, it's almost ready."

"We are? How?"

But he made her wait until he had served the chicken, rice and mixed vegetables. "Taste," he commanded.

She did and was ready to forgive him anything.

"So?"

"Fair," she said.

"Liar."

"All right, so it's better than fair. It's great." Making him, she thought, as sexy in the kitchen as he was in— No, she'd better not go there. "Now can we get down to— What exactly is it we're getting down to?"

"Trying to put together what we've learned today so we can save your agency." Between bites, he offered a scenario of Laura Hollister's secretive existence in the weeks before her death. "There's a pattern here and what repeats itself over and over, is Laura's need for money. It was an issue in her marriage and in her relationship with her sister."

Christy nodded. "Money to indulge a passion for expensive jewelry."

"Apparently. So where does she turn for those sums? There's Resurrection sitting out there along the river road, but what's left of the plantation isn't worth much, not surrounded as it is by those industrial storage tanks."

"And, anyway," Christy said, "her sister would never have agreed to sell the property, not when it's the resting place of Claiborne ancestors."

"No," Dallas agreed, "but there was something valuable in that crumbling house that Laura could sell."

"The architectural treasures we discovered in Dutch Vasey's warehouse."

"Exactly. And who would know she and Vasey were stripping the place when Monica probably never had a reason to go out there, or Glenn either?"

Christy nodded. "Which would explain all her visits to Resurrection, most of them at night. If it's true, then Vasey didn't steal all that stuff. He paid Laura for it."

"And maybe even got her involved in the profitable plundering of the old cemeteries. Could be they had a falling out over that. Suppose Vasey wanted to get his hands on the monuments in the Claibore plot, but that's where Laura drew the line. They argue, it gets violent and he kills her."

"Yeesss," Christy said slowly.

Dallas put down his fork and gazed at her. "And you are not satisfied by any of this."

"It all fits. It's just that…"

"What?"

"The voodoo. Where does it come in?"

"Who says it has to?" Before she could remind him of what she'd found in both the attic and the warehouse, he went on swiftly, "Yeah, I know, the gris-gris. They exist, but that doesn't mean they have any connection with Laura and her murder. Could be the cops are right about kids fooling around with voodoo. Maybe they got into the house before it was stripped and nailed a charm under the stairs and another one up in the attic."

Logic told Christy that his explanation made sense. Then why couldn't she get herself to accept it?

"Fun, huh?" he said, watching her struggle with doubt. "Afraid it gets even funnier, grits."

"How?"

"We don't have squat to prove any of this, which still leaves ol' Glenn facing a murder charge."

Christy lowered her fork. She was no longer hungry, maybe because that ache was there again at the back of her neck. She turned her head from side to side, trying to ease it.

"Your neck bothering you again?" he asked.

"Frustration, I guess. Wondering how we're going to get the evidence to save my client."

"Here, let Dr. McFarland cure you."

Before she could stop him, he rose from the table and came around to the back of her chair. "What are you—"

"It's all right. I'm not going to twist anything. Just a little gentle massage."

Which was exactly what she was afraid of, those seductive hands on her vulnerable flesh. "Um, listen, I don't think—"

"That's it," he said, his strong fingers soothing the back of her neck, "don't think. We'll get the answers we need. For now just relax, let the tension go."

How was she supposed to do that when his deep voice and sensual hands were the cause of her tension? On the other hand, his treatment did feel good. Awfully good. *Dangerously* good. But she didn't seem to have the will to resist him. He went on working his slow magic, stroking and rubbing until she felt so warm and languid she could have purred.

Her defenses were entirely gone when he leaned down to murmur in a husky voice, "Better?"

She felt his breath on her cheek. Turning her head, she discovered his mouth close to her own, his eyes smiling at her. That's when she realized it was more than just her body that was at risk from Dallas McFarland. Her soul was in equal jeopardy.

Chapter Seven

And she suddenly didn't care. She was fed up with pretending that she didn't want Dallas's arms around her, his mouth glued to hers. Because that's exactly what she did want, and had been wanting from the moment he had fished her out of that hole in the attic at Resurrection. As for her soul being in jeopardy—and, yes, her heart, too—well, she was prepared to risk both of them. It was time all right, long past time they did something about this sizzle between them. Except, as she just now realized, he *wasn't* doing anything about it. His mouth still hovered near her own, but that was all. No lips joined with hers to send liquid fire through her veins. What was he waiting for? Maybe her answer. She gave it to him in a silken whisper, a signal of encouragement.

"Oh, yes, I feel much better."

"Good," he said briskly, his face withdrawing from hers as he stood erect again.

Well, damn. After all her denials, all her resistance, was he no longer interested?

"Because," he went on, coming around to the side of her chair, "I wouldn't want to take advantage of a woman in pain."

"You haven't taken advantage of me," she accused him.

"I think I'm about to, though." Bending down, he scooped her into his arms, carried her effortlessly to the other side of the table, and settled on his own chair, cradling her in his lap. "Now, see, this works. Leaning over your shoulder like that was apt to give *me* a crick in the neck."

Ah, she thought, so that was the problem. "When are you going to be certain of it?" she asked, looping her arms around his neck. "About taking advantage of me, I mean?"

His glinting gaze met hers, searching for an invitation and finding something better than that. An eagerness for his kiss. "Just made up my mind," he said.

His head dipped, his mouth seeking and finding hers as he answered her longing with a potent kiss. A wanton business that involved his marauding tongue teasing every corner of her mouth. Christy responded with her own tongue, tasting the male essence of him, inhaling his clean scent and in the process, losing her last shreds of sanity. However, when he finally permitted her to breathe again, she did voice a token objection.

"You promised me faithfully that this wasn't going to happen again."

"I lied."

She hesitated, then nodded solemnly. "I can accept that."

That's when he began to kiss her again, treating her to another catalog of blissful sensations. Not all of them involved his mouth. In fact, some of the more interesting ones were connected with his hands. They had managed to find the path to her breasts by stealing under her T-shirt and climbing inch by sweet inch to her bra. Skillful fingers found and unhooked the front clasp, parting the fabric.

Her breasts were his after that, and there was no area of them that he neglected. He cupped, stroked, gently squeezed, and by the time he got around to slowly, torturously rubbing her tender nipples, Christy's bones had turned to mush.

She knew he was equally aroused. She could feel his hardness straining against her bottom, which was why his abrupt retreat was so surprising. In one minute he was kissing and fondling her, and in the next both his mouth and his hands had left the scene. Now what was going on?

"We can't do this," he said.

Oh, no, she groaned to herself, not again! Didn't this lout realize what it had cost her to finally acknowledge her desire for him? Didn't he have any sensitivity about abandoning her just when she was coming to a nice simmer?

"Why not?" she challenged him. And this better be good, she thought.

"Well, actually, we could, but chairs can be damn awkward."

She could have smacked him. Instead, she sagged against him in relief. "So this is all about positions again, huh?"

"Hey, I like to be comfortable. Allows me to concentrate on the important stuff." He jerked his head in the direction of her bedroom. "So, with your permission..."

"Be my guest."

She approved of his enthusiasm when, still bearing her, he surged to his feet and strode with her into the bedroom. She liked his eagerness when he placed her on the wide bed, stretched out beside her, and began to kiss her again. Not just on the mouth this time either but everywhere with hot, wet, lingering kisses. Of course, those occurred after he had helped her to shed her clothes before disposing of his own garments.

And she positively loved all the things he said to her that accompanied the stripping and the kissing. Raspy, sometimes ragged-voiced endearments like, "Look at you, grits. You're every man's fantasy. Both sexy and smart."

Smart? He actually thought she was smart *and* sexy? Oh, boy.

There were other things he told her, and she hated it that she didn't hear them, that they were all blurred. That was because by then his mouth had reached her breasts, and in between his whispers, his tongue performed the most exquisite maneuvers on her rigid nipples. How could she possibly understand him when he was lavishing that kind of attention on her?

The worst of it was, being in such a daze, she couldn't properly savor his own body. But she did her best. After all, it was such a splendid body, all sleek and swollen in the right places, not something to be neglected. So she branded what areas she could reach with her hands and mouth.

Dallas must have appreciated her performance, and not just because his thick groans assured her that he did. It was his hands again that expressed his satisfaction. They were down between her thighs. Centered, in fact, on the core of her womanhood. They were clever hands, their long fingers tenderly clasping, caressing, cherishing until she was raw with need.

"Christy?" His eyes were dark, urgent as they searched hers.

She understood him. "Yes, anything," she gasped.

"*Anything* means no turning back."

Was he afraid he would hurt her emotionally? Well, maybe he would, but she didn't care about that now. If there were consequences, she would deal with them later. Much later.

"I can handle this," she promised him. "I'm sexy and smart, remember?"

"And beautiful. Don't forget beautiful," he said, settling himself between her parted thighs with a slow, lusty smile that sent tremors coursing through her body even before he joined his hardness with her softness.

The feeling of his being inside her was incredible, something that was both powerful and tender at the same time. He gave her a moment to relish that pleasure, to adjust herself to him. Then he began to rock her with long, slow strokes. Winding herself around him, Christy answered his primitive rhythms.

Thrust by thrust, tempo increasing, he carried them ever higher. Up and up into a rarefied atmosphere where the light was radiant, blinding. And just when she thought she could endure no more, when every nerve ending in her body was raging, clamoring for relief, he released them on a pinnacle of roaring, mindless joy.

Somewhere between oblivion and the return of full awareness, while still clasped in each other's arms, she heard Dallas ask her something in a grave tone. She tried to focus on his words.

"There now, did that take care of it?"

"Uh, is it possible to be a little more specific here, please?"

"The ache in your neck. All gone, is it?"

"Oh, definitely gone," she purred. "I highly recommend your treatment."

"Yeah?" He sounded pleased. "Well, just remember, my office is open to you anytime." Planting a kiss on the tip of her nose, he rolled her to her side, snuggled against her tightly, and drifted off.

Christy lay there in the darkness that was relieved only by the soft glow of the lanterns out in the courtyard. She listened absently to the muted sound of jazz music somewhere down the street, a familiar evidence of the nightly revelry in her beloved Quarter.

Dallas didn't stir when she lifted a hand to his head, smoothing his tousled dark hair. She wished she could join him, sink into the same kind of deep, easy sleep. After this long, eventful day she needed that kind of rest. Not possible. Not just yet anyway, because those emotional consequences she'd been avoiding had just caught up with her.

Damn.

How had she gotten herself into this mess? It was all very confusing. At the start of this case, she had entertained some vague hope that when Laura's death had been solved, and following a decent interval, of course, she and Glenn might find each other again. But now Glenn Hollister was no more substantial for her than a bayou fog.

And what about the man beside her? She gazed at his strong, handsome face, a yearning inside her, and decided that *he* was very real and that out of nowhere she had these feelings for him. Trouble was, she wasn't exactly clear what those feelings were. She tried to define them.

From a mere phone call her shrewd father had determined the solid worth of Dallas McFarland. It wasn't that easy for Christy. So what was she willing to give him? He was sexy. No question of that. He was funny. Also a definite. He was a cuddler. Always good. *And* he could cook. That alone could recommend him for the all-time title of Mr. Right. Of course, it didn't hurt that he also seemed to care for her, though just how much was yet to be determined.

So why was she holding back? Why wasn't she head over heels in love with the man and ready to shout it? Maybe because there was…well, something she still didn't trust, but for the life of her she couldn't imagine what it was.

DALLAS GAZED at her across the table, looking like a kid whose favorite yo-yo has just been taken away from him. Which, in his case, was certainly possible.

"Let me get this straight," he said, reaching for one of the blueberry muffins he had whipped up for their breakfast. "We just spent a night in paradise, and all you want to talk about is business?"

"I'm worried."

Dividing the muffin, he slathered butter on both halves, offered her one and began to eat the other between swallows of coffee. "This had better be good, because I've got to tell you I expected to listen to nothing but praise this morning. Lots of it."

"One of these days you're going to drown in that ego of yours. And this *is* important."

"Okay, let's hear how important."

She ignored her muffin and described her concern. "Except for the voodoo part, everything we put together yesterday about Laura and Dutch Vasey seemed to fit so perfectly. That's why I couldn't understand why something about the whole explanation kept nagging at me."

"You think we left something out?"

"We did," she insisted, "and when I was blow-drying my hair just now, I remembered what it was. Something Glenn said when he first told me about his wife's murder. That one of the reasons the police suspect him is because two of Laura's close friends were worried about her in those last weeks before she died. She was behaving as though she was frightened of something and when they asked her about it, she said she was scared of her husband."

"And being ol' Glenn we're talking about, that's pretty laughable."

Christy let that one pass. "But if they're right, and she

was frightened, *really* frightened to a point of desperation—''

''Then her connection with Dutch Vasey wouldn't be enough to explain it. There was something more going on than stripping Resurrection and plundering cemeteries. Mmm.''

Christy watched him as he pushed back from the table. He was no longer interested in blueberry muffins or dwelling on his talents in the bedroom. Those expressive black eyebrows were knit in a frown of concentration. Dallas McFarland was once again wearing the skin of a dedicated private investigator.

''You think,'' he finally asked her, ''that you could persuade your client to trust you with his late wife's jewelry collection for a few hours?''

Christy was baffled. This was not what she'd expected to hear. ''Why? What are we going to do with it?''

''Laura must have had a favorite jeweler whose reputation she trusted. Find out who it is. I want him to value the stuff for us.''

''What on earth for?''

''Not sure, but I think your instinct thing is contagious, and I may have caught it. Let's just see what the jeweler has to say.''

She was inclined to think his idea was a waste of time, but for want of a better plan she was prepared to humor him. ''I'd better give Glenn a call and tell him we're on our way and why.''

Dallas stopped her as she started to shove back from the table. ''Tell you what. Why don't you go on alone and I'll meet you outside the Hollister house afterward. I should check in with my office, and in case you haven't noticed, I could use a change of clothes and a shave.''

As a matter of fact, she had noticed the dark stubble on

his jaw. Noticed it and considered it damn sexy. *Watch it, Christy. You go on like this, and you'll be dragging him back into that bedroom.* Which wasn't a bad idea, except she had a client to vindicate and her agency to save.

"All right," she agreed.

He reached across the table and caught her hand in a proprietary way. "Just remember that all you want from ol' Glenn is the loan of his wife's jewelry."

Was she hearing right? Was Dallas McFarland actually jealous? Interesting. No, had to be more than merely interesting since a little thrill was chasing around inside her.

THE CREAM-COLORED convertible was waiting for her at the curb when she came away from Glenn's house an hour later lugging the leather case that contained Laura Hollister's jewelry. Dallas was leaning against the fender, looking gorgeous in a pair of cargo pants and a fresh knit shirt that emphasized his masculinity. And wouldn't you know, she'd be wearing her usual uniform of Cubs cap and long shorts. One of these days she was going to have to start making a more impressive fashion statement.

"Any problem?" he wanted to know.

"No, and Glenn wasn't worried about lending us the collection, but it makes me nervous being responsible for all these gems. Wait until you get a look at them! Must be a fortune in here. Oh, he did wonder if either of us was planning to attend the funeral."

"This afternoon?"

"No, tomorrow afternoon." She nodded when Dallas lifted his eyebrows. "I know. I figured, too, that it would be scheduled for today since the wake was yesterday. But they've delayed it for another day to allow an elderly Claiborne aunt to get here. I feel so sorry for Glenn. All this waiting and wondering if at any minute the police are going to come banging on his door.''

For once Dallas didn't make a joke about it. In fact, his expression was very much on the sober side, almost anxious actually. ''Must be hard on the little girl, too, huh?''

''Daisy? I think she's too young to understand what's going on. Anyway, I didn't see her this time. Are we taking my car or yours?''

''I'll drive. You get the place?''

''Purreau's. It's on Carondelet just off Canal.''

When they arrived at the address minutes later, and Christy saw that it was one of those small, exclusive establishments that had probably been in business for the last two centuries, she regretted even more that she was in shorts and running shoes. However, they were greeted courteously by a silver-haired woman who conducted them without question into the workroom of the jeweler who had served Laura Hollister.

What Christy expected was an older gentleman with the exquisite manners of an antebellum Creole, something out of the same mold as her neighbor, Alistair St. Leger. What she and Dallas got was Buzz Purreau, with a ponytail and a skinny frame, who didn't look old enough to vote. Christy didn't feel so bad now about her shorts and running shoes.

''How you doin', folks? Help you?'' he inquired, lowering the volume on a radio tuned to a rock station.

Buzz believed in advertising. He had a diamond stud in one ear, a gold ring in the other and several gold chains around his neck. But since the longest of those chains bore a jeweler's loupe resting on his chest, Christy assumed he knew his business.

Dallas introduced them and explained their visit, adding an earnest, ''Anything you can tell us about Laura Hollister's collection may help our investigation.''

"Sure, glad to be of service. Let's see what you've got."

Christy placed the leather case on the work table in front of him. "There's a note inside from Mr. Hollister authorizing you to provide us with the value of the pieces. We understand that the majority of them came from Purreau's."

"She did buy a lot from us over the years. I created some of the original pieces myself. She never wanted anything but the best."

Seating himself on his work stool, Buzz unlocked the case and folded back the lid. Christy saw Dallas's eyes widen at the sight of the glittering array against nests of black velvet. The jeweler glanced at Glenn's note before fitting the loupe to his eye. Lifting out each piece, he proceeded to inspect them one by one. Christy began to have an uneasy feeling as she watched the frown on Buzz Purreau's face slowly deepen.

Finally removing the loupe from his eye, he lifted his head and met their anxious gazes. "Hate to tell you this, guys, but these are fakes. Except for the sapphire ring. It's genuine, but the stone has a serious flaw."

Christy couldn't believe it. "All of them? Are you sure?"

"My family has been in the jewelry trade since Noah loaded his ark. I'm sure all right."

"But the pieces you created for her—"

"They're here all right. Not original, though. Copies, every one of them. Pretty decent copies, actually, but none of it more valuable than costume jewelry."

"Her husband said she'd been adding to the collection lately. Things she might have bought elsewhere. What about those pieces?"

"Flashy, but basically worthless."

Dallas had been silent during this exchange. Christy

glanced at him. There was no expression of surprise on his lean face, which meant he must have anticipated such a result or at least the possibility of it. It was why he'd wanted the jewelry collection examined.

"Sorry to disappoint you like this," Buzz apologized. "And I wish I could offer you an explanation, but I can't. Hey, though," he said, directing a twenty-four carat smile at Christy, "if you're interested in gems, I could show you some real beauties in our vault. A personally conducted tour, anytime."

It was nice to be flirted with, Christy thought, even when it was someone who had probably started shaving last year. Dallas didn't agree. "She'd probably get a real buzz out of that, Buzz, but I bet your girlfriend wouldn't like it."

"I don't have a girlfriend."

"Get one."

Poor guy, Christy thought, watching the young jeweler's Adam's apple bob nervously under Dallas's steely gaze. She ought to have been annoyed with Dallas for assuming he had the right to stake her out as his personal territory, but it was pretty hard to be angry at the same time you were experiencing a warm glow.

At least Dallas had the courtesy to thank the jeweler for his help, even if he was a little effusive about it. "Buzz, it's been a real pleasure. And if we're ever in the market for diamonds, we know just where to come."

"'Preciate that," Buzz mumbled, hastily closing the leather case and returning it to Christy.

"You take care now," Dallas drawled to the jeweler as he cupped Christy under the elbow and steered her out of the workroom.

She ought to have lectured McFarland when they got back to the car, except she kind of liked him all possessive and protective like this. Up to a point, that is. Anyway, she had another subject that demanded attention.

"Guess I don't have to be nervous about this thing anymore," she said, slinging the jewelry case into the back seat of the convertible before facing Dallas accusingly. "You might have told me what you suspected about the collection."

"It wasn't a suspicion, only the wildest guess that something might not be right about that jewelry. Probably because we kept hearing Laura was desperate to get her hands on funds."

Christy nodded. "In other words, too desperate to be explained by a passion for jewelry. What does it all mean then?"

Dallas lifted his broad shoulders in a small shrug. "For starters, I think we can safely say that what the lady did, maybe over a period of time, was to sell off the valuable pieces while replacing them with copies that were close enough to the originals to conceal what she was doing."

"And," Christy added, remembering what Glenn had told her yesterday morning, "to make the deception even more believable, she added to the collection. Things that were flashy but obviously inexpensive. Which means she needed money, a lot of money. More money than she was getting from selling Vasey those architectural treasures from Resurrection. But why, if it wasn't to buy expensive jewelry?"

"You tell me."

As a matter of fact, Christy suddenly realized that she could do just that. Maybe. "Yes! I said earlier it could be the explanation. And then, of course, after what Glenn discovered about the collection being even bigger, I had to go and forget that possibility. But now it makes perfect sense!"

"You wanna ease off on the excitement there, grits, and try to be a little more specific?"

"Blackmail payments! That's why Laura had to have all those sums. She was paying a blackmailer. I mean, think about it, Dallas. She's behaving strangely, she's afraid of something. Her friends notice that she's afraid, and to protect her secret she tells them the lie about being scared of Glenn. And all those visits to Resurrection…could be they weren't just to strip the house. Could be she was meeting the blackmailer out there, and if she finally couldn't take anymore and they argued…well, you see how that could have turned out. So what do you think? Does it work for you this time? Huh? Maybe?"

Dallas was silent as they stood there beside the convertible.

"McFarland," she pleaded, "give me something. I'm dying here."

"Grits," he said slowly, "you are scaring the hell out of me. If you keep on coming up with inspired deductions like this, I'm gonna have to turn my list of clients over to you and close the doors of my agency."

He exaggerated the value of the solution she had just proposed, but who was she to complain? No siree, he could go right on praising her in those terms. Of course, he *would* have to go and temper the compliment with a dry, "Have to warn those clients, though, that they'll be getting themselves a P.I. with attitude."

"Look, before you go out of business, can I get just one opinion out of you?"

"Which one would that be?"

"Do we know now just why Dutch Vasey was so scared that he locked us up in his warehouse and then did a vanishing act?"

"Sounds like we do."

"So we agree that Vasey is the best candidate for Laura's blackmailer and her killer. Seems to me then that it's time for us to talk to that nice homicide detective again."

Dallas grinned and chucked her under the chin. "You go and do that. I'll drive you there and drop you off."

"What will you be doing?"

"Hunting up bail for you when he throws you in a cell."

Christy made a face. "I see your point. The police aren't going to listen to us when we don't even know why Vasey was blackmailing her."

"Yeah, I'd suggest we go and scare up a little evidence first."

Christy gazed at him. He was leaning now against the door of the car, legs crossed at the ankle, thumbs hooked into the pockets of his pants and wearing an expression that gave her a sinking feeling. "Oh, you're not proposing we go back to Vasey's store and break in through a window again? Not after what happened to us there yesterday?"

"Certainly not. This time I intend to bring a professional set of lock picks."

"You wouldn't!"

"No, you're right. Insane thing to consider trying in broad daylight. We'll wait until after dark."

"Dallas—"

"Okay, so it's a long shot, but if Vasey was in a hurry, the evidence of that blackmail could still exist somewhere inside that store. You in?"

Did she have a choice? Obviously she didn't, not if she still wanted to clear Glenn and save her agency.

Dallas drove her back to her car waiting outside the Hollister house in the Garden District. "I'll pick you up at your place after sundown," he said, pulling over to the curb.

He had told her on the way over that he would be spending the rest of the day helping one of his operatives sort out a problem on another case. Christy couldn't imagine what it would be like to have an agency so successful that you had to deal with more than one client at a time. Nor did she want to depress herself by trying.

Jewelry case in hand, she started to slide out of the convertible, but he stopped her. "When you give that back to ol' Glenn…"

"Yes?"

His eyes got dark and his voice deepened as he leaned toward her. "Just make sure that's all you give him. And in case there's any question about that…"

Christy suddenly found herself hauled up against him. Her mouth opened in surprise. He must have thought she was about to object, which she certainly had no intention of doing. In any case, he silenced her by covering her mouth with his own.

The blistering kiss that followed informed her quite plainly just who, in his opinion, was entitled to be intimate with her. And should she have any lingering doubt about that, he convinced her otherwise by deepening the kiss so dynamically that Christy was robbed of both air and reason.

She was shaken by the time he released her. He was maddeningly calm, parting from her with a confident, "Hey, give my regards to ol' Glenn, will you?"

Reaching around her, Dallas opened the door for her. Christy managed to stagger out of the car. She stood on the sidewalk in a daze, staring after the convertible as it sped away down the street. Damn him anyway for leaving her in this state!

Struggling to restore her sobriety, Christy headed for the front door of the Hollister house. She forbade herself, tempting though it was, to attach too much meaning to what had just happened. Even so, it was awfully hard to focus on her meeting with Glenn in his parlor a few seconds later, when her brain was still reeling from Dallas McFarland's possessive, totally sizzling kiss.

Glenn was shocked about both the jewelry and the possibility that his wife was the victim of a blackmailer. To Christy's disappointment, he could offer no helpful information on the subject, either who the blackmailer might be or what Laura could have done to be blackmailed for.

"I guess the truth is," he said sadly, "Laura and I didn't have much of a marriage. If she was being blackmailed, I didn't have a clue because I never knew what was going on with her or what she was really thinking. She seemed to want it that way."

"Have you finished going through her things? There may be some explanation there."

He shook his head. "Right there is an example of what I mean. Most husbands would have a pretty good idea of the belongings their wives left behind. But Laura guarded her privacy, which leaves her personal stuff a mystery to me. There's so much of it, but I'll go on sorting and searching."

Christy had permitted herself to be so dazzled by that kiss that she'd failed to realize until this moment that Glenn himself was distracted. "What is it, Glenn?" she asked him gently. "Has there been some new development?"

He nodded glumly. "It looks like I won't be the only one looking. I just got off the phone from my lawyer. The police succeeded in getting that warrant to search the house and grounds. It feels like they're closing in on me, Christy."

"We're going to save you, Glenn." She offered him words of encouragement. She reminded him that the investigation was finally producing results. Promised him they would catch Laura's killer. And by the time she left the house, she'd convinced Glenn everything would come out right. She just wasn't sure *she* believed it.

CHRISTY INTENDED to spend the afternoon preparing for their evening raid on Vasey Antiques and Architectural Salvage. There were a number of things on her mental list that would help to prevent another disastrous performance like yesterday's.

Her gun should be cleaned and the batteries in her cell phone tested so that both were primed for action. Then, to be sure she was in peak condition herself, she needed to run for a couple of miles along the levee, maybe practice some of those tactics she'd learned in a defense class last month. She might even take a nap so that she'd be fresh and alert tonight. Any one of these activities would be useful.

What Christy did instead was try on clothes. In fact, just about every garment in her wardrobe got an audition. By midafternoon her bed and every chair in her apartment were piled with rejects. Nothing satisfied her. Her only certainty was that she was not going to Magazine Street in shorts, running shoes and a baseball cap. Not this time, no way.

Ah, now this was a decided improvement.

She stood before her full-length mirror, scrutinizing the latest entry. A little black number that qualified as a power suit. Very effective with the clingy skirt well above her knees and her feet clad in four-inch heels.

"Nuh-uh," came the voice of judgment from behind her.

Christy looked over her shoulder to find Denise lurking in the doorway. "I'm sorry. I must have forgotten that I invited you up here to cast your vote."

"Girlfriend, you're gonna go and make a real fashion statement chasing bad guys in that."

''Who said I'm chasing bad guys? I'm not chasing any bad guys tonight.''

Denise rolled her eyes. ''You sure are after somebody all tarted up like that. Wonder who it can be?''

''It's no one. This is strictly business. And why aren't you down in the office tending to yours?''

''Huh, what have I got to be busy about? I don't see no bills to be sent out to customers. Don't see no reports to be typed up and filed away. Nothing like that.'' She pointed to the bed. ''Wear them dark pants and that gray shirt there. Good for nighttime undercover work. He'll like you in them pants. Does things for your butt.''

''Denise?''

''I'm here.''

''Don't be. Go away.''

Denise turned and ambled toward the stairway. ''Guess it can affect some women like that,'' she said loudly when she reached the flight and started down. ''Guess being in love can make 'em real testy.''

Christy ran after her, calling down the stairway, ''I don't know why you're on his side anyway. He stole your pralines.''

''I noticed that. Been wondering what for. Must've been for something *real* sweet.''

Denise laughed and went on her way. Christy waited until she was out of sight before she dropped weakly on the edge of the nearest available chair. Oh, God, Denise was right! The unthinkable had crept up on her and sucker punched her when she wasn't looking. She was in love with Dallas McFarland!

Well, damn. What was she supposed to do about it? For one thing, he had yet to utter a single word telling her how he felt about her, except if actions counted, he had already spoken volumes. Not the same as a commitment, though. Did she want a commitment? She didn't know about that.

Why didn't she know? What was making her hesitate? It wasn't like he was all wrong for her, not when she admired qualities in him she would never have guessed a mere two days ago existed in that gorgeous body. Under his playful humor and sham arrogance, there was a depth and sensitivity to him. Okay, so maybe some of the arrogance was genuine, but that didn't take away from his innate decency.

Then why didn't she completely trust him? Could be because she didn't seem able to shake the small, but persistent feeling that Dallas was keeping something from her. Probably her imagination, but still…

In the end, there was only one thing Christy was decisive about. She was going to wear the black slacks and the gray shirt. That was a definite. Unless, of course, a blue top looked better. And maybe jeans instead of the slacks? Or—

Chapter Eight

"Used to be very good at this kind of thing in my younger days," Dallas bragged, inserting the pick into the cylinder lock of the back door to Dutch Vasey's store. "I don't imagine I've lost my touch."

"Uh-huh. I suppose that means you have a long record of breaking and entering." Christy was annoyed with him. She had finally settled on the trim black pants and gray shirt, and for all the notice he had taken of her classy outfit, she might have worn hip-waders.

"Certainly not. I only used my skill to help old ladies get into their houses after they'd lost their keys. Hold that flashlight steady."

She wished he'd hurry. There wasn't so much as a security light burning in either the store or the warehouse behind them, which must mean Vasey hadn't been back since he'd fled the scene. But the absence of any lamp made the area so dark that the glow from their flashlight was making her nervous. What if its gleam was so obvious that a neighbor spotted it and called the police? She didn't think they'd be so forgiving this time.

"What's taking you so long?" she whispered.

"Hey, this is delicate work."

"I just hope that old lady isn't looking out her window again."

"Not a chance. She's only interested in nudies, remember, and how can she spot those after the sun goes down?"

He was right. Daylight was much less safe for an activity like this, but it was a lot friendlier. It gave her a creepy feeling imagining that anything could be lurking here in the blackness ready to pounce on them.

"Getting into the warehouse was a lot easier," she observed, careful to keep her voice down.

"Thought we agreed this was a much better possibility. What the hell is the matter with this thing?"

He had been fishing in the lock with both confidence and patience. They seemed to have deserted him. He rattled the pick with exasperation.

"Well, you can't force a window this time. Not with those bars on them."

"I know that," he muttered. "Don't you think I know that?"

He attacked the lock again, grumbled a lot and swore some more. Christy stood it as long as she could.

"Move out of the way," she commanded him.

"Excuse me? Did I just hear that somebody actually thinks her touch is more magic than mine? Look, if I can't tumble this lock, you don't imagine you—"

"Watch and learn."

Seizing the pick from him, she shoved the flashlight into his hand and went to work.

"I'll be damned," he murmured, observing her progress with the lock with amazement as he stood close behind her, directing the beam of the flashlight down over her shoulder. "You do look like you know what you're doing."

"I have three brothers, all P.I.s. They taught me a few useful things, this being one of them. It's all a question of raising the pins and drivers so that the breaks are lined up with the joint between the cylinder and plug. Once you manage that— What are you doing!''

"Holding the light for you," he said innocently.

"You just nibbled the back of my neck."

"Actually, it was more of a nuzzle. Mmm, nice scent."

It wasn't easy to get tough with him. Not anymore. Not when his merest touch made her insides all squishy and yearning for more. But if he went on tasting and sniffing her like this, they were going to end up on the floor of this alley. Not the best way to acquire the evidence they were seeking.

"Ever have a lock pick jab you in a vulnerable spot, McFarland?"

"Maybe I'll just stand over here."

Satisfied when he'd moved safely off to the side, Christy resumed her surgery on the lock. A few seconds later she felt the plug beginning to rotate. "I think maybe...yes, that does it." There was the soft snap of the latch sliding back. "We're in!" she announced triumphantly.

"I'm beginning to wonder why I'm even here," Dallas complained.

"Don't be silly. You're very useful to this operation." Removing her gun from her bag, she slapped it into his hand. "Because you get to go in there first in case Vasey is hiding behind that door."

"That's what I like about you, grits. Always putting my needs ahead of yours."

Gun in one hand, flashlight in the other, he spread the door open and moved cautiously into the building. Christy followed close behind him. To her relief, there were no surprises waiting for them.

"Where are we?" she whispered, unable to tell in the darkness. At that second she stumbled over what felt like a broken chair. "Oh—storeroom, I guess." The flashlight moved away from her. "What are you doing?"

"Closing the door and pulling the shades down at the windows. Hold on while I find a light switch."

"Should we risk it?" Too late. Dallas had already located the switch. Fluorescent lights overhead flickered into life.

"There's no danger," he assured her. "Shades are drawn, and if anyone notices the light, they'll just assume Vasey is in here or that security lamps came on."

Christy surveyed the room. It was a storeroom all right, containing a jumble of battered furniture that might once have passed as second-rate antiques, but now had a hard time qualifying as respectable junk. "This doesn't look very promising."

"No, but this does," he said, leading the way into another room located behind the showroom at the front of the store.

By the time Christy joined him he had the lights on. There were no windows in here to betray them. The place looked like a combination of office and—well, she wasn't sure. There was a TV on a scarred desk, a cot against one wall and a bathroom whose fixtures looked like they hadn't seen a scrub brush since the last Administration. For all she knew, Dutch Vasey had not only worked here, he'd lived here. That would explain an odor that smelled like too many bad take-outs.

"What now?" she asked.

"You get the pleasure of conducting a search."

"Uh-huh. Plan on stretching out there on the cot while I perform this search, do you?"

He wagged the gun in his hand. "Somebody has to play guard dog."

Christy had no argument with that. It would have been

foolish to let themselves be surprised a second time on these premises. She just hoped, since his own gun was still with the police, that he was a better shot with the Glock than she was. She also hoped it wouldn't be necessary for him to prove it.

"All right, what am I looking for?"

He had taken up a position in the office doorway where he could keep an eye on both the front and back entrances to the store. "Could be anything. Photos, letters, that sort of thing."

This wasn't going to be easy, Christy thought. "Where do you suggest I start?"

"Your call."

A lot of help he was, she grumbled to herself. She took another visual tour of the room's furnishings. There was a tall metal filing cabinet in one corner. Filing cabinets meant paper. Mountains of it. Convincing herself the desk was more interesting, she passed on the filing cabinet.

She knew her choice was a good one when she rounded the desk and discovered what was fastened by black ribbon to a handle of one of its drawers. "Nasty thing," she muttered.

"What have you got?"

"Another gris-gris. What do you want to bet it's here to warn intruders away from the desk? Means he's hiding something inside."

"Go for it."

With a sense of growing excitement, Christy started with the deep drawer to which the gris-gris was attached. It contained two items. One of them was an almost empty pint of whiskey, evidence that Dutch might not be a blackmailer, but he was certainly a drinker. The other item was a half-eaten sandwich, which must have been there a long time since it had something fuzzy and green growing on it.

It was a miracle the thing hadn't attracted vermin. And why did she have to go and think of that she wondered, glancing around with the kind of apprehension she reserved for mice.

"Anything?" Dallas asked.

"Yes. Dutch has disgusting habits." She tried a second drawer. "Oh, look, you have something in common with him." She held up a yo-yo.

"You're not having much luck, are you?"

"I'm not through."

She pawed through the contents of the other drawers. One of them yielded the kind of reading material that confirmed her opinion Dutch Vasey was a slob. And in the last drawer—

"Oh, my!"

"Find it?"

"Not unless these belonged to Laura Hollister, and somehow I don't think they did." With thumb and forefinger, she held up a pair of lurid, red, bikini panties. "This guy is into more vices."

"Maybe he's a cross-dresser. That could be fun. Shame, though, that nothing you've turned up so far is illegal."

"I know," she said in disappointment, "the desk is a washout."

There was no avoiding it. She would have to tackle that filing cabinet. Like everything else in the place, it was in a sorry condition, the metal case dented and rusting.

"I don't think the man owns anything that's new," Christy said, "which either makes him a cheapskate or not the well-heeled blackmailer we hope he is."

She started with the top drawer. As she'd anticipated, it was filled with paper, all of it consisting of old invoices. The second drawer was no more interesting or incriminating. Just more files related to business. The only letters were from buyers or sellers of antiques, the only photos were those that depicted legitimate salvage pieces.

"Nothing," she reported when the third drawer in the stack proved to be just as discouraging in its contents.

"Guess that means no more naughty stuff either, huh?" Dallas said from the doorway.

"Not even that, but *this* might be more entertaining." She had reached the bottom drawer and it refused to move. "It's the only one that's locked." She rose and started to move away from the cabinet. "Where did we put those picks?"

Dallas swiftly crossed the office. Before she could stop him, he delivered a powerful kick into the top of the drawer that resulted in the snapping of metal inside. "Now it's unlocked."

"Oh, fine. If Dutch Vasey proves to be innocent—"

"Then I owe him a new file cabinet," Dallas promised, returning to his post.

"We'll never know," Christy said dismally. She had crouched again in front of the cabinet and rolled out the drawer. "It's empty. Guess it wasn't locked, just stuck."

Not surprising. None of the old drawers had slid smoothly, including this one. When she tried to shove it back into position, she met with further resistance.

"There's something stopping it," she said.

"Maybe something that jumped out over the back end when I kicked it. Take the drawer out and look."

Christy did as he directed, removing the drawer from the case and ducking her head to peer into the cavity. There in the dust on the floor was a box the size and shape of a book. She withdrew it with hands that trembled and got to her feet.

"Oh, Dallas, it's a videotape! And if that drawer *was* locked, and it must have been, then this means—"

"That you shouldn't start celebrating before we view it. With our luck and Vasey's tastes, it could be an adult movie."

"A VCR! We need to get to a VCR!"

"Turn your head and look."

He nodded in the direction of the TV on the desk. She noticed it then. The TV was one of those units that came equipped with its own VCR. Removing the cassette from its sleeve, she approached the TV.

"Here, you work it. I'm so anxious, I'll just mess it up."

Too eager himself to worry about his vigil in the doorway, he joined her at the desk. "No label," he said, glancing at the cassette when she handed it to him. "That means it's probably not a commercial tape."

"But," she warned him as he popped the cartridge into the player, "if this does turn out to be an adult movie—"

"I know. Watch my mouth, watch my hands."

"Well, at least until we get home."

He looked at her before punching the play button on the machine, an unmistakable gleam in his eyes. "Oh, yeah? Then maybe I hope this thing does end up being X-rated."

But it was not that kind of video. It was something far more disturbing. The two of them stood in shocked silence, watching the vile images on the screen. There was everything to tell them that what they were seeing were the late-night rituals of a voodoo ceremony. The satanic variety.

The figures were gathered somewhere in an isolated clearing lit by torches and the flames of a bonfire—a cult of worshippers composed of men and women both black and white. There were perhaps a dozen of them weaving from side to side to the slow, steady beat of a pair of drums.

Facing them in front of a low altar was their priest wearing the mask of a serpent god. He chanted to them in a low, sibilant voice, using a language that sounded to

Christy like nothing but gibberish. But his followers must have understood him. They responded with moans and cries.

A variety of masks, feathered headdresses and face paint concealed the identities of at least half of the participants. The rest were hidden behind nothing. Their nude bodies wore only the ruddy glow of the firelight. One of those figures was Laura Hollister.

"It is her, isn't it?" Christy whispered.

"With the way the camera keeps focusing on her," Dallas muttered, "I don't think there can be any question of it."

It was awful, Christy thought. And it got worse. At a command from the priest, the drums quickened. The worshippers obeyed their calls with wild, feverish rhythms. Their naked bodies springing to life, they leaped, twisted, wound around each other in an obscene dance. Laura Hollister's performance was more frenzied than the rest.

When the priest raised a knife in one hand and a squawking, squirming chicken in the other, Christy could take no more. "You watch the rest," she murmured. Dallas made no objection when she fled to the doorway to take up his vigil.

"It's safe now," he reported a few minutes later, ejecting the tape from the player.

"How bad did it get?" she asked, rejoining him at the desk.

"Bad enough. I'll spare you the details. All you have to know is that the chicken was sacrificed and that Laura was one of those who drank its blood."

Christy shuddered. "Do you suppose she even knew what she was doing? It looked to me like she was in a trance."

Dallas nodded. "Either induced by the ceremony itself

or maybe some substance abuse. One thing's for sure. She couldn't have realized she was being videotaped like that.''

"She would have known it afterward, though, when Dutch Vasey showed it to her and began to demand his blackmail payments. Now we know what voodoo had to do with all of it. *And* we have the evidence we need,'' she said, taking the cassette from him and tapping its case.

"Looks like it.'' He didn't sound entirely satisfied.

"Dallas, you can't have any doubt about it. This thing would have ruined her socially, maybe cost her her marriage and her child, possibly even had her facing charges. And did you spot the columns in the background when the camera followed the dancers? That was the house at Resurrection, I'm sure of it. Those ceremonies were held out at the Claiborne plantation, which makes it even worse that Laura provided the setting.''

"It's serious,'' Dallas agreed, "but I wonder if it was serious enough to make her so desperate she caved in to the repeated threats of a blackmailer.''

He was silent for a long moment. Christy watched his right hand stirring restlessly, as if it longed to be spinning the yo-yo it didn't have. It was a sign of how intensely his mind was examining everything they had learned.

"The box,'' he said suddenly. "Did you check down inside the box when you removed the cassette?''

"No, it never occurred to me.'' She looked around for the cardboard sleeve. "Where did it get to?''

"Here.'' Dallas found it where it had slipped down behind the TV. She watched him peer into the carton. "Oh, yeah,'' he said, "I think this could be pay dirt.''

His fingers dug deep inside the jacket, withdrawing from its bottom end a tightly folded paper. Christy stood close beside him as he spread his discovery flat on the surface of the desk. It revealed itself as a story clipped from a newspaper dated several months ago. Leaning over the desk, they read the piece. It was brief, tragic and potentially damning.

When they looked up from the article, their eyes met in a mutual conclusion. "You were right," Christy said, "there was something more."

"Yeah," Dallas said solemnly, "and the lady must have been sick with worry about it. Playing around with voodoo is one thing, but the hit-and-run death of a teenager is pretty ugly stuff."

"I don't suppose there's any question Laura was at the wheel of the unidentified car that struck that boy."

"It all fits, Christy. The river road late at night, a woman under the influence of some drug she'd ingested at a mid-night voodoo ceremony, someone beside her a witness to the accident. Hell, Laura Hollister would have been willing to pay her blackmailer whatever he asked not to turn her in."

"And when she had no more to give him, they quarreled and he ended up killing her."

"Sounds about right."

"Do you suppose Dutch Vasey was the priest behind that serpent mask and that he's the one who got her involved with voodoo in the first place?"

"Guy's smarmy enough."

"But not really cunning, I didn't think. Not in that way. At least not so that he'd appeal to a woman like Laura Hollister. Still, it must have been him." She frowned. "It's funny, though."

"You having another of those instinct attacks, grits?"

"Just a tiny one. Just wondering why Vasey wouldn't have destroyed the cassette and the clipping before he ran. I know he was in a hurry, but it's odd he'd leave them behind."

"You're right and that leaves me wondering what else he might have abandoned. Rodents like him never limit themselves to one victim. If he was blackmailing others, chances are good there's more evidence in the place."

"Which," she said firmly, "we will leave for the police to find."

"That's no fun."

"Listen to the man. He loafs in the doorway playing cowboy with a trusty six-shooter while I do all the work. So who's having fun?"

"I'll help you look this time."

"Not smart. No one to stand guard."

"We'll stay alert. Come on, Christy, the more we can come up with, the stronger our case becomes."

That was true. They would need as solid an argument as possible this time to convince the police that Glenn was innocent and that Vasey needed to be found and apprehended. "And just where do we search? I've covered everything in here."

"There's still the storeroom and the showroom up front."

Christy groaned. They would be here all night! That settled it. Something was definitely wrong with her. No sane woman would allow herself to fall in love with a man who would do this to her. She blew out her cheeks in exasperation. "Where do we begin?"

"The showroom involves risking lights that would be pretty obvious from the street. We'll investigate it last if we need to."

Tucking the cassette and the clipping into her bag for safekeeping, she followed him out of the office and into the storeroom.

"You take that side," he directed as he separated from her, "and I'll go through the closet over on this end."

Christy eyed her portion of the room. It didn't look anymore promising than the first time she'd considered it. Just a lot of broken clutter through which she reluctantly waded. She did find a steamer trunk in the corner, but there was nothing inside it except the unappealing odor of mildew.

"You having any luck?" she called.

"Cleaning supplies."

Which, Christy decided, made Dutch Vasey a comedian as well as a blackmailer since dust coated everything in the place. There was certainly a healthy layer of it on the wardrobe that stood against the wall. It was one of those enormous old things with a massive cornice that looked in danger of collapsing. But not, she hoped, before she checked out the interior of the piece.

There were mirrored doors, and when she folded them back they disclosed a rod for clothes on one side and shelves on the other. All were empty. There was a drawer up on top, but it was stuck shut. She wasn't tall enough to get a good grip on the knobs.

Dallas was still rummaging in the closet, his back to her, when she dragged a stool into position. Lowering her shoulder bag to the floor to get it out of the way, she climbed onto the stool. The drawer was stubborn. So was Christy. She yanked on it so forcefully that the battered wardrobe shook and rattled in every seam. The front of the cornice parted company from the rest of the piece. Christy could hear it coming down.

Throwing her arms protectively over her head, she ducked low in an effort to escape a collision. The cornice grazed her hunched-up shoulders and went on its way, landing with a thump on the floor. Nothing else seemed to be descending, so she uncovered her head and stood erect again on the stool. When she opened her eyes, which had been scrunched shut, there was an arm directly in front of her.

Since it didn't seem possible that a human arm could be dangling from the top of the wardrobe, swinging like a slow pendulum a scant three inches from her face, Christy spent several seconds struggling with disbelief.

"What's the racket over there?" Dallas demanded. "Are you all right?"

Christy managed not to scream. She even managed to get down from the stool. Hey, it was no big deal. Just an arm. The fact that it must be attached to a body was something she didn't permit herself to think about. Not then.

"I think," she said, absolutely calm in her reply, "that it's possible I've just found another of Dutch Vasey's victims."

By this time Dallas had joined her on her side of the room. "When you go looking for evidence, you don't fool around, do you?" he said as she pointed up to the place where the front of the cornice had been. The arm was still hanging there, but to her relief it had stopped swinging.

"I suppose," she said, no longer sounding quite so calm, "that one of us ought to find out who it belongs to."

"Seems like a reasonable plan."

He wore a utility belt in which her gun was already tucked. The belt also carried the flashlight. Removing it, he climbed onto the stool she'd vacated. His greater height permitted him an eye level view with the flat roof of the wardrobe. With the aid of the flashlight, he visually examined what had been stuffed down into the gloom behind the tall front of the cornice that was no longer there.

Christy was feeling weaker by the moment as she waited for him. And by the time Dallas came down off the stool she was wilting fast. "Dead?" she croaked.

"Let's see. A bullet through the head, a body that's cold. Yeah, I think that qualifies as dead."

"Shot by Vasey, I suppose. Murdered, just like he murdered Laura Hollister."

"Don't think that's possible, grits. See—" he jerked his thumb in the direction of the ceiling "—the guy up there *is* Dutch Vasey."

Christy was too shaken by now to do more than stare at him. Dallas answered for her. "Uh-huh, it looks like Vasey wasn't running a blackmail racket all on his own. Looks like maybe he wasn't running it at all, but only taking orders from a higher-up. And you'd better sit down. You're sagging."

It sounded like a sensible suggestion. She lowered herself onto the stool. But since that seemed like a rather wimpy thing for a P.I. to do, she made an effort to focus on the newest twist in this case where nothing was turning out to be what it was supposed to be.

Hunched there on the stool, Christy thought about it a moment before offering a possible scenario for Dallas's approval. "Vasey was scared when he found us in his warehouse. After he locked us up, he came in here and called his boss. By the time whoever that is arrived on the scene, Vasey was in a real panic. He threatened to expose the real killer of Laura Hollister to save himself and that someone silenced him with a bullet. That's what you're thinking, isn't it, Dallas?"

"Until somebody comes up with something better anyway."

She nodded slowly. "It works. That's why Vasey didn't seem right to me. It *was* someone else behind that voodoo mask. He killed Laura Hollister and he killed Dutch Vasey. I suppose we have to assume it is a *he.*"

"Or a woman who had help. Vasey was a small man,

but it must have taken real strength to haul his body up a ladder and hide it behind that cornice.''

Christy had experienced outrage when she was convinced Dutch Vasey was a killer. But she'd never felt chilled, as she did now by the shadowy image of a cunning, cold-blooded killer prepared to go to any lengths to conceal his identity.

She knew Dallas could see how shaken she was. That's why he expressed his concern. ''You want to lie down, sweetheart?''

She shook her head. ''Give me a minute. I'll be okay. Uh, I could use some water.'' She didn't need the water, but she didn't want him hovering over her seeing what a pain she was being.

''Coming up. I think I spotted paper cups in that bathroom.''

She watched him go off to the office, hoping he checked the paper cup for bugs before he filled it. In this place, the presence of crawling critters was a definite possibility.

While she waited for Dallas, Christy tried not to think about the body squeezed up there on top of the wardrobe. She made an effort to occupy her mind with something more constructive.

The police, she thought. We'll have to phone the police. We should have done that straightaway. Anyway, they can't say now we don't have evidence of Glenn's innocence. They'll have to believe us when they read the clipping and watch what's in that tape. Of course, as she now realized, neither the tape nor the clipping would still be here if Vasey hadn't been killed.

Damn it, why did she always have to come back to that dead body? And what was keeping Dallas? Her aloneness here was beginning to spook her.

What time was it? She had to squint at her watch to see

that it was almost ten. The light was very poor in here. A couple of the overhead fluorescents had burned out and nobody had replaced them. Christy grumbled to herself about that.

Ten seconds later she regretted her complaint, because weak light was better than no light at all. And that suddenly was what she had, a total blackout. The office, too, must have been plunged into darkness. There was not so much as a flicker from that direction.

Had there been a power failure? If so, it seemed funny that she wasn't hearing from Dallas on the subject. He should have been calling out to her. She opened her mouth to shout to him, but something prevented her from doing that. Probably her sudden awareness of the silence. It was as absolute as the darkness. Christy had a bad feeling about that. A *very* bad feeling.

Why wasn't Dallas on his way back to her? Why wasn't she hearing him knocking into furniture and swearing about it? Where was the glow of his flashlight?

Coming slowly to her feet, she held her breath and listened. There was nothing but the awful silence. But a moment later, ears strained, she heard it. The soft, furtive sound of a footstep across the room. And she knew then that she'd been wise to keep still, to utter no cry that would have betrayed her position. Because Christy was no longer alone in the storeroom. Someone was in here with her. Someone who was hunting her.

Willing herself not to panic, realizing that without a weapon her only defense was evasion, she got down on her hands and knees, and began to crawl along the floor. Her intention was to conceal herself in the maze of junk, but if she plowed into any of that junk, the noise would reveal her location. She moved cautiously, feeling her way down the row.

There was also the chance that she would crawl smack into her enemy. Where was he now? She stopped to listen again and thought she heard the shuffle of footsteps somewhere off to her left. Why was he hunting her in a darkness that, logic told her, he must have caused himself? And what else was her stalker responsible for? Dallas! If Dallas wasn't here, then he must have hurt him, maybe even— No! She refused to name it. Instead, she prayed that nothing serious had happened to Dallas. He had to survive. She had yet to tell him that she loved him. Why hadn't she made the opportunity to do that? Why had she waited? If it should be too late now to let him know—

Don't think that. Don't even let yourself consider it might be too late.

She crept forward again, brushing by what felt like a wicker basket. Then she froze again, startled by the creak of an old floorboard. She waited, heart slamming against her ribs.

Seconds later came a soft, soft rustling. It wasn't several safe yards away this time. It was right here with her in the blackness! So close beside her on the floor that she could actually feel the heat of his presence!

Christy's flesh crawled with terror. Silence no longer seemed of any value. And since the situation now appeared to demand a shrill alarm, she drew a deep breath to scream. That's when a hand was clapped over her mouth.

Chapter Nine

Had she been able to get her teeth over the flesh of that big hand, Christy would have done her best to take a chunk out of it. Fortunately, before she could manage to do just that, a familiar voice hissed into her ear, "Don't bite. It's not nice."

It was the barest of whispers, but it must have been heard. A gun barked. By then she had been dragged down flat on the floor. The bullet struck wood somewhere over her head.

The hand that had been horrifying mere seconds ago was now so welcome, Christy was prepared to kiss it in relief. She would have done so except it had been removed from her mouth.

Her rescuer offered no further explanation. Silence was, again, of vital importance. As they huddled there on the floor, she heard their armed enemy on the move once more. He was coming closer.

Dallas must have seized some object from the junk around them. Must have raised it up and hurled it across the room. It landed with a thunk on the other side. The gun cracked again, sending its fire in that direction.

Their assailant was confused now, not knowing where to seek his target. His footsteps were no longer cautious.

Christy heard the noise of him stumbling over something and then came another long, taut stillness. It was followed again by the footsteps. This time they seemed to be hurrying away toward the front of the building. There was silence once more. An eternity of it.

Dallas finally risked another whisper. "He's gone, but just to make sure of it—"

Christy clutched at his arm as he started to get up. "Don't! He could be waiting out there!"

He removed her hand from his arm, squeezed it briefly in reassurance and scrambled to his feet. "Stay put."

And then he was gone, leaving her crouched there on the floor and wishing she *had* bit him. Damn him for his recklessness! He deserved to get shot! No, forget that. She didn't want him hurt. Unless, of course, she was the one doing the hurting. How could she go and fall in love with such a big goof?

Minutes passed. Anguished minutes in which she listened for the sounds of struggle, followed by gunfire. There was only more silence, which was just as bad. Then, as suddenly as they'd gone out, the lights came on again. Feeling instantly vulnerable, Christy shrank from their glare.

"All clear!" Dallas shouted from somewhere at the front of the store, presumably from the spot where he'd managed to locate and restore the power.

There had never been two words she was more grateful to hear. Picking herself up from the floor, she dusted off the legs of her slacks and went to recover her shoulder bag from where she had left it in front of the wardrobe. It was not there.

Christy experienced a sinking feeling as she remembered that their stalker had stumbled over something in the darkness. She could guess now what that something had been and why, after a tense moment, he had slipped away again into the night. He had gotten what he came for. If there was any doubt of that, Dallas eliminated it when he trotted into the storeroom a second later carrying her bag and wearing a glum expression.

"Found it pitched on the floor by the front door," he said, handing her the bag. "Don't bother checking. Everything's there but what we need to be there."

"That's why he was hunting me. He wanted the cassette and the newspaper clipping."

"We'd left the box on the desk in the office, so he knew one of us had them, and, uh—" Dallas paused to sheepishly clear his throat "—since he didn't find them on me, that left you."

Christy drew a slow breath and tried to look thoughtful. "Now I'm a little confused here. The last time I was clear about anything you'd gone off to bring me a cup of water, and about three, terrifying lifetimes later I don't get the water, I get my purse. Did something happen in between I should know about? Maybe a whole lot of something?"

"Well, yeah, kind of."

"Like to tell me about it?"

"Not particularly." He looked embarrassed. "See, on the way to the bathroom I sort of got conked on the head from behind. When I came to, the gun and the flashlight were gone."

"Are you all right?"

"I'm good. Except my head probably has a new hole in it."

"This *is* getting to be a habit with you, isn't it?" she said in reference to yesterday's episode in the cemetery when he had been ambushed and robbed.

"And I'm getting pretty fed up with it. I owe that bastard something, and when I catch up with him—"

"Hold it. I seem to remember it was a couple of punks who attacked you in the cemetery."

"Think about it, grits. Whoever this guy is, he's responsible either directly or indirectly for everything."

Dallas was right. The thieves in the cemetery, or at least one of them, if Brenda Bornowski was to be believed, had sold their loot to Dutch Vasey. And Vasey had taken his orders from the man who had killed him and had probably murdered Laura Hollister. The same man who hid behind the mask of a serpent god. And tonight in this room—

"That's the reason!" she exclaimed in sudden realization.

"I agree. Now tell me what reason we're talking about."

"Why he was stalking me in the dark. He didn't want me to see his face."

"Or take a chance on a little thing like being a lighted target for the gun you might have had."

"But how did he know I was back here?"

Dallas shrugged. "Probably heard me speak to you before I left to get the water."

"Which means he was already inside the building by then." Christy shivered at the thought.

"And since we didn't hear him break in—"

"We have to assume he had his own key to the front door. That he's so familiar with the place he knew just where the main power panel is and how to find his way around in the dark. He must have been livid to find us here and to learn we'd gotten our hands on that incriminating cassette. He had to have been searching for it himself after he killed Vasey, only he was interrupted when we were spotted on the warehouse roof and the police arrived. So he waited for a chance to get back here. And this time it had to be after dark because I imagine he also meant to remove Vasey's body."

Christy paused to mentally examine the jigsaw puzzle they had just assembled. Perfect. All the pieces were there. Everything fit. Who said she wasn't a kick-ass P.I.? Then how come she was suddenly feeling less than supremely confident about the whole thing?

"Dallas."

"Yeah?"

"Do we know what we're talking about?"

"I think we do, grits. Only you know there's this one tiny little thing…"

"Uh-huh. None of this is any good without the cassette and the newspaper clipping to back up our story."

"Let's just say it's going to be a hard sell when that homicide detective starts grilling us."

Christy's gaze drifted unhappily in the direction of the wardrobe on whose roof Dutch Vasey's body still rested. "I suppose one of us should phone the police."

"Yeah, one of us should."

"They're not going to be very happy about any of this, are they?"

"Have a feeling they're not."

IT WAS A BRUTAL ORDEAL for him. The lights were so hot that his face glistened with perspiration. He kept mopping at the beads on his flushed forehead and cheeks, but the sweat continued to flow. And still the questions were asked, a relentless stream of them.

Might they not be exaggerating the contents of this mysterious, missing tape?

Could it even be an invention, maybe as imaginary as their phantom intruder?

Was it just possible, in fact, that one of them had killed Dutch Vasey?

His shoulders drooped. It was obvious he was fighting

exhaustion under this pitiless, punishing barrage. Christy could finally take no more of his cruel suffering. She leaned forward, speaking to him across the table with a gentle note in her voice.

"Lieutenant, you look ready to drop. It's understandable. I heard one of your officers say you'd pulled a double shift. Why don't we take a break before you drain yourself? Then when you feel refreshed, we can get back to it. It's not as though Dallas and I are going anywhere."

She looked to Dallas for support, but he hadn't a word of sympathy to offer the beleaguered homicide detective. He simply went on sitting there beside her, cool and relaxed and with a serene answer for every question.

The exasperated lieutenant slapped a heavy hand on the surface of the table. "No breaks! We're going to stay here until I'm satisfied, if it takes all night!"

Suit yourself, Christy thought. Really, it was no wonder the man was flushed and sweating and weary what with all the weight he was carrying on that body. You'd think the police department would insist that their people keep in better shape.

The detective's promise was no exaggeration. This time unable to talk their way out of the stew in which they had landed themselves, they were held all night at police head-quarters. They spent the last hours snoozing in a cell after the lieutenant finally surrendered to fatigue.

Two things won their release—the arrival of Dallas's lawyer and the medical examiner's report indicating that Dutch Vasey's death had occurred yesterday afternoon while they had been guests of the police. Therefore, they could not have killed Vasey, but their theories were still regarded as so much wild speculation. The police could hardly ignore a dead body, of course, but it was clear to Christy they meant to treat Dutch Vasey's murder as a separate problem that might or might not have any connection to Laura Hollister. Meaning, they intended to continue focusing their investigation on Glenn. It was an infuriating outcome.

"Hang in there," Dallas encouraged her as he drove her back to her apartment on Royal Street. "We're not licked. Experiencing a little setback maybe, but not licked. We'll see to it yet that ol' Glenn walks off into the sunset."

Christy turned her head to look at him. How did he do it? All night in a police station sparring with an unfriendly homicide detective, inadequate sleep, and he still managed to look gorgeous, even in rumpled clothes and with a growth of whiskers shadowing his jaw. The right gene pool, she supposed. She wondered if that same pool was also responsible for his unfailing optimism.

Although, even with defeat staring them in the face, it was difficult not being cheerful on a morning like this. The newly risen sun was burning its way through a haze that veiled the streets, which were almost empty at this early hour. It was going to be another balmy day, the kind where you could smell oleander and sweet olive on the air, and think that life was good in New Orleans. Providing you weren't a millimeter away from being charged with your wife's murder. Poor Glenn.

And if we don't solve this case, poor me and my agency.

At which they had now arrived, Christy noticed. Dallas pulled over to the curb in front of the mouth to the carriageway and left the engine of the convertible idling.

"I know you're dying for me to come in," he said, stretching one arm along the back of her seat as he turned to face her.

"I am?"

"Well, sure you are. And I intend to oblige you, but you're going to have to be patient for a couple of hours while I go home and get cleaned up and we both snatch a little sleep.''

''After which you will show up at my apartment.''

''With a late breakfast.''

''That's the plan, huh? And then what?''

''Sweetheart, you're not with me. Think about it. We have to consider some moves.''

''Where to go next on the case, you mean?''

''That, too.''

''Then we're not talking here about just the case. So what other moves did you have in mind?''

''Let's see—'' He paused to think about it while she watched one of those expressive black eyebrows lift in a manner that was unmistakably suggestive. ''Could always show you some moves with my yo-yo. I can do remarkable things with my yo-yo.''

''I'll just bet you can. You're terrible, do you know that?''

''And you just love it,'' he drawled in that slow, mellow voice that had her insides turning over.

''Yes,'' she said softly, ''I guess I do.''

The arm along the back of her seat curled down around her shoulder, drawing her toward him. ''How much? Show me.''

And she did, her mouth lifting to his. A woman crossing the street on her way to work had a tantalizing view of the kiss that followed. After that, the convertible could have been surrounded by a crowd of spectators and Christy wouldn't have been aware of them. She was far too engrossed by then in what Dallas McFarland's talented mouth was doing to hers.

Marvelous the way his lips could take such sweet possession of her senses. The way he could draw out a kiss until nothing else mattered but the hot taste and feel of him, rough morning beard and all. And the way his tongue stroked hers in concert with his hands skimming the sides of her breasts.

She was shamefully aroused by the time he released her. And wishing he hadn't released her. Wishing, too, that she didn't have to wait two hours until he showed up in her apartment.

"That was quite a performance," she congratulated him. "Even without the yo-yo."

"I'll bring it with me when I come," he promised with a meaningful grin, leaning across her to open the door for her.

"I'll look forward to that," she said.

He stopped her when she started to slide out of the car. "And, uh, maybe we'll talk, huh?" There was a look now on his face that said he had something to discuss with her, something that mattered deeply.

"That sounds serious. Not like you, McFarland."

"Yeah, well, it can wait until breakfast."

DALLAS DROVE away with a troubled frown on his face, his guilt gnawing at him.

He could no longer keep this secret inside him, even though he'd convinced himself that his silence had been necessary. Christy deserved to hear the truth. But it wouldn't be easy sharing it with her, not with these growing feelings he had for her. Not when he feared her reaction.

Yeah, he was going to tell her over breakfast. And until then, all he could do was hope she would understand and forgive him. It would be hell if she didn't.

CHRISTY WAS IN A DAZE when she reluctantly parted from him, crossed the courtyard, let herself into the office and climbed the stairs to her apartment. She blamed her state on a combination of fatigue and that blinding kiss. But this wasn't the explanation, and she knew it. There was something he wanted her to know that would change the course of their relationship. That was why she was reeling. She was experiencing the excitement of anticipation.

Of course, she could be mistaken. Maybe he wasn't going to tell her that he had fallen in love with her, just as she'd fallen in love with him. Maybe it was something else entirely. Like if she didn't switch her loyalty from the Chicago Cubs to the Atlanta Braves he couldn't go on seeing her. But she didn't really believe it would be anything less than an extraordinary declaration of his feelings.

Oh, this was dopey. As bad as high school when she'd worked herself into a state wondering if Bud Prouty was going to ask her to go steady. Willing herself to forget about it, she fell across her bed, intending to treat herself to at least two hours of uninterrupted sleep.

Impossible. How could she rest when Dallas McFarland was inside her head doing things to her emotions that made Bud Prouty a pathetic amateur? Wonderful things that exhilarated her and at the same time unnerved her. As a P.I., Dallas challenged her, taught her to trust in her own investigative abilities. As a man, he challenged her on another level, a glorious one in which he taught her the essence of her womanhood. But this level was so elevated that sometimes it made her dizzy scaling it, leaving her unsure of her balance.

You are not going to fall, Christy Hawke. And if you do, Dallas will be there to catch you.

Uh-huh. And when he gets a good look at the mess he's caught, he'll drop it. Are you going to lie here and let that happen?

Christy decided that she was not. Much too expectant to sleep anyway, she rolled out of bed and headed for the bathroom to correct the appearance of a woman who had just spent half the night eluding a killer and the other half answering questions about it.

She bathed, she worked on her hair and nails. She wondered what scent Dallas might like or whether he didn't like perfume at all. She tried on outfits and hoped that this time Denise wouldn't catch her at it. She knew that at some point Denise had arrived. She could hear the sound of her favorite jazz station down in the office.

Christy must have been working on herself a good hour or more when the image of the woman in the long mirror, face flushed, eyes shining, startled her into a sudden awareness.

Oh, my lord, you know what you're doing, don't you? You're getting ready for the prom and the most important date of your life. That's what you're doing.

Well, so what? A woman deserved to look good when the man she loved was—

"Hey, girlfriend!"

Christy went to the head of the stairs. Denise was at the bottom, hands on hips. "What's up, Denise?"

"You got yourself company down here."

Dallas, she thought, her pulse accelerating. "Thanks, Denise. Send him up."

Denise looked uncertain. "That's what you want, huh?"

"That's just what I want." She started to turn away. "Oh, and no interruptions please."

Muttering to herself, Denise went back to the office to inform their visitor that Christy was waiting for him. Christy was grinning like a kid on Christmas morning as she hurried into the kitchen alcove to check on the coffeemaker. She heard the tread of feet on the stairs.

"Be right out," she called. The coffee had finished brewing. "Do you take sweetener in your coffee or not? I can't remember."

"Thank you, Christy, but I don't have time for coffee."

It was not Dallas's voice. She put down the napkins she had taken from the basket on the counter and walked out of the kitchen. No wonder Denise had been surprised by her request. Her visitor standing there at the top of the stairs was Glenn Hollister.

Christy tried not to register her disappointment, but it must have been evident just the same. "I guess you were expecting someone else," he said.

"Uh, yes, but it's all right." She looked around for a chair to offer him.

"I can't stay. There's a couple of last-minute arrangements I have to take care of for the funeral this afternoon. I just stopped by for a quick minute to—"

He didn't go on. That's when Christy noticed that his thin face and gray eyes were deeply troubled. She felt an immediate guilt. She'd been so busy mentally gushing over Dallas that she had forgotten all about her client and his desperation.

"Has there been another development, Glenn? Are the police—"

"They're at my place now, searching the house and grounds. But that isn't why I'm here. It's because of something more I found, this time buried in the bottom of Laura's desk." He withdrew an envelope from inside the breast pocket of his suit coat. "I left the originals with my lawyer. These are photocopies I made for you. I thought that you...well, that you ought to have them."

Christy had an unpleasant feeling in the pit of her stomach as Glenn handed her the envelope, a sensing that something was about to go very wrong. She stood there for a few seconds holding the envelope, unwilling to open it.

That infernal instinct of hers was telling her that, once she examined the envelope's contents, nothing would ever be the same again.

This was silly. What did she think she was running away from?

As Glenn watched her with a grave expression on his face, Christy quickly lifted the flap and removed what the envelope contained. There were two sheets of paper. The first was a cover letter from a private laboratory in New Orleans, dated almost four years ago. It indicated that the accompanying report was the result of the blood test that Laura had hired them to perform.

Sliding the letter under the second sheet, Christy read the lab report itself. Its subject was the infant Daisy Hollister. Although somewhat technical in language, the conclusion was clear enough. The man who had requested and cooperated with the blood test was not the father of Laura's daughter. That man was Dallas McFarland.

Glenn was still looking miserable when a stunned Christy lifted her gaze from the report. Did she look as equally miserable? And was that pity she read in his eyes because he'd somehow guessed she had fallen in love with Dallas and that at this moment she was experiencing a wrenching sense of loss?

"You didn't know, did you, Christy?"

Anxiety. That's what she was seeing in his eyes. Glenn needed to hear that she hadn't been any part of this lie. That she hadn't betrayed him. Her emotions were still safe. "No, Glenn," she numbly managed to assure him, "I never had a clue."

He smiled bitterly. "I should be feeling nothing but gratitude that I'm still Daisy's father, but I can't get past that report. You know what its existence means, don't you?"

"Yes," she said hoarsely, the words sticking in her

throat, "Laura had an affair with Dallas McFarland just before she came back to you."

"She had to have been sleeping with both of us, and maybe she wasn't sure who Daisy's father was. Anyway, McFarland must have heard about the baby eventually and insisted on a blood test."

"And you never guessed that—that she was seeing someone else?"

Glenn shook his head. "I had no idea until I found that thing that she and McFarland even knew each other."

"Why did Laura keep the report? Why didn't she destroy it long ago?" Because if she had, Christy thought, I wouldn't be hurting like this now. I'd still be living in innocence with Dallas's deception.

"God knows. Maybe just to taunt me with it someday. Laura was capable of that, and when a marriage was crumbling like ours..."

"I'm sorry, Glenn." For both of us.

"There's one thing I don't understand, though," he said. "McFarland must still have some feelings about this whole business, maybe even strong ones. Then why did he agree to help with my case?"

Christy wondered that herself. She knew she ought to promise Glenn that she would secure an explanation for him, ought to provide him now with an update on the progress of the investigation. Assure him all over again, that she wouldn't rest until he'd been vindicated. She could do none of those things. All she could offer him, while wanting him to go away so that she could deal with her pain in private, was a lame, "Try not to worry, Glenn."

To her relief, he glanced at his watch and expressed a need to leave. Carrying the letter and the lab report which she had placed back in the envelope, she walked with him down to the office. He remembered something before he turned to go.

"I haven't paid you a dime yet for your services. I should write you a check."

"Later," she said. "We'll get together and sort it all out."

"Will you be coming to the funeral this afternoon?"

"No, I don't think so." *Please, just go.*

Thankfully, he did, but when the door closed behind him she was left with Denise. The scowl on her assistant's face could have melted rock.

"You must be sick, girlfriend. Must have caught a bad fever that's attacked your brain. Can't think of any other reason why you'd go and turn down that man's check. Do you know how long it's been since any kind of money's come into this—"

Denise didn't go on. By now she'd become aware of the anguish in Christy's eyes, perhaps even understood it. Her manner immediately softened. "Huh, so that's how it is. You really don't feel so good. You wanna talk it out?"

Grateful for the offer, Christy placed a hand on Denise's arm and shook her head. "Thanks, girlfriend, but this one I have to work out on my own."

She didn't want to be here when Dallas arrived. All right, so she was a coward, but she couldn't face him. Not just yet, maybe never. "I'm going out. Give this to McFarland when he shows." She passed the envelope to Denise. It was all the explanation that Dallas would need.

Christy left the office without another word and walked rapidly through the streets of the Quarter. She had a destination in mind. A place where she could release the ache that was tearing her up inside.

Chapter Ten

It was a good place to be when you were deeply troubled. Christy had always thought so, anyway. Maybe because there was so much here to soothe a wounded spirit.

Park benches had been placed all along the broad walkway on top of a section of the levee known as Moon Walk. She sat on one of them, an anonymous figure among the vendors peddling souvenirs, the strolling street entertainers and the ever restless streams of tourists. The river, too, was an artery of constantly shifting traffic. Christy liked gazing out over its brown expanse at the tugs, tankers and enormous container ships. Liked the odors here that were peculiar to New Orleans—moss and damp earth, roasting coffee and the pungent fumes of the river itself, all of them mingling on the warm, humid air.

This morning, however, the magic of the levee failed her. Probably because the wound in her spirit was much too raw for any simple cure. Dallas was responsible for that and she was both disappointed and angry with him. Angry with herself as well for so blinding herself with love that she'd failed to see all the signs of his deception.

And those signs had been there from the start. Dallas so eager to be a part of this case. Dallas standing outside the iron fence that first morning, an odd intensity in his manner as he gazed at the Hollister house. Dallas concerned with Daisy's welfare, asking her about the child. While Christy, sensing all along that he was withholding something from her, had gone and naively trusted his every denial. How could she not have guessed? How could she have been so—

Wait a minute. If the blood test was proof that Daisy *wasn't* his daughter, and Laura must have shared the results with Dallas, then why was he so interested in Daisy? Unless… Yes, Dallas must have a reason to feel there was still a chance Daisy was his. It would explain his interest in the case, provide an answer to Glenn's puzzlement. Or did it? She wasn't sure.

Oh, what difference did it make? He had lied to her, used her to win a connection to Daisy. And she, fool that she was, had fallen for a pair of brash green eyes, a country boy drawl and a wicked humor sexier than any set of broad shoulders. Fallen so hard that she was sitting here in a skirt and heels because she'd wanted to please him, show him how feminine she could be.

Christy was looking down at those heels, disgusted with herself that they weren't running shoes, that her honey-colored hair wasn't crammed under the familiar baseball cap, when his deep voice startled her.

"Guess this is your form of a yo-yo, huh?"

Her gaze shot up to find Dallas standing beside the bench she occupied. Damn. How had he found her? Oh. Denise, of course. Denise knew this was where she came whenever she was deeply troubled. She would have something to say to her assistant on the subject of misplaced loyalties when she got back to the office. Meanwhile…

"I'm in no mood for another riddle from you, McFarland."

He removed his hands from the pockets of the black jeans he wore and jerked his thumbs in opposite directions, indicating both Jackson Square behind them and the river in front of them. "I work a yo-yo whenever I'm having a bad time and need to think. Looks like maybe this place does the same for you."

She hated it that he was so perceptive about her.

"Can I sit down?" he asked.

"No."

He sat anyway, settling his tall figure beside her on the bench. "There are two things, Christy, that are not going to go away. Me and the problem we have. Let me know when you're ready to discuss them." Prepared to wait, he stretched his long legs out in front of him, folded his hands across his middle, and gazed out at the river.

Christy had three choices of action. She could smack him for his nonchalance, which he richly deserved. She could surge to her feet and walk away, which would also be effective. Or she could talk to him. Since the last of those three actions was probably the more mature choice, as well as ultimately inevitable, she supposed, she went with it.

"Fine," she said, turning to him, "let's dialogue. Where shall we begin? Maybe with how you deceived me from the start for a motive of your own. Whatever it might be. I'm not exactly clear about that. In fact, there are a lot of things I'm not clear about."

"You're really annoyed with me, aren't you?"

"Understatement, McFarland. A *large* one."

"All right, I don't blame you. I should have told you the truth long ago. So here it is now. Five years ago I had an affair with Laura Claiborne."

"Yes," she said dryly, "that part was kind of obvious from the lab report. Were you in love with her?"

Not that it mattered, Christy thought. After all, given his age and his masculine allure, there must have been a lot of women in his life. Laura was simply another of those relationships long in the past. The only thing that Christy minded was his failure to be honest with her and the shock of learning about that secret connection. That's what she tried to tell herself, anyway.

"Yes, I was," he said, and everything Christy had just convinced herself didn't matter was canceled by the pangs of a foolish jealousy. Until, that is, he added a careless, "For about five minutes."

"Oh." Now that she had no reason for it, she regretted the jealousy. It had been weak of her to even momentarily feel it.

"Look," he went on, "it was one of those things that never should have happened. She was on the rebound from Glenn and looking for some excitement when we met at this fund-raiser and I guess I was flattered that a woman from her part of town was interested."

"That's all, huh? Just a brief fling. Only she got pregnant."

"Which could have happened before she quarreled with Glenn."

"But you weren't certain of that."

"Laura insisted it was Glenn's baby, but the times were so close I don't see how she could have known for sure. I think it was a matter of her choosing the guy who would make the most manageable father. And if nothing else, ol' Glenn is that."

"So she went back to Glenn and you were still her secret."

"Yeah, I know, and I should have left it at that because she and Glenn had been married for months before I learned about the baby. Hell, I didn't want to hurt anyone, but if there was a chance the kid was mine…"

"You needed to know." Christy guessed she could understand that part. "How did you get Laura to agree to the blood test for you and Daisy?'' She couldn't imagine that Dallas would have threatened to go to Glenn. Even if he was a skunk, that simply wasn't his style.

"Laura didn't put up much of a fuss about it when I went to her. I suppose she figured that if she didn't satisfy me, there was the risk that she'd never be rid of me.''

"So you and Laura with the baby sneak off to this private lab and the results are conclusive. You are not Daisy's father. Then why didn't it end there? Why, four years later, are you still hanging on to it?''

He didn't answer her. He stared off into the river where a rusty looking Greek freighter was anchored. One of the excursion boats that toured the port chugged into view, tooting its whistle. A deckhand on another freighter appeared at the rail and tossed scraps to a pair of pelicans. And still Dallas was silent.

"Okay,'' he finally admitted, drawing himself up on the bench, hands dangling now between his parted legs, "so even with the proof, I was never able to completely shake the feeling that Daisy might still be mine.''

"Some kind of paternal instinct at work? Is that what you're trying to tell me?''

He laughed. A wry laugh. "Yeah, I know. A real hoot for a clown like me, huh?''

It was tempting, that one. It would have been so easy for Christy to be sympathetic. And, after all his deceit, so very wrong. "But you never acted on it.''

"How could I with the lab report telling me how wrong my feelings were? So I managed to bury those feelings, until—''

He turned his head, looking at her again, a grim expression on his mouth. "That lab we went to…there was this cute little scandal there last week. Evidence that a technician had been bribed to falsify a test in a custody case.''

Yes, Christy thought, searching her memory, there had been a report on the news about a lab scandal. She understood where Dallas was going. "You think that Laura might have paid someone in that same lab to fake the results of your own blood test."

"It's possible, but before I could go to Laura about it she was murdered."

"And her case fell right into your lap and me along with it," she said, unable to help the resentment in her voice.

"Try to understand," he pleaded with her. "This was my chance to connect with the kid who might be mine, to be there for Daisy if Glenn was dangerous and did turn out to be Laura's killer. Hell, I don't know, maybe I even thought I owed it to Daisy to solve her mother's death."

"Oh, I understand all right. You used me as a pipeline to Glenn and his daughter. That's all I ever was, a channel of information for you, because I could get next to Glenn and Daisy and you couldn't. Okay, I can accept that. But you know what stinks, McFarland, what *really* stinks? That you never once, even after all we shared, trusted me with a truth I should have been told at the start."

"What if I had told you? You would have felt bound to go straight to your client with it, and ol' Glenn would have immediately shut me down by having his sister-in-law remove me from the case."

"And you couldn't take that chance, could you, Dallas? Even now after the magic we had, or *seemed* to have, you didn't have enough faith in me to confide your secret."

"I *was* going to tell you over breakfast this morning. I swear that's the truth."

He must have thought this admission would ease the hurt she was feeling. He couldn't know that he'd just made it worse, that his words were like a steel band around her heart.

It was her own fault. She'd done this to herself, because Dallas had promised her nothing when he'd dropped her off earlier, only that he had something important to discuss when they met for breakfast. It was she who had convinced herself he meant to express his love for her, but all he had ever intended— Oh, what a giddy, absolute fool she had been!

"I believe you, Dallas," she said, trying not to let him see just how bad the ache was. "But your timing is lousy. All this should have been said long ago."

Christy got to her feet. He didn't love her. That was what she had to remember, painful though the reality was. He didn't love her, because if he had he would have trusted her to know. In the end it was as simple as that. Which meant that she had to part from him. Now and permanently, before she made any greater fool of herself.

"Grits," he appealed to her earnestly, understanding her intention, "don't do this to us."

"Why?" she said, looking down at him unhappily. "Because together we make a solid team? But that isn't so. You never believed in my potential as a P.I. That was just a sham to keep me near you so that you'd know what was happening with Glenn and Daisy."

Dallas came to his feet beside her, his face tight with anger. "Fine. I'm a bastard guilty of a treachery you can't forgive or forget, but the truth stops there, babe."

"Are you accusing me of—"

"That's right, a few inventions of your own. Like me not thinking you're good and growing better all the time. See, I happen to be convinced that, with or without me, you're going to make a great P.I. That is, if you ever stop putting beliefs into the heads of people that were never there to begin with."

"Anything else?"

"Yeah, start believing yourself that you're worth something, because you are. Now get out of here before I do something that's going to get me arrested again, like pitching that obstinate little fanny of yours into the Mississippi."

Christy went, willing herself not to look back over her shoulder as she walked rapidly in the direction of her agency. It would have been so easy to fall for his compliments, to go on working with him. But she couldn't make that mistake again and survive it. She *couldn't,* not loving him as she did and knowing he didn't share that feeling. Not when she didn't trust him or his praise.

Although, to be fair about it, he had all along pushed her to be the best she could be. Even when she had resisted that pushing. Oh, she didn't know anymore what to think! She was too confused in her misery to sort it out.

That anguish was still with her when she reached the office. Denise needed only to glimpse her face to understand that her meeting with Dallas had been a disaster. Christy knew that her assistant had an opinion on the subject, probably several of them, but for once Denise had the wisdom to keep them to herself.

"No calls, please," Christy ordered.

With no further word of explanation, she fled upstairs to the sanctuary of her apartment. And wouldn't you know, the first thing her gaze fell on as she marched in the direction of her bedroom was that damn red cloth voodoo doll she had tossed on the desk the other day. It was too poignant a reminder of the man Camille Leveau had intended to lure to Christy's bed. She knew that as long as the silly thing remained here in plain view it would nag her without letting up.

Wanting to bury any reminder of Dallas, she opened a bottom drawer. She was ready to shove the doll out of sight to the back of the drawer, but there was something else there that caught her attention. An open shoe box bulging with small rocks. Not ordinary rocks. Each one bore the imprint of a fossil.

Forgetting about the doll, Christy lifted the old shoe box out of the drawer and placed it on the surface of the desk. Its contents, unlike the doll, had pleasant associations for her, and she needed those kind of memories right now.

Dipping into the box, she sifted through the collection, permitting herself to remember how her brother Mitch had patiently taught her about the fossils that had so fascinated her when she was a kid. She had been closest to Mitch, maybe because out of all of her family he was the one who had seemed to best understand her. Still did.

Before the voodoo doll had detoured her, Christy meant to hide herself away from a cruel world, or at least one man in it, by crawling under her bed covers and whimpering. The shoe box, however, urged something else.

She glanced at her watch. Mitch would have arrived by now at his own P.I. office in San Francisco. She suddenly had a longing to unload all her current woes on a big brother. A sympathetic one, she hoped.

He answered on the first ring, his familiar voice deep and steady, already offering her the comfort she sought. ''Hawke Detective Agency. Mitchell Hawke speaking.''

''Mitchell Hawke, I am sitting here holding in my hand the fossil of a shell. Cambrian period, if I remember correctly.''

He chuckled with recognition. ''You still hanging on to those things, brat?''

Christy assured him that she was and within seconds she was telling him everything, including the fool she had made of herself over Dallas McFarland. She finished her story with an eager, ''Help, please.''

"You want me to come down there and beat this guy up for you?"

"That might be nice."

"Or I could offer you a piece of advice."

"Like?"

"With or without him, get on with the case."

"How? I seem to be flat out of leads."

"Hell, you sound like a funeral, you might as well go to one."

She knew he was referring to the funeral for Laura Hollister this afternoon. "You think that could be useful?"

"Probably not, but it's something to try. And that's what a P.I. has to do, keep trying. Look, all the mourners will be people who were connected with her in some way. Pay attention to them. One of them could be her murderer."

Mitch was right. No whimpering under bed covers. No more feeling sorry for herself. Glenn was counting on her and there was also the small matter of the renewal on her lease. Either she put her backside in action or she lost her agency.

"And, brat?"

"Yes?"

"Your McFarland might be a stinker, but he is right about one thing. You are good and you need to have confidence in that."

"I think I left my heart in San Francisco. Thanks, Mitch. Now go back to whatever it is you were doing. I've got to see if I have anything sober enough to wear to a funeral."

A YO-YO WOULDN'T have helped this time, even if he'd had one with him. Dallas needed a much stronger release for his frustration. That was why he strode rapidly along the top of the levee, hoping to wear off his explosive emotions.

The savage obscenities he muttered to himself must have

been audible, because people hastily got out of his way as he passed. Even the pigeons took flight. He didn't care. He was too angry for that.

Damn it, women never got under his skin, especially the small, blond ones! He just didn't permit it to happen! Then what was Christy Hawke doing under his? And what did it matter anyway since he'd gone and lost the brainless little—

Lost her.

The full understanding of that shocked him, brought him to a standstill. He turned and gazed out at the river where a pair of snowy egrets skimmed over the surface of the muddy waters. The sight of them gave him a feeling of aloneness, a sudden, awful emptiness. He didn't want to acknowledge the reason for that.

Dallas tried instead to tell himself he was better off without Christy, except the argument wouldn't work. Not when his brain was filled with animated images of her, all the things he would miss. Already missed. Like the rapid-fire way she talked when she was excited, bouncing all over the place. That dumb baseball cap at which she was forever tugging. Those sweet blue-green eyes burning holes in him. The lush little figure that made his groin thicken with the memory of it. And when he thought about himself buried deep inside her, her legs wrapped around his, he went a little crazy. Crazy?

Well, hell, he realized with a jolt, he was in love with her. Wildly, thoroughly in love. And why hadn't he understood that before he'd gone and messed it all up? He should have told her the truth long ago. Now she was gone, and he was on his own.

But he didn't want to be on his own. What he wanted was to rush back to her place, take her in his arms and tell her that, okay, maybe there had been a parade of women in his life, but none of them had been substantial. None of them solid and real until her.

That's what he longed to do, but the little sense that was left to him in his euphoria insisted it would be another mistake. Feeling as she did, she wouldn't let him near her. But if he stayed away, gave her time to cool down, then maybe...

Yes, maybe. He clung to that hope.

In the meantime, with or without Christy, there was a case for him to solve. And, if it should come to that, a child for him to safeguard who might or might not be his.

Dallas turned back, his long legs carrying him swiftly in the direction of his car. He had work to do, work which would permit him no time to dwell on his fear that it might be too late for Christy and him.

CHRISTY GUESSED THAT, since your remains had to spend eternity somewhere, this was as pleasant a spot as any for them. Parking her Escort in the shade of a live oak, she headed for the chapel where Laura's funeral service was to be conducted.

No Claiborne had been interred in the old cemetery at Resurrection in several generations. Claibornes these days were laid to rest in a family mausoleum inside a memorial park out beyond Riverbend. The mausoleum was located close to the chapel itself in sight of the soaring Huey P. Long Bridge.

Christy was late. The chapel was already packed with mourners. She managed to find a standing place in a corner at the back. A good position for observing the crowd, which, after all, was why she was here.

It was a restless crowd, but that was understandable. Modern though the chapel was, its air-conditioning must have failed. Even with the windows wide open, the place was uncomfortably warm, and made worse by the suffocating perfume of the flowers blanketing the casket. Christy longed for her familiar shorts instead of the midnight blue silk dress that clung to her damply.

An organ played softly, and prayer cards fanned faces as the gathering waited for the service to begin. Christy used the opportunity to scan heads. She had a clear view of Glenn down front. Even from here, she could see how tired and worried he was. His sister-in-law was close beside him. Slim and lovely, Monica Claiborne was the only cool-looking woman in the room.

Christy saw no sign of Daisy. They must have decided to spare the child her mother's funeral. Good thing, too.

She went on casting her gaze around the chapel. From the corner of her eye, she caught a movement at the entrance. Another late arrival. She swung her attention in that direction and wished she hadn't. Her heart missed a beat at the sight of Dallas.

What was *he* doing here? Same as her probably, checking out the attendees, which meant either Glenn had not asked Monica to remove Dallas from the case or else she'd refused his request.

And wouldn't you just know, McFarland would turn up looking absolutely gorgeous in a dark gray suit that had every female in the place eyeing him. Including her, damn it.

Too late for Christy to hide herself behind one of the other mourners. His gaze, searching the room as he stood there, found her and locked on to her own gaze. Her senses immediately betrayed her, longing for him in ways that she knew she shouldn't. It was all the fault of those sinful green eyes and that bold, sensual mouth. A mouth that experience had taught Christy was so enticing with its hot kisses, it could persuade her to reveal state secrets. Providing she knew any state secrets.

She was afraid Dallas would try to approach her. He didn't. Saluting her with a little nod, he turned away, finding a place for himself on the other side of the chapel. Christy didn't know whether to be relieved or hurt. She probably felt a bit of both, actually.

With an effort, she forced her attention away from Dallas and her painful love for him. She needed to focus on her assignment. Now that the service was commencing, she was able to concentrate on the crowd without risking any particular notice. There was more than one surprise among them.

Christy supposed there was nothing unexpected about the attendance of the young jeweler, Buzz Purreau. After all, Laura had been one of his major clients. She could even understand why her neighbor, Alistair St. Leger, was here. Alistair had never had a connection with Laura herself, but he did know Monica and his old-fashioned code of ethics would require him to pay his respects to her.

What did startle Christy was Marty Bornowski. What on earth was the asphalt king doing here? Even more astonishing was the presence of Camille Leveau. The voodoo queen had insisted Laura Hollister had never visited her store. Then why was Camille attending Laura's funeral? Camille, who Christy couldn't help noticing had the height and strength of a man.

Whatever the explanations for Marty and the voodoo queen, they would have to wait. In the meantime, Christy found herself interested in another figure. With his dark hair pulled back into a tight club and his massive girth, it would have been hard to overlook him, even if he hadn't been a latecomer. What piqued her were his actions. He joined Glenn and Monica at the front of the chapel, where they welcomed him without hesitation. Throughout the remainder of the service, he exchanged a series of whispers with Glenn. Christy didn't recognize him.

"The man up there beside Glenn," she murmured to the woman standing next to her. "Do you know who he is?"

"Edgar Evers," the woman murmured back. "He's Glenn's lawyer."

Which accounted for his immediate acceptance by Glenn, but not what the two men were whispering about so earnestly. The explanation of that, and Christy was in no way prepared for it, occurred after the service adjourned to the family mausoleum outside, where a brief ceremony of interment was performed.

She hung back in the shade of a magnolia afterward, watching as the mourners filed past Glenn and Monica to offer their condolences. She didn't see Dallas again. He must have already slipped away.

She waited to express her own sympathy until the last of the crowd climbed into their cars and departed, leaving only Glenn and Monica with Edgar Evers still beside them. But Christy hadn't been the only one waiting for the end of the funeral. As she started forward, a pair of police cruisers rolled up to the front of the mausoleum.

Dumbstruck, she watched several officers converge on Glenn and Monica with warrants in hand. It was all so fleeting that it was over before Christy had time to react. Both Glenn and Monica were charged with Laura Hollister's murder, read their rights and bundled into the police cruisers. The cruisers sped away, the lawyer following them in his own car.

Christy stood there all alone on the edge of the lane, trying to comprehend what she had just witnessed. Monica? *Monica Claiborne?* Why?

What was going on? She didn't know, was too staggered

to even begin to sort it out. But she damn well intended to understand it. And there seemed to be only one person now who could provide her with answers to the questions that churned in her mind.

Swinging around, she walked swiftly in the direction of her own car. Glenn's eyes had briefly met hers just before he was hustled into the police cruiser. There had been a look of desperation in them. A haunting appeal which Christy couldn't ignore.

PULLING INTO the first gas station she saw, Christy filled her car and then asked the young attendant if she could borrow his phone book. There were so many lawyers listed in the Yellow Pages directory that it took her a few minutes before she was able to locate Edgar Evers. Jotting down the particulars, she returned to the Escort and headed back into the heart of the city.

The address she wanted was on Esplanade on the other side of the Quarter. She had no trouble finding it and was even lucky enough to get a parking spot. The imposing building was a nineteenth century three-story townhouse that had been converted into suites of offices. Evers's office was located at the rear of the ground floor overlooking a gem of a courtyard.

Before the woman at her computer in reception could ask, Christy hastily informed her, "No, I don't have an appointment with him, but it's very important I see Mr. Evers."

The receptionist looked doubtful. "He's out and I don't know when he'll be back."

Christy expected that. The lawyer would be with Glenn wherever they had taken him, protecting his client's rights. And that could be a lengthy business. "I'm prepared to wait."

"Even if he does come in, I can't promise that he'll see you," the receptionist warned her.

"I'll wait," Christy insisted.

She gave the woman her name and settled in a chair where she had a view of the lush vegetation in the courtyard. It should have been a soothing scene. It wasn't. She was too anxious for that. She needed an explanation and until she had it, there was no point in speculating.

The minutes crawled by as the receptionist tapped at her keys and answered the phone. Christy tried not to wonder about Dallas, where he'd gone after leaving the funeral or what he might be up to. But her mind couldn't seem to shake the image of him.

Forget him. Concentrate on Glenn and how he needs you.

An hour passed. She used her cell phone to call Denise, telling her not to wait for her and to close the office when the time came because she didn't know when she'd get back. Denise wanted to hear about the funeral, but Christy said she'd have to wait. She rang off and went back to her own waiting.

The long afternoon was ending before Edgar Evers finally arrived. Christy got to her feet as he came through the door, thinking that he looked more like a sumo wrestler than a lawyer. He was even sweating like one.

She thought he would be annoyed to find her there and was surprised by his reaction when the receptionist introduced her. "Ms. Hawke, you've saved me from having to look you up. Come on into my office. I imagine you need to talk to me as much as I need to talk to you."

Christy followed him into the paneled office, perching on the chair he indicated. Mopping at his brow, Evers lowered his bulk into his own chair behind his desk. "Before

I tell you what I know you want to hear," he said, "there's a favor I need to ask."

He had a high-pitched voice that also was not in keeping with the image of a courtroom lawyer. But none of that mattered, Christy thought. The intelligence that was in his eyes did.

She leaned forward on her chair. "You're bargaining for a favor in exchange for information?" She couldn't imagine what she had that he could possibly want.

He smiled. "Cutting deals is what lawyers do best, Ms.— Can I call you Christy?" She nodded. "Anyway," he continued, "I'm negotiating on behalf of my client, not me."

"But Glenn must know that I'm already doing everything I can to clear him of—"

"No," Evers cut her off, "it's nothing to do with your investigation. The favor Glenn is begging is for his daughter."

"Daisy?" Here was yet another surprise.

The lawyer explained the situation. "Glenn is behind bars, and until I can manage otherwise, and I haven't so far, he's going to stay there. Monica Claiborne's own lawyer will probably win her release, but that isn't going to occur until sometime tomorrow, if then. That leaves Daisy with no one to look out for her."

Christy was bewildered. "Glenn is asking me to— Wait a minute, this doesn't make sense. Who's caring for Daisy now?"

"Monica's housekeeper. But the woman is so distraught, she refuses to remain on the job. You'll understand why after I tell you what you came here to learn. Look, it will be just for the night. Glenn has a brother over in Lake Charles, but a family emergency kept him from coming to the funeral. He thinks he can get away tomorrow morning and then he'll come by your place to pick Daisy up to take her back to Lake Charles.''

''*My* place?''

''Glenn feels it would be better if Daisy is removed from a scene that's been in such an upheaval since her mother's death, and I agree.''

''Yes, but why me? There must be—''

''Only an elderly aunt of Monica's and she's already on her way back to Miami. Besides, she never related to Daisy and I'm told that you did when you met the child. There's no one else that Glenn trusts, Christy.'' The lawyer shifted around in his chair, waiting for her answer.

She thought of the little girl, of how alone and vulnerable she was with her mother gone and both her father and aunt in jail. How could she refuse?

''I'll watch out for her,'' Christy agreed. ''Now suppose you tell me what's going on?''

''Some rather bad results, I'm afraid. The police searched Glenn's property and turned up what they were looking for in his tool box in the garage. A hammer that had been carefully cleaned, except their lab found traces of Laura's blood on it. The medical examiner agreed it was the murder weapon since it had left its impression on the victim's skull.''

''Okay, so they got the evidence to arrest Glenn for his wife's murder. But Monica?''

''Yes, it gets worse, I'm afraid. She was taken into custody because she's suspected of being his accomplice.''

''Is this supposed to make sense?''

''It did to the police after they talked to the housekeeper. She's one of those people intimidated by authority. She caved under their questions and told them that Monica and Glenn had been having a secret affair. Now all she wants to do is get out of that house. And that leaves the police with the classic three—means, opportunity and now the motive. At least that's how they see it.''

Christy stared at the lawyer, unable to believe what she had just heard. ''But can this be true about Monica and Glenn?'' she asked him numbly.

''I'm afraid it is. When I conferred with Glenn after he was charged, he admitted he and Monica are in love. But he swears that he didn't kill Laura.''

It had been a day of revelations, one shocking surprise after another. Now here was this latest blow. Christy struggled with it and found she was able to accept it, but it left her deeply disappointed in Glenn.

He had used her, just as Dallas had used her. Had intimated he still cared for her in order to win her help. That, of course, was why he had come to her in the first place, because if a man meant something to a woman, she was bound to fight for him. That's what Glenn had wanted Christy to do for him while all along, he had been involved with his sister-in-law. Monica, who hadn't trusted Christy to clear her lover and had chosen Dallas McFarland instead, on the pretext of solving her sister's murder.

Not that any of this mattered in the end since, worst luck, it was Dallas that Christy loved. Which, she supposed, left her minding nothing but Glenn's dishonesty.

She was suddenly aware of Edgar Evers watching her shrewdly as she digested his information. ''And now that you know the truth,'' he asked her quietly, ''are you going to drop his case?''

Glenn deserved to lose her. He had lied to her, disillusioned her with his weak character. She ought to turn her back on him, throw him to— Oh, hell, he was still her client, wasn't he? Anyway, for all his flaws, she still didn't believe him capable of murder.

She shook her head. "I promised to save him. I won't go back on that, but what are his chances now?"

The lawyer rubbed his heavy jowls. "In my opinion, none of what the police have is that solid. But juries have convicted on less."

"Meaning that something had better get turned up to prove Glenn didn't do it."

He smiled at her as he heaved himself to his feet. "A miracle wouldn't hurt. While you're deciding where to get one, I'll have my assistant phone the Claiborne house to let the housekeeper know you're on your way to collect Daisy."

Chapter Eleven

What was the saying about being fresh out of miracles? Whatever it was, it applied to Christy. She didn't have the miracle Edgar Evers needed to vindicate Glenn. Or, for that matter, any idea how to go about getting one.

In any case, she decided as she drove across town through the evening rush hour traffic, her investigation would have to go on hold while she cared for Daisy. She couldn't help thinking about it, however, wondering who had framed Glenn by planting the murder weapon in his garage. The unknown intruder who had stalked Dallas and her in Dutch Vasey's store? If she could learn his identity...

Tomorrow, Christy promised herself. Tomorrow, when Daisy was safely on her way to Lake Charles with her uncle, she would tackle the case again. That she would be investigating on her own this time, without Dallas at her side to guide and protect her, was something she wouldn't permit herself to think about.

Monica Claiborne's housekeeper must have been looking through a window, anxiously waiting for Christy's arrival. She had the front door open and was standing there in the entry by the time Christy mounted the steps to the gallery of the Garden District home.

"You are Ms. Hawke?" The woman was small and dark,

her voice betraying a slight accent. Something Asian, Christy thought.

"That's right."

"Come in."

Once inside the foyer, Christy faced the housekeeper. The woman was plainly relieved to see her.

"Daisy is in the kitchen. I'll bring her to you. Wait, please." She started to go and then turned back, looking both worried and guilty. "I can't stay with Daisy. I have to leave. They explained this to you?"

"Yes, I understand."

She nodded, satisfied that Christy accepted her need to flee from a situation that unnerved her. Then she hurried away into the back regions of the house. Left to herself, Christy examined her surroundings.

An archway framed the living room, which was tastefully and elegantly furnished. No surprises there. Monica Claiborne was a woman of style. Christy guessed she could understand why Glenn had fallen in love with her. And her sister before her.

There was a silver-framed photograph of Laura on the grand piano. Christy went over to look at it. Auburn hair and the flawless features that men would find intriguing. Men like Dallas.

It was a formal portrait. Laura wore the jewelry she'd loved. Diamonds at her ears, more diamonds studding the brooch at her throat. It was a distinctive brooch in the sunburst style. That was why it jogged Christy's memory. She had seen the piece before. In the collection she and Dallas had brought to Buzz Purreau for his appraisal. But, of course, she corrected herself, what she had seen was the copy. Laura would have disposed of the real brooch along with the other valuable gems.

There was the sound of voices from the long hallway

behind the foyer. Christy turned away from the piano as Daisy and the housekeeper came through the archway. The woman carried a small suitcase. The child cradled in her arms the stuffed panda bear that had been her mother's.

There was something so forlorn in the sight of the four-year-old standing there, gazing up at her with an expression of uncertainty on her small face, that Christy felt her throat tighten with emotion. Daisy had lost her mother, which was enough of a tragedy to bear. But now her father had been taken away from her, and though she might be too young to understand what was happening, she had to realize that something was wrong. On top of all that, she was being handed over to a woman she had met only once.

I know, Daisy. It stinks, doesn't it?

She approached the little girl with care, not knowing what to expect. Her teacher training hadn't prepared her to handle children at this level. What if she made a mess of it? What if Daisy refused to go with her?

Christy's eyes met the housekeeper's over Daisy's head. The woman understood her silent question and nodded. Daisy had been told she would spend the night with Christy at her apartment. But did she accept the arrangement?

"Hi, Daisy." She crouched down in front of the child. "Do you remember me?"

"Uh-huh."

"I'm really happy you're going to be visiting me for the night. I see you're all ready to go."

Daisy eyed her in silence and though she didn't back away, she looked worried. Christy had an inspiration.

"It's going to be a real adventure. We'll have a pajama party. You did remember to pack your pj's in that suitcase, didn't you?"

Daisy looked interested. "What's a 'jama party?"

"What? You never went to a pajama party? Then you've

been missing a lot of fun. See, what we do first is have supper. Afterwards, we put on our pj's, pop some popcorn and then we get to play games and tell stories.''

The child's eyes brightened. ''Does George get to be there, too?''

Christy considered the panda bear in Daisy's arms. ''I don't know. Does he have his pj's with him?''

''He doesn't have any. He just has an ache in his side. See?'' Daisy indicated a seam on the side of the stuffed bear that was beginning to part where the stitches were separating from age and hard use.

''Poor George. He's going to lose his insides if we don't do something about it. Guess I could try repairing him tonight. That is, if you and George are coming to the pajama party.''

Bonding with Daisy after that was no longer a challenge. The four-year-old chattered freely and cheerfully on the drive to Royal Street. She was asking Christy what they would fix for supper as they strolled through the carriageway.

The tunnel was dim with twilight except for the glow of lamps from the side window of St. Leger's Antiques, which had closed for the day. It was this rectangle of brightness that caught Christy's attention, stirred something in her memory. She stopped to peer into the window at the merchandise that was displayed both there and in the glass cases beyond. But what she sought was nowhere in view.

''Tell me what it is and I'll be happy to hold it for you.''

The voice startled Christy. She turned to face its owner. He must have come from his upstairs apartment across the courtyard from her own apartment. She could see from the rather formal way he was dressed that he was on his way to a function.

''Sorry, Alistair. I didn't see you there.''

He chuckled. "Obviously my window was more interesting. Are my displays that good or am I on fire in there?"

"It was just that I remembered—" She stopped and shook her head. "Never mind, it isn't important."

"Something wrong?"

"No, really, it isn't anything."

He regarded her for a few seconds and then he noticed Daisy. "And who do we have here?"

"This is Daisy. She's come to have a pajama party with me."

Alistair smiled. "Ah, those are the best kind. I'm afraid the party I'm going to will be very dull and I'm already late for it. Have a good evening, ladies."

He went on his way through the carriageway to the street outside. Christy watched him disappear around the corner. Then, with a last glance at the shop window, she took Daisy by the hand and led her across the courtyard.

It was the brooch that had jarred Christy's memory all over again. The brooch in Laura Hollister's photograph. The lighted window had reminded her of exactly where she had seen the memorable piece. Not in Laura's jewelry collection, but in Alistair St. Leger's shop where she had admired the piece the other afternoon while she and Dallas waited to speak to Alistair.

For a moment the connection had jolted her. But she realized now there was nothing remarkable about it. Either Alistair had acquired the brooch from the dealer to whom Laura had sold her jewelry or else the brooch in his shop was simply similar to the original that had belonged to Laura. Whatever the explanation, it had no bearing on the case.

Christy turned her attention to the more vital subject of their supper. Daisy was still waiting to hear about that. "Well, now let me see," she said, pondering the matter as she unlocked the office door and turned on lights. "What would George like?"

"He thinks peanut butter is good."

"What would he say to macaroni and cheese?" Christy suggested, leading the way upstairs.

"He would like it," Daisy agreed, validating Christy's hope it was a dish that still pleased most kids, as it had in her own childhood.

Twilight deepened into darkness outside as they ate their meal. Christy caught herself studying Daisy's face across the table, searching for some evidence of Dallas in the child's delicate features. She could see no likeness. But then Daisy didn't resemble Glenn either. Her coloring and structure were her mother's.

Are you her father, Dallas? Is this your child I'm caring for?

The mere possibility seized Christy with a sudden, terrible longing for the man with whom she had so unwisely fallen in love. Where was Dallas now? What was he doing? And, damn it all, she wasn't supposed to care where he had gone or what he might be up to. She wasn't supposed to want him here beside her.

Resolutely putting him out of her mind, she gave her attention to Daisy. The little girl had finished the macaroni and cheese on her plate, dutifully drank her milk and was gazing expectantly at Christy.

"Is it time now for the party?"

Christy consulted her watch. "Oh, my, we're late. We should have been in our pj's long ago. Let's hurry before George starts kicking up a fuss about it."

An excited Daisy slid off her chair and rushed into the bedroom where her suitcase had been deposited. Christy followed, and minutes later, the two of them emerged from the bedroom wearing their pajamas.

"You pick out a CD to play," she directed the child, giving her several to choose from, "while I start the popcorn."

Leaving Daisy to solemnly inspect the offered CDs, Christy went on to the kitchen. She had popped the corn and was filling her largest bowl with the result when she realized that her guest was being awfully quiet. Leaving the bowl on the counter, she went to check on her.

The CDs had lost their appeal for Daisy. Something else had claimed her interest. She was playing with it on the floor below the desk where Christy had so carelessly left it this morning.

That damn voodoo doll.

Innocent or not, the thing didn't belong in the hands of a child. She went and knelt on the floor beside Daisy. "Sweetheart, let's not fool with this. There's other things that are more fun."

"What?"

Yes, what? Christy wondered as she gently removed the doll from Daisy's possession and got to her feet. The answer came to her in the form of the shoe box, which she had also left out on the desk.

"This," she said with enthusiasm. Tossing the voodoo doll off to one side, she got back down on the floor with the box, displaying its contents to Daisy.

"Rocks," Daisy said in disappointment.

"Not ordinary rocks. These are magic rocks. Well, kind of a magic. Look, here's a shell and here's the leaf of a fern…"

Daisy was soon eagerly finding the fossils on her own. Christy brought the popcorn from the kitchen and put on a CD. They snacked on the popcorn, listened to Ricky Martin, played three games of fish and told each other stories.

Daisy had nodded off before Christy finished "The Little Mermaid."

Scooping the child into her arms, Christy carried her into the bedroom and tucked her in. She hadn't realized that caring for one four-year-old could be so exhausting. But Daisy wasn't finished with her.

"Don't forget what you promised," Daisy mumbled before she laid her head on the pillow.

"I did? Oh, that's right. I have to make George all better."

"Uh-huh."

Daisy went to sleep and Christy went to work. Finding a needle and some stout thread, she settled on her rocking chair in the living room with the fossils strewn across the carpet and the panda bear in her lap.

"George, my friend, you do look like you could use some help."

The strained seam in the old bear's side had apparently suffered during the trip from the Garden District. The stitches were no longer threatening to pull away from the fabric. They had already done so, and now the cotton stuffing was coming out of the open wound. A closer inspection explained the problem.

"Aha, you've had surgery before in this area, haven't you, George? Hate to tell you, but you had a lousy doctor. No wonder you're spilling your guts."

The earlier mending of the seam had been a poor one, with hasty, awkward stitches that were spaced too far apart. Christy planned to correct that.

"But first let's get your insides back where they belong before you lose that handsome shape."

She began poking the cotton stuffing back into the gap, using her forefinger to work it tightly into the cavity of the bear. One of her deep thrusts encountered resistance in the shape of something hard and flat.

"George, have you got a secret in your tummy?"

Bemused, Christy used thumb and forefinger to wriggle the object loose from the batting packed around it. Its shape and size had a familiar feel, and that was verified when she finally withdrew it from the split into which it had been inserted.

A floppy disk! What on earth was a computer disk doing inside a child's panda bear?

Silly question. Obviously, someone had lodged it there for safekeeping. Who and why? The *who* wasn't difficult. According to Glenn, the bear had belonged to Laura, a cherished plaything she'd kept from her childhood. She couldn't have known when she used it to conceal the disk that Glenn would find it among her things and give it to Daisy.

As for the *why*...well, only the contents of the disk could tell her that. One thing was for sure. Whatever those contents were, they had to be explosive if Laura had gone to the trouble of burying them where they were least likely to be found.

Christy was on fire with excitement as she laid the bear aside, left the rocking chair and went to her desk. Clearing away the clutter, she drew her computer forward and placed herself in front of it, praying the disk was compatible with her machine.

It was, and within seconds the disk was displaying its contents on her screen. She had no trouble recognizing them. She had seen too many files like this not to be familiar with them, had written her own share of them.

What she was seeing was the case report of a private investigator to his client. That client had been Laura Hollister. Laura had hired the Atlanta detective to research the background of—

Christy scrolled down to the line where the subject was identified. The name leaped out at her from the screen. Unbelievable, shocking and, as she read on, chilling in its matter-of-fact description of a secret existence.

OF COURSE, he thought to himself, she had no idea that he could see into any room of her apartment. No reason to suppose he might want to. She assumed that the bougain-villea sprawling so luxuriantly along his balcony protected her privacy by screening his view. And it did. From all his windows, that is, except one. The small window in the place where his personal altar was hidden behind a locked door looked through a gap in the bougainvillea and directly across the courtyard into her living room. Not at all effective by day, but at night like this, standing here in the darkness and with a pair of powerful binoculars trained on her lighted window…oh, yes, he could see everything.

And he needed to see what she was doing. He was worried about his little friend. He hadn't missed the fleeting uneasiness that had crossed her face when he had caught her looking into his shop window. Now why…

That's what he'd wondered all the way to the preview party for the Crescent City Antique Show. The question had continued to nag at him while he endured the tedious affair. What could have troubled her? He was always so cautious, so careful to keep this role he played separate from his other existence. Never any mistakes. Except…

Could that be it? The diamond brooch his fool of a clerk had displayed without his knowledge? The piece had been in the glass case less than a day before he'd discovered it there and immediately removed it. But that was the day Christy and McFarland had been in his shop. Had she noticed the brooch, somehow connected it afterward with Laura and then this evening remembered that—

It wasn't a serious error. Nothing that couldn't be comfortably explained should he ever be challenged over his possession of the brooch. No reason whatsoever for him to be concerned. But the animal cunning of a survivor hadn't permitted him to be entirely convinced of that.

He had made his excuses and left the party early. He needed to be here across the courtyard from her. Needed to monitor her activities from the darkness of this little room where he had stationed himself. A darkness which had always protected him in its soothing familiarity.

Besides, the child she was caring for interested him very much. He remembered she was Laura's child and how faithful a follower Laura had once been. And wondered if her daughter had the same potential…

He went on watching her. She had been mending something in her lap and now suddenly she was at her computer. There was an intenseness in her manner that he didn't like. What was she seeing on that screen?

No chances. He could take no chances with her. If she presented any danger, he would deal with it. Tonight was crucial. Nothing must threaten it.

ALISTAIR ST. LEGER.

That was the name that assaulted Christy like a physical blow, left her so shaken that she needed a few seconds to recover before she was able to continue reading.

Alistair St. Leger, her distinguished, oh-so-respectable neighbor. Alistair, the subject of the P.I.'s case report. Only in Atlanta he hadn't been Alistair St. Leger. He had been—

She peered at the screen. Harrison Cross. Same man, same vile activities. The blackmail of a wealthy widow whose grandson had gone to the police, rumors of a satanic cult. He had disappeared from the scene before he could be arrested, later created a new identity for himself in New Orleans. One that the police in Atlanta, where he was still wanted, were not aware of.

Why not? Christy wondered. If the P.I.'s investigation, along with whatever information Laura had been able to provide him, revealed that Harrison Cross was now masquerading as Alistair St. Leger, why hadn't the Atlanta police been informed of that?

There was no answer to that question in the case report itself. But, because the P.I. had been thorough, the file also contained every piece of correspondence exchanged by Laura and the detective during the course of his investigation.

Scrolling down through the contents of those letters, Christy learned that Laura's elderly aunt had browsed through St. Leger's Antiques during one of her stays in New Orleans. She had afterward remarked to her niece that its proprietor bore an uncanny resemblance to the owner of an art gallery she had visited on a trip to Atlanta two years earlier.

Which, Christy realized, explained what had alerted Laura, motivated her to contact an Atlanta-based private detective. But as for the other—

Wait! Here it was in Laura's last letter to the investigator. "You assured me when I hired you," she wrote, "that you preserve complete client confidentiality. Therefore, I am instructing you to destroy any and all material you've collected on Harrison Cross, aka Alistair St. Leger, and to mention your findings to no one. I'm adding a bonus to your final fee to guarantee that." The file ended there.

Christy sat back from the computer, trying to bring order to the thoughts that were chasing in a frenzy through her head. What did she understand now? That Laura hadn't

wanted Alistair exposed. Made sense when she considered
it. The result of such an exposure would have meant
Laura's own ruin. All of it would have been revealed—her
connection with a voodoo cult, the theft of cemetery art,
her involvement in a hit-and-run death.

What else did Christy know? That Laura must have been
desperate to free herself of Alistair's blackmail. And what
better way to break his cruel hold over her than with a
counter-blackmail? That was why she had used the Atlanta
P.I. Once equipped with his information, she'd have gone
to Alistair with a threat to contact the Atlanta police unless
he let her go. And then—

Christy had no way of knowing exactly what followed
in that confrontation. But she could guess, and the image
of it left her horrified as she sat there in front of the computer, struggling to accept it.

Alistair, her friend who was not kind and gentle, who
was evil, a murderer. Alistair, who—

Oh, dear God, he'd been here all along! Just steps away,
with nothing but a courtyard between them! He could be
out there, even now!

Shoving away from the desk, Christy rushed to the window, her flesh crawling as she stared into the night. There
was no sign of light anywhere in his apartment. He was
still out for the evening. But that didn't make her feel any
safer, even after she swiftly lowered the blinds at her window.

Vulnerable, she thought. She and Daisy were vulnerable
as long as they remained here. Nor would she risk waiting
for the police. She had to take Daisy and leave before Alistair returned, and only when they were out of here, with
Daisy secure, would she act on her knowledge.

But there was one call that she did have to make before
they fled the scene. Sensible or not, the urgency she was

feeling for that contact would not permit her to delay it.
She wanted Dallas, *needed* Dallas. Never mind what she
had told both him and herself this morning. None of that
mattered. Not now when all she could think of was having
him close beside her, his arms wrapped around her offering
his strength and protection. Because, of course, he meant
everything to her. It was just that simple.

*Oh, Dallas, how could I have been such a fool to send
you away?*

Her purse! Where had she left her purse? There, on the
table! Christy pounced on the bag and tore through its contents, extracting the slip of paper she needed. Bless Denise
for having learned and written down the numbers for both
Dallas's home and his office. Her assistant had forced the
slip on Christy that first morning she'd gone out to meet
Dallas, explaining it with one of her typically sassy obser-
vations. ''There are times, girl, when a woman has got to
call even the Prince of Darkness.''

Reaching for the phone on the wall, Christy dialed Dallas's apartment, praying he would be there. She waited
tensely through four rings and then to her deep disappointment, his answering machine kicked in.

''Dallas, if you're there, please pick up! It's important!''

Silence. He wasn't there. She left her earnest message.

''Listen, I'm at home and I have Daisy with me. We're
leaving here and going to—'' Where? Where could she take
Daisy that she would be safe for the night? It occurred to
her then, the only refuge she could think of. ''—Denise's
place. Denise Rawlins. You'll find her in the phone book.
I'll explain everything when you get there. And, Dallas,
whatever you do, don't try to contact my neighbor about
any of this.''

Ending that call, she punched in the numbers for his
agency on the chance that he would be there, even though

it was long after office hours. Once again she got the answering machine. This time, not wanting to waste precious seconds, her message was brief.

"Dallas, if you turn up there before you go home, check in with the answering machine at your apartment. It's important."

There was nothing more she could do to try to reach him. She didn't know the number for his cell phone, had no idea where he might be. She was on her own. It was up to her to guard Daisy and herself. Time to prove her worth as a P.I. and her courage as a woman. A challenge she couldn't afford to fail.

Hurrying back into the living room, she retrieved the vital disk from the computer, slipped it into her bag and went on into the bedroom where she threw on jeans and a shirt.

Daisy hadn't stirred. She was still asleep when Christy leaned over the bed. She hated to disturb her, feared the child would be alarmed by the necessity of leaving in the middle of the night. No choice. But maybe if she carried her...

Daisy was small for her age. Christy thought she could bear her weight, at least as far as the car. No need to bother with her clothes. It was a mild night. Daisy would be warm enough in her pajamas.

The child awakened, but only briefly, when Christy slid her hands beneath her body and scooped her up into her arms. Her eyes fluttered open and she murmured a drowsy, "Where we going?"

"Just for a little ride. It's all right, sweetheart. Go back to sleep."

And, thankfully, Daisy did just that as Christy carried her out of the bedroom, through the living room, down the stairs and across the darkened office to the front door. Then came the awkward business of holding on to both Daisy and her shoulder bag while she fumbled with the lock.

The bolt snapped and she opened the door, easing it back with her foot. There should have been nothing waiting on the other side but the route to safety. Instead, there was Alistair St. Leger. A very lethal Alistair, who stood there with a gun in his hand, his eyes gleaming with diabolical amusement in the soft glow of the courtyard lanterns.

"I was right to be worried, wasn't I?" he said, his voice low and deceptively pleasant.

Christy stared at him, her heart kicking in fear.

"The window," he explained. "You left the computer and rushed to the window to lower the blinds."

Then he *had* come back! Had been out there the whole time watching her!

"So I was right to be worried." He gestured with the gun, indicating the stairway behind her. "We'll go back up to your apartment now, Christy. We'll learn exactly how much there is for me to be worried about."

No choice, not with that gun he was waving. She turned, her heart now in her throat, and climbed the stairs. Daisy had grown heavier in her arms. She had to be careful not to drop her, careful not to wake her.

"Put her on the sofa," Alistair commanded when they reached the living room. "That's right," he said as she gently placed Daisy on the cushions and hovered over her protectively. There was a smile on his face when he looked down at the sleeping child. "Such a little angel, isn't she? Looks so much like her mother."

Christy gazed at him. He was not the Alistair she had known. That Alistair had been stripped down to the hard reality hidden beneath a mask of silver-haired congeniality. A reality which exposed a brutality in the thin, pale face, a cruelty in the cold blue eyes.

But Christy refused to be daunted by him, not when there was this threat to Daisy. She faced him squarely. "If you dare to hurt her—"

"I wouldn't dream of it. I have plans for young Daisy. But those are in the future. At the moment there's another matter that demands my attention. Empty your bag on the table there." When Christy hesitated, he wagged the gun in his hand, reminding her of its deadly presence. "Now, please."

She complied, spilling the contents of her purse on the table. The disk lay among them.

"Take it to the computer," he ordered. "Show me what's on it."

He stood behind her, watching as she inserted the disk and brought the file up on the screen.

"Why didn't I realize that Laura would cheat me in the end?" he said angrily as he scanned the report contained in the file. "I should have known when she gave me the original that she would keep a copy." He glanced down at the floor where Christy had placed the panda bear. "And, of course, she concealed it inside the bear you were repairing. That's what had you so excited when you found it. I've seen enough. Go over there now and stand by the sofa."

When Christy obeyed, Alistair removed the disk from the computer and gazed at it thoughtfully. "No, I shouldn't have trusted Laura. But then this disk wasn't my only mistake, was it? Telling you and McFarland about the traffic in stolen cemetery art was another. Still, if I hadn't told you, some other dealer would have."

Tucking the disk into his pocket, he moved toward the window. "The brooch, though, was a more serious error. I really shouldn't have kept the brooch. I should have disposed of it, just as I disposed of the rest of Laura's jewelry that she handed over to me piece by piece. But then I couldn't bring myself to part with it, not with this weakness I have for antiques that are unique. Ah, well, everything will soon be corrected.''

He'd reached the window. Parting the blinds, he looked out into the night. "The moon will rise in another hour," he said. "By then, you and I and the child will have joined the others waiting for me at the plantation. The rites are always better by moonlight. And you'll watch me, Christy, you'll be a part of the last ceremony I conduct at Resurrection." He turned away from the window and smiled at her. "Only appropriate, I think, that it should end where it all began."

There was an eagerness in his smile, an excitement on his narrow face that sickened her. How could she have ever thought it aristocratic, when it was the face of a savage predator?

No, Christy thought as she watched him with fear and disgust, Alistair wasn't the only one who'd made mistakes. She had made a bad one in her decision not to contact the police until she got Daisy safely away from this scene. She should have phoned them immediately. But she'd never guessed that the danger was already present.

Regrets were pointless. She needed to act, find some means of help. If only—

"It's time to go," he informed her abruptly. He gestured toward the sofa with the muzzle of the gun. "Carry the child."

Her own gun was gone. Had been gone since the night it was taken off of Dallas by the intruder in Dutch Vasey's store. Alistair, of course. But her cell phone was still there on the table with the other articles from her purse. And if that phone accompanied her...

She started toward the table, intending to collect the bag

and its contents, but Alistair stopped her. "You won't need any of that."

Desperate now, Christy cast her gaze around the room, searching for some last form of deliverance. Hope came to her in the sight of the objects scattered on the floor below her desk. It was the remotest of chances, but it was all she had.

"Where are you going now?" he demanded sharply as she crossed to the desk.

"The panda bear," she said. "It will calm Daisy if she has it with her when she wakes up."

He apparently decided, just as she'd prayed he would, that keeping Daisy quiet was desirable. "Be quick about it then."

Christy crouched down to retrieve the bear from the floor. The voodoo doll, which she must have brushed off the desk when she'd slid the computer into position, was there beside the bear. Near them were the fossils she had produced to entertain Daisy.

Using her body as a shield from the eyes that she knew were watching her, Christy swiftly placed the fossil of the fern on the breast of the red voodoo doll. It was a wildly obscure message, but if Dallas came to the apartment when he didn't find them with Denise, and he *must,* there was the possibility he would discover her clue, somehow manage to decipher it.

Dallas, please come. Please understand the message I've left for you.

It was a litany Christy repeated to herself over and over as she picked up Daisy, preceded Alistair down the stairs, across the courtyard and through the gate that opened onto the alley where the tenants parked their cars.

Alistair unlocked and opened the back door of his black

Mercedes sedan. "Lay the child across the seat," he instructed her.

"I'll hold her in the front."

He shook his head. "No, you won't. I want you at the wheel while I keep an eye on you with this." His forefinger tapped the side of his gun, reminding her not to try anything.

There was nothing to do but obey him. She ought to be belted, Christy thought as she stretched Daisy across the length of the back seat. On the other hand, if she made Daisy sit up, the child was bound to wake and Christy wanted to keep her innocent of their plight as long as possible.

As it was, Daisy stirred again as she placed her on the seat, mumbling a groggy, "Where's George?"

"Right here, sweetheart."

Alistair, who had taken charge of the stuffed animal, thrust it at Christy, and she gave it to the child. Satisfied, Daisy hugged the panda bear against her cheek and promptly went back to sleep.

"Now drive," Alistair commanded her.

And Christy drove, taking them through the traffic of the city, across the bridge and up the river road toward Resurrection, and the depravity of a voodoo ceremony. Nowhere along the route did they encounter a police car. Even if they had, she wouldn't have dared to signal it. Not with that gun at his side, not with Daisy in the back.

It was a nightmare of a journey, made all the more hideous by the rantings of the man beside her. "Most of them were like Laura," he gloated of his victims. "Silly, bored creatures craving new thrills. Eager to be one of us. But they were never serious about my dark religion. Never one of the truly faithful, as I was and will continue to be.

"I'll be gone from here before tomorrow. Back to Haiti

where it all began for me, where it's still possible to find the pure religion. I'll start over, but this time it will be different. Laura's daughter will be with me. The very young are malleable material. I'll train her, teach her to be my obedient disciple, and in time…''

Christy knew that Alistair didn't intend for her to survive this night. Otherwise, he wouldn't be sharing all this horror with her. Daisy *would* live. She ought to be thankful for that, but the image of the obscene existence Alistair planned for the child sickened her. Christy couldn't bear it.

Find us, Dallas. Come to us before it's too late.

Chapter Twelve

Where the hell could they be?

Denise hadn't seen them. They had never turned up at her place. Denise hadn't heard a word from Christy. Had no idea what was going on.

"You want me to call the cops?" she had offered as a distracted Dallas stood at her front door, plowing a hand through his black hair.

Dallas had told her no, assured her that if necessary, he would call the police himself after he'd checked out Christy's apartment. He had hopes that she was still there, though she hadn't answered her phone when Denise tried to ring her for him.

It was the tone of urgency in the message Christy had left for him on his answering machine that Dallas thought about now as he sped across town in the direction of the French Quarter. He didn't like it one bit. Why was Daisy with her? And what did Christy's neighbor have to do with any of it? It was that part of her message that worried him the most, had him exceeding every speed limit on his drive to Royal Street.

If only he'd been there when her call came. But he'd been out all day, attacking the case in an effort to keep himself from thinking about the woman he loved and feared he might have lost. It hadn't worked, of course. He'd spent most of the afternoon and evening missing her, wanting her, making himself miserable with his longing. And with the images of having her just where she belonged, naked in his bed with his arms around her holding her close, his hands stroking her sweet flesh, his mouth on hers. But, hell, he would have taken her without the sex just for the chance to be with her again, if that's the way it had to be.

The traffic was worse than usual. Dallas cursed it in his impatience to reach Christy's apartment. Where were they, she and the kid? What was it all about? Had Christy managed to learn the answers they had been searching for? Dallas hadn't, though he had been pursuing them on his own ever since Laura Hollister's funeral.

Three people had attended that funeral who oughtn't to have been there. Had their presence been in any way significant, connected somehow with Laura's murder? Dallas had tracked them down afterward, one by one. A tedious, lengthy business, and ultimately disappointing.

Buzz Purreau had been nervous with him. Something to hide? "Look," the young jeweler had defended himself, "I didn't want to go to the funeral. But my family insisted. Said it would look bad and reflect on the business if I didn't show respect for a woman who'd been one of our important clients. And why wouldn't I be nervous with you after the way you threatened me over your girlfriend when the two of you were in here the other day?"

Dallas's interview with Marty Bornowski had produced no better result. "Okay, so I went to her funeral. You wanna know why? It's because I've been feeling guilty. I mean, what if this craving I had for illegal cemetery art contributed somehow to the woman's death? Least I could do was pay my respects."

Camille Levau's explanation had also been understandable. "Sugar, think," the voodoo queen had pleaded with him. "If it was evil voodoo that destroyed this poor woman, then only the presence of my good voodoo at her funeral could save her soul from everlasting damnation."

A wasted effort, all of it. Instead of following dead-end leads, he ought to have stuck with Christy. Should have insisted, whatever her objections, that she remain at his side, even if that meant handcuffing her to him and throwing away the key. Because if anything had happened to her…

But Dallas didn't want to think that. *Refused* to think it. And then found, when he finally reached Royal Street, that he couldn't not think it. It was the courtyard that concerned him first. He didn't like its silence, its feeling of desertion.

There were no lights in St. Leger's apartment. But there was a glow behind the blinds of Christy's living room window. That should have reassured him. It didn't, not after he tried her front door and found it unlocked. It ought to have been locked for the night. Why wasn't it?

He went into the unlighted office and called up the stairway. "Christy, are you there?"

Silence and again that sense of desertion. A fear clenched now at his gut as he took the steps two at a time. It intensified when, reaching the empty living room, the first thing he saw was her abandoned shoulder bag on the table, its contents spilled across the surface.

He checked the kitchen area, then the tiny bedroom where he noticed the open suitcase and a child's clothing. Daisy must have been spending the night with her. He kept thinking about that shoulder bag. Christy wouldn't have left without her purse. Not willingly. He could no longer tell himself that something wasn't wrong. *Seriously* wrong. Just what had happened here after she had made that phone call to him? And who had made it happen?

Christy's warning about her neighbor. It all came back to that, didn't it? Had she learned something alarming about Alistair St. Leger? Were she and the child missing because of him?

Dallas went to the living room window, parted the blinds and gazed across the courtyard at St. Leger's unlighted apartment. The more he thought about the antiques dealer, the more convinced he became that somehow, unlikely though he was, Alistair St. Leger was the explanation for everything. The killer they had been searching for.

And, my God, he must have grabbed Christy and the child!

Where? Dallas asked himself as he swung away from the window, casting his frantic gaze around the living room as though it could provide him with the answer. Where had St. Leger taken them?

His eyes went to the glowing screen on the other side of the room. The computer. Had Christy been using her PC this evening? Was there a chance that it could tell him what he needed to know?

Dallas started eagerly toward the desk. His foot crunched on something. He looked down. Rocks. There were small rocks scattered about the floor. What on earth—

And then he saw it. The red voodoo doll that had been a gift from Camille Leveau. It was there just below the desk and something had been placed on it. Dallas hunkered down to examine it. One of the rocks. Only they weren't ordinary rocks. He could see that now. They were fossils, and this particular fossil—

A fern. The fossil of a fern resting on the breast of the voodoo doll. Was it a happenstance or deliberate? He took the rock in one hand and the doll in the other, weighing them in his palms. A fern and voodoo. Voodoo and a fern.

Meaningless, or could Christy have intended them as a message?

If ever he needed his P.I. skills, it was now. He applied them to the problem, his mind burning in a struggle to unlock the riddle. Fern and voodoo, voodoo and fern. What could—

And then in a burst of insight it struck him. The resurrection fern that was so common in southern Louisiana! The Claiborne plantation had been named for that fern! Resurrection, where midnight voodoo ceremonies had been held!

The bastard had taken them to a voodoo ceremony at Resurrection. Dallas was sure of it. Or at least certain enough to lose no time in racing out of the building and through the courtyard to his car. And if he was wrong, if they weren't at the abandoned plantation—

But he wouldn't permit himself to consider that possibility. They *had* to be there and he *had* to reach them in time to prevent whatever atrocity St. Leger intended.

Dallas had crossed the Mississippi and was tearing up the river road on the west bank before he remembered that he hadn't called the cops. He reached for his cell phone and, to his frustration, discovered he had no signal. The phone was dead. Since he'd had no occasion to use the instrument after the police recovered it for him following the episode in the warehouse, he could only assume that Dutch Vasey had abused the phone when he'd seized it from him.

The hour was late, and what few businesses existed along the back route he traveled were long closed. He was nearing Resurrection before he found a public phone in a roadside bar. Dallas made his urgent call and then was on the road again.

He had no intention of waiting for the police. Who knew

how long it would take them to reach the plantation. And Christy needed him. He was terrified for her and the child. If St. Leger or his followers hurt either one of them, he would tear the bastards to pieces limb by limb. But that couldn't happen. He couldn't fail Christy, not when he'd promised her father that he would make sure she was safe, not when she meant everything to him.

Hang on for me, grits. Whatever happens, hang on.

ALISTAIR WAS EXULTANT as he addressed the writhing snake that represented his demonic deity. "Master," he intoned, holding the snake aloft in both hands, "the sacrifice we offer you tonight will please you like no other."

The leaping flames of the fire that blazed in the center of the clearing revealed the bloodlust in his eyes behind the serpent mask he wore. Glowing eyes that were directed with unmistakable meaning at Christy huddled on the ground. Surrounding her were Alistair's followers who chanted an obedient response, their swaying figures casting grotesque shadows.

Christy's arms tightened protectively around Daisy. The whimpering child clung to her, burying her face against Christy's breasts. It was a foul scene, made all the more loathsome by Alistair's insistence that Daisy be there to witness the rites. For that alone, Christy wished him in the hell he served.

Yet, when the time came, when he seized that sacrificial knife waiting beside the skull on the altar behind him, she was prepared to plead with him. Not for her life. That would be useless, and a humiliation to which she would never lower herself. But Daisy...she would beg him to spare Daisy the horrifying sight of her death. Perhaps that much he would grant her.

But that time had yet to arrive. They were waiting for

the moon to clear the trees, to pour its light down into the clearing. And until it did, until their filthy ceremony demanded the ultimate climax, Christy had a chance to survive. But how? Escape was impossible. Four members of the cult, armed with rifles, had been posted around the perimeter of the clearing to guard against the approach of any outsider. She knew they wouldn't hesitate to bring her down, and Daisy with her, if she made any attempt to flee. Nor, as yet, could she think of any way to outwit them.

I love you, Dallas McFarland. If I never see you again, I need you to know that.

Daisy was weeping in earnest now. Christy rocked her in her arms and murmured soothing reassurances in her ear. "It's all right, sweetheart. Everything is going to be all right…"

Christy knew that it was far from all right. That to expect deliverance was useless. But she also knew that, as long as the blood pumped in her veins, as long as her brain was capable of functioning, she could not and would not abandon hope.

IT WAS THE BEAT of the drums and the rattle of their gourds that guided Dallas to the clearing behind the graveyard. He had left his car back in the lane in order to steal silently through the trees. Now, exercising every caution, he crept forward. Crouching in the thick undergrowth, he peered out into the firelit circle.

It was an eerie scene that met his gaze. A scene that both disgusted and outraged him. There were almost a dozen of them in wigs and masks and face paint dancing around the fire with moans and savage howls. Whipping themselves into a frenzy induced, he suspected, by drugs as well as by the goading of the sinister figure who was their high priest.

He didn't have to see the face behind that ugly serpent mask to realize it belonged to Alistair St. Leger.

But what maddened Dallas more than all the rest was the sight of Christy there on the ground in the middle of all this insanity, surrounded by them, trapped by them. Helpless, yes, but defiant, too, daring them with her stubborn chin and angry eyes to touch the child she clasped securely in her arms. He was both proud of her and afraid for her.

Where the hell were the cops? Why weren't they swarming into the clearing? He couldn't wait for them. He had to act. Had to save Christy and the kid from whatever roles they would be forced to play in this gruesome spectacle. How? He didn't have his gun. The police back in New Orleans had kept his piece. It wouldn't have been of use, anyway, against the rifles of those four alert lookouts.

Dallas searched his mind for a method of rescue. A distraction. He had to create a distraction. If he could lure enough of them away from the clearing for the few moments he would need to slip in there and snatch Christy and the kid…

What? What could he use?

He turned his head, his gaze raking the area on both sides and behind him. The moon had cleared the horizon. He could see its pale light on the columns of the plantation house several hundred feet off to his right. He looked at the ruin and then he knew what he had to do.

Making his way back through the tangled undergrowth until he was in the clear again, he turned and sprinted through the grove of live oaks. When he reached his car, he dug into the glove compartment until he found the book of matches left behind from the days when he'd smoked. His hand also closed on something round and hard but with enough weight, he hoped, for his purpose.

Armed with the two articles, Dallas raced around to the back of the mansion. There was a stand of tall pine trees in the weedy yard, their crowns forming such a dense canopy that the carpet of needles at their feet remained dry. He spread his coat on the ground and worked feverishly, scooping up handfuls of needles until the coat was loaded. Then he took his bundle and carried it through the gap in the boarded doorway of the house.

The only light inside was a weak glow from the moon finding its way through the hole in the roof. But it was enough, along with his touch and sense of smell which told him that, where the rain hadn't managed to penetrate, the house reeked of dry rot. The floorboards in the center hall were like tinder. He knelt on them, dumping the pine needles in a heap.

Dallas regretted the necessity of sacrificing the old mansion, but the crumbling structure was beyond rescue anyway. It took only a single match to ignite the needles. The mound flared like a torch. By the time he squeezed back through the gap, the flames were already licking up the walls.

The whole effort had required no more than minutes and within another two minutes, he'd worked his way around to the back side of the clearing behind the graveyard. The voodoo ceremony was still in progress as he crouched in the shrubbery and waited.

It seemed like a lifetime to Dallas, but in reality, it was only a matter of seconds before the house erupted like a volcano. The roar of the flames bursting through windows and roof, their hot glare a nova against the night sky, couldn't fail to produce a stunned silence in the clearing. Almost immediately, it was followed by a stampede as the cult members, with cries of excitement, crashed through the undergrowth toward the raging mansion.

They left behind a single sentinel to guard an astonished Christy, who still huddled on the ground with Daisy in her arms. And that's when Dallas went into action. He knew it would be a mistake to try to rush his enemy. That deadly rifle would defeat him before he could overwhelm his target. He held back until the guard, unable to resist the lurid spectacle of the burning mansion, turned his head in that direction.

Dallas tightened his grip on the metal disk he had removed from the glove compartment. His talent with a yo-yo had never been anything more than recreational, an amusement to relax him. Now it was vital, demanding his accurate delivery.

With a prayer and a powerful thrust, he sent the disk flying into the clearing. It connected with the skull of the guard. Stunned by the blow, the man sank to his knees. Dallas was on him like a linebacker.

But the guard was tougher than he'd anticipated. And determined. He clung to the rifle, resisting Dallas's struggles to wrest it from him while he yelled his head off. The other cult members heard his shouts for help. Some of them were already turning back. The rest were bound to follow.

"Take Daisy and get out of here!" Dallas ordered Christy, who was already on her feet with the child desperately clinging to her.

There was only one direction for Christy to run. If she headed for the road, she would be cut off. That left the wilderness at the back of the clearing. Dallas turned his head to make certain she was fleeing that way through the shrubbery. Mistake. The guard took advantage of his carelessness to heave against him, breaking his hold. Before Dallas could drag him down again, the man scurried off into the undergrowth at the front of the clearing. He still had the rifle.

Dallas did the smart thing. He got out of there. A bullet sang past his ear as he plunged into the shrubbery after Christy. The growth on this side was like a jungle. He plowed through it, searching for some evidence of Christy's presence, not daring to risk calling out to her.

He could smell the sweet fragrance of honeysuckle vine and the sour odors of the perpetually damp earth of southern Louisiana's subtropical climate. He pushed on through the tangle. The moonlight revealed an opening past the mossy boles of the tall slash pines. It was another clearing, a much smaller one. She was waiting for him there in the shadows.

Dallas hadn't exactly counted on a tearful embrace, especially since her arms were full of Daisy. But then neither did he expect what he got. Managing to free one hand when he joined her, she closed it in a fist and walloped him on the chest.

"What was that for?" he demanded.

"For almost getting yourself killed back there."

"Of all the ungrateful—"

"Don't worry, McFarland. The minute we get out of this mess, I plan to climb all over you with expressions of my gratitude."

Now *that,* he thought, was a promise that definitely had interesting possibilities, one that had him longing to take her in his arms right now and kiss her until she was limp. Instead, he had to settle for a fast, "Make them friendly enough and you've got a date. In the meantime…"

He didn't have to go on. He knew she realized they were still in peril. From the direction of the voodoo clearing they could hear their enemies calling out to each other as they spread out, thrashing through the growth to flush them out.

"He won't give up," Christy said and Dallas knew she

was referring to St. Leger. "I know too much now and he has to get me back."

And those rifles, Dallas thought grimly, make us prey running from hunters. "Then we have to avoid them until the cops get here." And what was keeping them? he wondered.

She accepted that without the need for explanation and started to move on, but he stopped her. He could see that her burden was growing too heavy for her. Daisy kept slipping down in her arms. "You'd better let me carry Daisy."

"No!" the frightened child objected, clutching at Christy.

"It's all right, sweetheart. He's going to help us."

Daisy was, plainly, not convinced of that.

Dallas, tapping his memory, had an inspiration. "Hey, you can trust me, Daisy. I'm a friend of George's."

Impressed by his claim, Daisy permitted herself to be handed over to Dallas. It gave him a funny feeling having her small, warm body nestled against him. A feeling of almost fierce protectiveness. Whether this was in any way paternal, or whether he might be entitled to such an emotion, he didn't know. Nor was there time to examine his reaction. They needed to move.

Setting the pace, he led them across what had once been a cultivated field but was now a wilderness of palmettos and banana plants that had gone native. When he wasn't pushing aside fronds, he was slapping at mosquitoes.

Christy finally spoke, asking softly, "Is Daisy asleep?"

Dallas looked down. The child's eyes were closed, her head resting against his shoulder. "Yes."

"Poor baby. She's exhausted."

There was another moment of silence between them and then Christy began to talk to him in a low, urgent voice. "Alistair intended for me not to leave that ceremony alive.

That's why he felt safe telling me everything on the way to Resurrection. Why, he entertained himself by watching me squirm while he gloated. He's a maniac, of course. Do you know that he actually believes he can achieve immortality with his voodoo?''

"Christy, save your wind. There's no need for you to tell me any of this. Not now.''

"There is," she insisted. "You have to know it all in case I don't survive and you do.''

"I don't want to hear that kind of talk," he growled. "We're all three going to make it.''

She didn't listen to him. She began to speak again, rapidly explaining how she had discovered the computer disk, what it contained and how Alistair had forced her to take Daisy, and accompany him to the plantation.

Dallas, coming to a halt, interrupted her account. "Listen.''

They stood there, straining to hear any sounds of their pursuers behind them. Except for the whine of insects, there was nothing but silence. No shouts, no noise of bodies beating through the heavy growth.

"Have we lost them?" she asked hopefully.

He shook his head. He didn't know. But he didn't like it. He could smell mud and rotting vegetation, and the ground had grown soggy under their feet. He understood why when, urging them forward again, they suddenly came to water. A dark expanse of it gleaming in the moonlight.

"We're trapped," she said as they stared at the cypress swamp that stretched away on either side without any sign of dry land.

"Maybe not," he said, spotting something long and low drawn up on the bank a few yards away. "Here, take Daisy.''

Passing the child back to her, he went to investigate. It

was a pirogue, one of those homebuilt crafts used for fishing in the swamps. The long shaft for poling it was tucked down inside.

"It's either this," he said, "or turn back and take our chances. Unless, of course, you'd like to try a moonlit swim."

Christy decided that she would not. By the time she joined him, he had floated the pirogue. He saw her settled in the bow with the still sleeping Daisy. Then, standing in the back of the craft, he dug in with the pole and shoved them away from the bank.

"Uh, I don't suppose you…"

"Not a clue," he said, knowing that she was asking him where they were going. "All I care about is putting distance between us and that pack back there."

Satisfied with that, she was quiet as he wove a passage for them through the ranks of the cypress trees. Depending on your mood, Dallas thought, the swamp with its trailing strands of Spanish moss and a light mist that caressed the knees of the cypress was either romantic or sinister. Given the moonlight and the woman who was with him, romantic would have been better, but he supposed that under the circumstances sinister was more appropriate. Christy must have thought so since after a moment she felt impelled to go on with St. Leger's unsavory revelations. This time he let her, knowing that she needed to get it all out.

"It was Laura's expensive tastes that got her in trouble," she said, checking on Daisy to make certain she couldn't hear her. "She always needed funds and for a while, she got them from Alistair and his band by letting them use Resurrection. The plantation had everything they needed— isolation, the fresh graveyard dust their rites demanded, even a Claiborne ancestor who'd been a famous practitioner of the black arts buried there."

"Sounds cozy. When did it all change?"

"When Alistair enticed her into joining them in their ceremonies, then turned around and began to blackmail her. Well, we saw why that night at Dutch Vasey's store."

The videotape and the newspaper clipping that incriminated Laura in a hit-and-run death, Dallas remembered.

"It all went," Christy said. "Her bank account, the fittings that Vasey stripped out of the house, her best jewelry. Laura even helped them with the thefts of cemetery art until in the end—" Breaking off, she asked nervously, "What was that?"

Dallas had heard it, too. A soft splashing in the water a few feet away. "Probably just a turtle." A turtle seemed far more preferable than a hungry alligator or an aggressive water moccasin, both of which were possible. He reminded himself to handle the pirogue with care. The thought of overturning them wasn't very appealing.

"In the end," Christy continued, "Laura fought back with the disk I told you about. She had the original with her that afternoon she asked Alistair to meet her in the Claiborne cemetery at Resurrection. She was prepared to give him the disk in exchange for his promise that he and his partner would never again try to bleed her."

"Why the cemetery at the plantation?" Dallas asked.

"Because there was something else she wanted from Alistair. And she was willing to buy it back by giving him the only thing she had never permitted him to touch in a place that was still sacred to her. There was a sleeping marble cherub on one of the family tombs. Alistair admired it. He could have it if he returned the one favorite piece of her jewelry he hadn't sold, the diamond brooch."

"Am I right in guessing that a hammer has something to do with this part of the story?" He recalled the alleged murder weapon.

"And a chisel," Christy said. "Laura brought them from Glenn's tool box to chip the cherub off the tomb. Except Alistair wasn't in a mood to negotiate. He was furious that Laura dared to challenge him."

"So he ends up killing her with the hammer."

"And manages to return both tools to the box in Glenn's garage."

"Where the police find them."

"As they were meant to do. Are we sailing in circles? I could swear you poled us past that same log over there a few minutes ago."

"That log is not at all like the other one," he said confidently.

Hell, he didn't know. The swamp would be bad enough to navigate by day. At night, like this, it was impossible. Everything looked the same. But it didn't matter as long as he kept them moving away from the danger.

Christy took up her story again. "Alistair was cunning. He made his partner keep the blackmail tape. That way, if anything went wrong, the evidence wouldn't be found at his place. But it all backfired on him when Dutch Vasey caught us in his warehouse and panicked. He called Alistair and when Alistair arrived on the scene, Vasey threatened to save his own neck by exposing Alistair as Laura's killer."

"At which point," Dallas figured, "St. Leger promptly killed his partner and hid his body."

"And then looked for that video to destroy."

"Which he didn't find," Dallas said, "because his search was interrupted by the cops who had turned up to cart us off to jail for indecent exposure on a warehouse roof."

"Exactly. Alistair did a fast exit, deciding to come back at night to find the tape and deal with the body, only— Well, you know the rest." She turned her head and peered through the cypress trees. "McFarland, I hate to complain again, but there's a shoreline ahead and it looks awfully familiar."

"It's not the one we left," he insisted. "We're probably clear on the other side of the swamp by now. Look, see that spit of land? You don't remember that, do you?"

"No, I guess not."

He poled them toward the point. If it proved to be solid and safe, he would land them there. They couldn't go on winding through the swamp all night. They needed to find their way out of this wilderness, get to a phone or at least a road.

He scanned the dense growth on the shore as they neared the point. It was silent, still. Satisfied, he dug in the pole and thrust the pirogue up onto the bank where it grounded in the mud.

"Stay here," he instructed Christy, "while I check it out."

Leaving her in the pirogue, he stepped ashore. He was bending over to lay the pole on the ground when a figure detached itself from the thick shadows where it had been lurking, waiting for them to land.

Alerted by Christy's gasp of warning, Dallas lifted his gaze to the sight of Alistair St. Leger. Mask removed, he wore a triumphant expression on his narrow face as he slowly approached them in the moonlight with gun in hand. Dallas was infuriated with himself. He had made a very grave mistake. He hadn't listened to Christy. He had brought them back to the same shore from which they had fled.

"Put it down," St. Leger ordered him, referring to the long shaft that Dallas still clutched in his hand. "*Now,* before a bullet makes the decision for you."

His sharp voice must have penetrated Daisy's unconsciousness, alarming her with its chilling tone. She awoke suddenly in Christy's arms and cried out. Startled by her wail of fear, Alistair's attention was diverted for a second.

That second was all Dallas needed. The stout pole flashed in his hand, the end of it striking Alistair's wrist with all the force and swiftness of a javelin. The gun jumped out of St. Leger's hand and went sailing off into the reeds. Before he could make any move to recover it, Dallas launched himself up the bank and slammed into him. Both of them went down under the impact.

Grunting and cursing, the two men rolled in the mud, each struggling for the advantage over the other. But Alistair was no match for the enraged Dallas. In the end, straddling the winded St. Leger, Dallas gripped him by the collar and shoved his face into his.

"This," he said, biting off the words, "is for me and that night in Dutch Vasey's store." He smacked Alistair's head against the ground. "And this," he said, his fist connecting with Alistair's jaw, "is for Christy and Daisy."

Dallas had the supreme satisfaction of hearing the high priest of the serpent god groan twice before he slid into unconsciousness. By the time he rolled off of St. Leger and got to his feet, Christy had climbed out of the pirogue and found the gun. She turned it over to Dallas and went back to the pirogue to collect a bewildered Daisy.

"She okay?" Dallas asked when Christy, carrying the child, rejoined him.

"She's going to be fine. Aren't you, sweetheart?"

"Can we go home now?" Daisy asked.

Before Christy could answer her, Dallas held up one hand. "Listen," he said.

There was a long moment of silence and then Christy murmured a puzzled, "I don't hear anything."

"That's the point. No yells, no feet pounding through the trees and St. Leger was alone."

"Does that mean the others gave up and scattered? I hope."

"Either that or the cops finally arrived and managed to round them up."

Christy issued a sigh of relief. "Then it's all over."

"Not quite, grits." He grinned down at her, his teeth gleaming wolfishly in the moonlight. "You still owe me those expressions of gratitude and I mean to collect on every one of them."

Chapter Thirteen

Christy had every intention of paying her debt. Was eager to pay it. But, to the frustration of both her and Dallas, there was a necessary matter that demanded their attention before they could get around to satisfying her obligation. The officer in charge of the scene seemed to expect a full explanation from them.

They gave it to him as the three of them stood beside Dallas's car in the oak grove, talking in low tones in order not to disturb Daisy. Reunited with George, the child was safely asleep under a blanket on the back seat of the car.

The police sergeant nodded after they'd provided him with the essentials. "We'll need complete statements from both of you, but they can wait until tomorrow."

He'd assured them earlier that most of the cult had been apprehended, and he was confident the rest would be found and charged. Alistair St. Leger was already on his way to New Orleans in handcuffs.

The sergeant closed his notebook and looked contrite. "Sorry for our delay in getting here, folks, but there was a car accident on the road that had to be cleared away before we could get through."

"Apology accepted," Dallas said. "That is," he added, tilting his head in the direction of the smoking rubble which was all that remained of Resurrection, "if you're willing to accept mine. I'm sorry about the fire, but I needed something spectacular enough to draw them away from the voodoo ceremony."

"Shame about the old place," the officer said, "but under the circumstances, I can't imagine that Ms. Claiborne won't forgive you."

"There's one thing you can say about it anyway," Christy said.

"What's that, ma'am?"

"That this is one plantation burning they can't blame on us Yankees."

Chuckling, the sergeant went off to check on his men who were still busy securing the scene.

Dallas turned and faced Christy. "So now that we're finally alone..."

"Yes?"

"I'm waiting for those expressions of gratitude."

"Of course." She extended her arm in an indication that she was prepared to shake his hand. Her offer was accompanied by an address of mock formality. "You have my deepest thanks for coming to our rescue."

"Uh-huh." He reached for her hand, grasped it tightly and hauled her forcefully up against his chest. "You can do better than that, Yank. *Much* better."

"Yes," she murmured, gazing up into the strong face that was now so accommodatingly close to her own. "I guess I can."

"Show me," he demanded.

And she did. Withdrawing her hand from his, she lifted both of her hands and locked them behind his head to draw his face down to hers. Their warm breaths mingled and became one as she closed her mouth on his. Her kiss was light, teasing. Until, that is, he slid his arms around her and deepened it.

It became an intense business after that. A prolonged matter involving his sensual tongue stroking hers, his hands shifting to caress the sides of her swollen breasts, his hardness squeezed against her with an unmistakable yearning.

Christy was limp when he finally released her. She was barely able to croak a careless, "Is that sufficient?"

"Hell, that was just a down payment." He groaned. "But I guess the rest will have to wait until we get home and behind a locked bedroom door."

She shook her head. "We have a problem."

"What problem? There's no problem. How can there be a problem when we're in love?"

"We are?"

"I am and you'd better be. Hey, you are, aren't you?"

The anxious expression that was suddenly on his face delighted her. "I'm afraid so."

He grinned in relief. "Then what's to worry about?"

"My brother, Mitch. Mitch is very fond of me. He's threatened to come to New Orleans and beat you up. He'll probably bring Devlin and Roark with him."

"Three brothers?"

"All of them big suckers."

She watched Dallas's face as he thought about it. "Think I know of a way to pacify them."

"How?"

"We merge our agencies. That ought to please them. The McFarland-Hawke Detective Agency. Sound good?"

"Hawke-McFarland is better."

"You come from a tough family, grits. Okay, Hawke-McFarland."

"That might help."

"Not enough, huh? You're right. I've got to find some

sure way to keep you close by my side so that you don't get into any more scrapes like tonight. Because I've got to tell you, grits, I have no intention of ever being that scared again. I guess the only way to make certain of that is for us to get married.''

"Do I have a choice about this?''

"I wouldn't recommend any argument,'' he warned her.

Christy sighed. "It looks like I'm going to be paying that debt to you for the rest of my life.''

She offered no objection when his arms went around her again. "If I were you,'' he said, just before his mouth angled across hers, "I'd count on it.''

Epilogue

Nothing should have troubled her. Not on her wedding day. That's what Christy kept telling herself as she stood in front of the full-length mirror, critically examining the image that gazed back at her.

The problem, of course, wasn't in her appearance. But, hey, why shouldn't she look good? No baseball cap, no shorts, no running shoes. She had traded that uniform for a creamy confection that was full-skirted, filmy and utterly feminine. Her lustrous, honey-blond hair was piled on top of her head. At the moment her mother was weaving small, pale blue and yellow flowers through its mass of curls.

"My darling," Moura cautioned her, "if you don't hold still I'm going to end up wounding you."

"Ma, you need another pin over here," Eden advised.

And that was another thing, Christy reminded herself, all of her family were here for the wedding. Her sister, Eden, and Denise were to be her attendants. It was great. Everything was great, including the setting.

She and Dallas had chosen to be married aboard the *Dixie Belle,* a classy replica of a paddle wheel steamer that cruised the broad expanse of Lake Pontchartrain. The boat had provided refreshments, a Cajun band on deck and a lavish display of flowers. There were even flowers here in the Victorian-style cabin where Christy was readying herself for the ceremony.

Perfection, all of it. Not a thing for her to be worried about. But Christy was worried and with good reason. What if Dallas couldn't accept the result of what they were about to learn? What if it turned out to be something he didn't want to hear? She couldn't bear it if he was unhappy, even though he had promised her that either way it went he was prepared.

Their wedding day. Why had he insisted on being provided with the outcome on their wedding day? Why couldn't he have waited? "Sweetheart," he'd tried to explain his decision to her, "when I stand beside you and pledge my vows, I don't want there to be a question about anything. I want us to begin our lives together without a single shadow. That's why I have to hear the truth as soon as it's available, even if that means just before the ceremony and it looks like that's just when it will be."

Christy had tried to understand, but she couldn't shake the feeling this was a mistake.

The cabin door opened and Denise appeared. She had volunteered to post herself as a lookout on the open deck. Christy turned from the mirror and met her gaze. The expression in Denise's eyes reflected her own tension.

"They're here," Denise reported. "Just pulling up to the dock."

Christy started for the door, but Eden stopped her. "You can't go out there," she objected. "It's bad luck for the groom to see the bride before the ceremony."

"I think," Moura said quietly, "that this is one occasion when custom can take a back seat. Christy needs to be there with him when he gets the news."

Eden, remembering then what Christy had shared with

the family, nodded her understanding. ''I'll have the bridal bouquet for you when you're ready for it.''

Christy thanked her mother and sister, accepted hugs from both of them, as well as Denise who murmured a quick, ''Good luck out there, girlfriend,'' and left the cabin.

The spacious deck of the *Dixie Belle* presented a lively scene. The Cajun band played toe-tapping selections while waiters circulated through the ranks of wedding guests with trays of drinks. One side of the vessel offered views of the dazzling, sun-spangled waters of Lake Pontchartrain. Off the rail on the other side, rose the majestic skyline of New Orleans.

Christy searched the crowd composed of friends and family, which included Dallas's own clan who had arrived in force that morning from Baton Rouge. She finally located Dallas standing near the bow with her father and brothers. They all seemed to be enjoying one another's company. At the moment they were busy laughing over some story that Camille Leveau's father, Chester, recounted with appropriate gestures.

Christy was reluctant to approach them. An interruption proved to be unnecessary. Her father looked down the length of the deck and discovered her. With a simple wink, Casey Hawke told his daughter how proud he was of her. She knew her whole family was pleased that she had managed to save her branch of the agency and that she was marrying the man who had helped her to win that victory.

Christy smiled her appreciation and managed to silently convey to her father her need to see Dallas. Casey nodded in understanding and turned toward Dallas, signaling his attention.

Slipping away from the group, Dallas strode toward his bride.

She watched him weave his way through the guests, tall

and handsome in a dark blue suit, every female gaze turning in his direction as he passed. Her heart swelled with love, making her hate her nervousness as she waited for him.

Those wonderful green eyes of his widened in admiration when he stood in front of her. "My God," he said, voice husky with emotion as he gazed down at her, "you take my breath away."

Damn it, Christy thought, she didn't want to have to do this. She wanted instead to have him go on telling her how beautiful she was, wanted to let him know how happy he made her. Wanted nothing but joy. But in this moment she owed him something else.

"Thank you, darling. Uh, they've just arrived."

"Yeah?" His face sobered. "Then let's go and meet them."

He took her hand when she fell in step beside him, squeezing it to let her know she had nothing to be concerned about, that he was ready to accept whatever he was about to hear. But Christy still worried that he could end up feeling a loss, perhaps a deep one, which was why she was prepared with some news of her own. She had deliberately saved the sharing of it until now when it might be needed to soften a serious letdown. She just hoped it would be sufficient.

By the time she and Dallas reached the boarding stairway, the new arrivals had left their car and were ascending to the deck. Christy stood at Dallas's side and waited for them, a smile of welcome on her face as she watched them approach.

Glenn and Monica looked like a couple who belonged together, perhaps because they no longer had to hide their love for each other. They would be married themselves within a month or two. Daisy was with them, which already made them a family unit. Christy was happy for them, but if Dallas suffered—

"Welcome to our wedding," she greeted them as they arrived on deck.

Monica thanked her and offered her best wishes with a warmth that made Christy wonder why she had ever thought the woman was haughty. The men shook hands. There was a sober expression on Glenn's face, but that was no indication. He could be feeling bad either for Dallas or himself.

Daisy was excited. "I have a new dress!"

Christy bent down to admire it and expressed her regret when she was informed that George had been left at home. Devlin's wife, Karen, who was expecting their second child and looked it, appeared on the scene as Christy had requested.

"You must be Daisy," she said with a delighted smile. "I have a little girl just about your age. Her name is Livie. I know she'd love to meet you." She glanced at Glenn, who nodded his approval. "What do you say, Daisy? Shall we go and find her?"

Christy sent her sister-in-law a look of gratitude as Karen took Daisy's hand and led her away.

"Let's go back here," Dallas suggested, leading the way toward the stern of the vessel. "It's less crowded."

The *Dixie Belle* had rumbled to life now that the last guests were on board and was already moving away from the shore as the four of them reached an area where they could be reasonably private. The passengers, squeezed against the rails to watch their departure, paid no attention to their earnest conversation.

"You have it?" Dallas asked.

Glenn nodded. "It came by messenger just before I left

the house. But I wish you hadn't insisted on having it now. Not on your wedding day. It could have waited.''

''No, it couldn't.''

Dallas's tone indicated he had already waited long enough. It had taken him more than two weeks to persuade Glenn that another test, this time from a reputable lab, was necessary.

Monica laid her hand on Glenn's arm. ''He deserves to know the truth. Both of them have earned it.''

''You're right. If it hadn't been for Christy and Dallas, I'd be the one still sitting in a cell facing a murder trial instead of Alistair St. Leger. I can't thank you enough for that.''

''Yes, you can,'' Dallas said, holding out his hand.

Glenn reluctantly complied by withdrawing an envelope from the inside breast pocket of his suit coat and handing it solemnly to Dallas. Christy stood close beside him, holding her breath as Dallas removed the contents of the envelope. Together they read the result of the blood test that had been performed yesterday afternoon.

Dallas was not Daisy's biological father. That connection still belonged to Glenn.

Releasing her breath, Christy anxiously searched Dallas's face. There was no stricken expression there, nothing to tell her what he might be feeling.

''For your sake,'' Glenn said, ''I wish it hadn't come to this, but I can't pretend I'm sorry. I don't know what I would have done if Daisy—''

Dallas cut him off with a sharp, ''Damn it, Hollister, do you think I would have tried to take her away from you when you were the only father she's ever known? Okay, maybe I would have asked for visitation rights, the chance to know my daughter, but that's all.''

''Yes,'' Glenn murmured, ''I should have realized that.''

"Look," Christy interceded, "whatever the outcome, we're happy that both of you are here to share our wedding day."

Monica tactfully came to her aid. "Come on, darling," she said, linking her arm with Glenn's, "let's go and join the other guests."

The couple moved away, leaving Christy and Dallas alone at the rail. Neither of them spoke. The Cajun band went on playing while the *Dixie Belle* lumbered out across the lake, its paddle wheel churning the blue waters.

After a moment Dallas became aware of Christy's worried, sympathetic gaze fastened on him. He turned to her with a reassuring smile. "It's all right, grits. I'll be a father later on." He paused and suddenly looked anxious. "I will, won't I?"

"Well, actually…" And that was when she told him, stretching up on tiptoe to whisper it into his ear.

He stared at her, his eyes gleaming. "Yeah? You're sure?"

"Unless the double pink line on the stick is wrong and I have every reason to believe it isn't, then you've got a nursery to build."

His arms slid around her, drawing her close. "Forget the champagne they're serving," he said with a big grin. "I'm already drunk on joy."

Christy was glowing herself. She thought how much she loved this man, of how he had helped her to achieve her potential, both as a P.I. and a woman. There was nothing she couldn't be with Dallas McFarland beside her. *Together.* There was a real magic in that simple word, wasn't there?

He started to kiss her, but Eden, arriving on the scene with her bouquet, interrupted them. "Hey, you two, you don't get to do that until the man says, 'You may now kiss the bride.'"

Dallas released Christy long enough to issue an urgent, "Then let's take care of that right now."

Flinging an arm around her waist, he headed them toward the flower-smothered nuptial altar that had been erected on the broad deck of the bow where the guests had congregated. Christy, laughing, just managed in passing to grab the bridal bouquet from her sister's hand as Dallas hurried her toward the future that waited for them.

This Mother's Day
Give Your Mom
❁ A Royal Treat ❁

Win a fabulous one-week vacation in
Puerto Rico for you and your mother at
the luxurious Inter-Continental San Juan
Resort & Casino. The prize includes round
trip airfare for two, breakfast daily and a
mother and daughter day of beauty
at the beachfront hotel's spa.

❖

INTER·CONTINENTAL
San Juan
RESORT & CASINO

Here's all you have to do:

Tell us in 100 words or less how your
mother helped with the romance in your
life. It may be a story about your engagement,
wedding or those boyfriends when you were
a teenager or any other romantic advice
from your mother. The entry will be judged
based on its originality, emotionally
compelling nature and sincerity.
See official rules on following page.

Send your entry to:
Mother's Day Contest

In Canada	**In U.S.A.**
P.O. Box 637	P.O. Box 9076
Fort Erie, Ontario	3010 Walden Ave.
L2A 5X3	Buffalo, NY
	14269-9076

Or enter online at www.eHarlequin.com

All entries must be postmarked by April 1, 2002.
Winner will be announced May 1, 2002. Contest open to
Canadian and U.S. residents who are 18 years of age and older.
No purchase necessary to enter. Void where prohibited.

PRROY

HARLEQUIN MOTHER'S DAY CONTEST 2216
OFFICIAL RULES
NO PURCHASE NECESSARY TO ENTER

Two ways to enter:

• **Via The Internet:** Log on to the Harlequin romance website (www.eHarlequin.com) anytime beginning 12:01 a.m. E.S.T., January 1, 2002 through 11:59 p.m. E.S.T., April 1, 2002 and follow the directions displayed on-line to enter your name, address (including zip code), e-mail address and in 100 words or fewer, describe how your mother helped with the romance in your life.

• **Via Mail:** Handprint (or type) on an 8 1/2" x 11" plain piece of paper, your name, address (including zip code) and e-mail address (if you have one), and in 100 words or fewer, describe how your mother helped with the romance in your life. Mail your entry via first-class mail to: Harlequin Mother's Day Contest 2216, (in the U.S.) P.O. Box 9076, Buffalo, NY 14269-9076; (in Canada) P.O. Box 637, Fort Erie, Ontario, Canada L2A 5X3.

For eligibility, entries must be submitted either through a completed Internet transmission or postmarked no later than 11:59 p.m. E.S.T., April 1, 2002 (mail-in entries must be received by April 9, 2002). Limit one entry per person, household address and e-mail address. On-line and/or mailed entries received from persons residing in geographic areas in which entry is not permissible will be disqualified.

Entries will be judged by a panel of judges, consisting of members of the Harlequin editorial, marketing and public relations staff using the following criteria:
- Originality - 50%
- Emotional Appeal - 25%
- Sincerity - 25%

In the event of a tie, duplicate prizes will be awarded. Decisions of the judges are final.

Prize: A 6-night/7-day stay for two at the Inter-Continental San Juan Resort & Casino, including round-trip coach air transportation from gateway airport nearest winner's home (approximate retail value: $4,000). Prize includes breakfast daily and a mother and daughter day of beauty at the beachfront hotel's spa. Prize consists of only those items listed as part of the prize. Prize is valued in U.S. currency.

All entries become the property of Torstar Corp. and will not be returned. No responsibility is assumed for lost, late, illegible, incomplete, inaccurate, non-delivered or misdirected mail or misdirected e-mail, for technical, hardware or software failures of any kind, lost or unavailable network connections, or failed, incomplete, garbled or delayed computer transmission or any human error which may occur in the receipt or processing of the entries in this Contest.

Contest open only to residents of the U.S. (except Colorado) and Canada, who are 18 years of age or older and is void wherever prohibited by law; all applicable laws and regulations apply. Any litigation within the Province of Quebec respecting the conduct or organization of a publicity contest may be submitted to the Régie des alcools, des courses et des jeux for a ruling. Any litigation respecting the awarding of a prize may be submitted to the Régie des alcools, des courses et des jeux only for the purpose of helping the parties reach a settlement. Employees and immediate family members of Torstar Corp. and D.L. Blair, Inc., their affiliates, subsidiaries and all other agencies, entities and persons connected with the use, marketing or conduct of this Contest are not eligible to enter. Taxes on prize are the sole responsibility of winner. Acceptance of any prize offered constitutes permission to use winner's name, photograph or other likeness for the purposes of advertising, trade and promotion on behalf of Torstar Corp., its affiliates and subsidiaries without further compensation to the winner, unless prohibited by law.

Winner will be determined no later than April 15, 2002 and be notified by mail. Winner will be required to sign and return an Affidavit of Eligibility form within 15 days after winner notification. Non-compliance within that time period may result in disqualification and an alternate winner may be selected. Winner of trip must execute a Release of Liability prior to ticketing and must possess required travel documents (e.g. Passport, photo ID) where applicable. Travel must be completed within 12 months of selection and is subject to traveling companion completing and returning a Release of Liability prior to travel; and hotel and flight accommodations availability. Certain restrictions and blackout dates may apply. No substitution of prize permitted by winner. Torstar Corp. and D.L. Blair, Inc., their parents, affiliates, and subsidiaries are not responsible for errors in printing or electronic presentation of Contest, or entries. In the event of printing or other errors which may result in unintended prize values or duplication of prizes, all affected entries shall be null and void. If for any reason the Internet portion of the Contest is not capable of running as planned, including infection by computer virus, bugs, tampering, unauthorized intervention, fraud, technical failures, or any other causes beyond the control of Torstar Corp. which corrupt or affect the administration, secrecy, fairness, integrity or proper conduct of the Contest, Torstar Corp. reserves the right, at its sole discretion, to disqualify any individual who tampers with the entry process and to cancel, terminate, modify or suspend the Contest or the Internet portion thereof. In the event the Internet portion must be terminated a notice will be posted on the website and all entries received prior to termination will be judged in accordance with these rules. In the event of a dispute regarding an on-line entry, the entry will be deemed submitted by the authorized holder of the e-mail account submitted at the time of entry. Authorized account holder is defined as the natural person who is assigned to an e-mail address by an Internet access provider, on-line service provider or other organization that is responsible for arranging e-mail address for the domain associated with the submitted e-mail address. Torstar Corp. and/or D.L. Blair Inc. assumes no responsibility for any computer injury or damage related to or resulting from accessing and/or downloading any sweepstakes material. Rules are subject to any requirements/limitations imposed by the FCC. **Purchase or acceptance of a product offer does not improve your chances of winning.**

For winner's name (available after May 1, 2002), send a self-addressed, stamped envelope to: Harlequin Mother's Day Contest Winners 2216, P.O. Box 4200 Blair, NE 68009-4200 or you may access the www.eHarlequin.com Web site through June 3, 2002.

Contest sponsored by Torstar Corp., P.O. Box 9042, Buffalo, NY 14269-9042.